DEATH TOLL

Short Thriller Fiction, Full Length Adrenalin

A Thriller Fiction

Anthology

EM.C PRESS

Los Angeles, Worthing
An Imprint of EspionageMagazine.com, LLC
www.deathtoll.co.uk

WHAT DO PEOPLE THINK OF OUR SHORT THRILLER FICTION ANTHOLOGY

DEATH TOLL?

"Meet the boys! And these boys are good. Espionage Magazine has put together a collection of stories for the aficionado or the newcomer to the genre. Some of my favorite writers offering thrilling entertainment in short bursts. I read it more than once, bet you do too." **–Harlan Wolff**, author of *BANGKOK RULES*

http://amzn.to/11UG0yp
http://expatsolutionsthailand.com

"You have a real treat in store for you here, my friends. These guys tell *great* stories; stories that feel so real you'll be looking over your shoulder. They just do it in an extraordinarily economical way." **–Jake Needham**, author of six bestselling novels, including *THE UMBRELLA MAN*

http://amzn.to/11UGlBa
http://jakeneedham.com/

Nothing excites me more than discovering new writing talent - and this book is bursting with it. **–Stephen Leather**, Britain's bestselling thriller writer with over thirty titles.

http://amzn.to/10ir2j6
http://www.stephenleather.com/

"...you like your murders raw?... your killings with milk and sugar?...your tortures on the rocks?... pick your poison, and grab a load of some of the best short, sharp offerings on the delights of physical elimination...welcome to the art of great fiction in

compressed form...the Death Toll anthology's for you... "
--**Seumas Gallacher,** Blogger of the Year and author of
VENGEANCE WEARS BLACK

http://amzn.to/11UJLnr
http://seumasgallacher.com/

An eclectic mix of authors, established and new, have been brought together and delivered a hard-nosed, pull-no-punches collection of crime stories. Miss this at your peril.
–**Rachel Amphlett,** author of WHITE GOLD and UNDER FIRE

http://amzn.to/14s5nM9
http://www.rachelamphlett.com/

"Everyone dies ... and it's no spoiler to tell you that some people die in these many fine stories. These are deaths fit for a fabulous thriller collection; by turns cruel, gruesome, professional, clean, mysterious, faked and, of course, tragic. The resulting death toll is all the evidence a jury would need to decide that the art of writing short stories is alive, kicking and in absolutely no danger. Read it, or weep." –**Mark Chisnell,** author of the bestselling, THE DEFECTOR and THE WRECKING CREW

http://amzn.to/1053EYX
http://markchisnell.com/

"Action, violence and cold-blooded ruthlessness, this compilation of thrillers has it all. Six authors, six different styles, one great read." --**Jack Silkstone**, author of the bestselling PRIMAL SERIES

http://amzn.to/14s5VS7
http://www.primalunleashed.com/blog/

Scary. It's one of those rare instances when the reader does not want to be transported onto the pages to live the lives of the protagonists; to be sure, their plight drew me in like a magnet, but the blurry line between fiction and truth scared me, and made me grateful for the safety of my couch. --**Jack King**, author of *AGENTS OF CHANGE*

http://amzn.to/16IgFAe
http://www.spywriter.com/

"When I was growing up I loved to read boys stories and this without a doubt is a wonderful collection of just that. This anthology is like reading a grown-up Boy's Own Annual stuffed full of conmen, an unsuspecting husband, spy craft, an assassin, Australian soldiers in Afghanistan, terrorism, and some old fashioned burglary. A thrilling ride through stories packed with adventure or misadventure." —**Cat Connor** author of FLASHBYTE

http://amzn.to/XPFcfC
http://catconnor.blogspot.com/

The stories contained in this collection are works of fiction. All characters, organizations, and events portrayed in this anthology are either products of each author's imagination or are used fictitiously.

EM.C PRESS
An Imprint of EspionageMagazine.com, LLC
Lurid Tales of Deceit and Betrayal, Mystery and Imagination

Death Toll, Copyright © 2013 by K.K. Chamberlain and EM.C PRESS. All Rights Reserved. Paperback printed in the United States of America. For information, contact EspionageMagazine.com, P.O. Box 7531, Long Beach, CA. 90807

www.DeathToll.co.uk

www.EspionageMagazine.com

All of the stories in this anthology appear courtesy of the authors listed and are reprinted with permission by the copyright holder.

The *DEATH TOLL* name and anthology concept created by Stephen Edger.

Cover design by Alex Shaw. Cover photo by Aaron Amat.

Edited by K.K. Chamberlain and Julia Gibbs.

ISBN-13: 978-0615803661
ISBN-10: 0615803660

For Jack and Emily

Death Toll

i	Introduction; Jake Needham
1	Hiatus; Stephen Leather
19	Hetman: Donetsk Calling; Alex Shaw
77	The Assassin's Mistress; J. H. Bográn
89	Best Served Cold; Stephen Edger
103	Goodbye Maria, Sorry; Howard Manson
133	Predator Strike; Liam Saville
205	Under Cover of Death; Howard Manson
217	Breaking In; Stephen Leather
232	Death Toll Authors

INTRODUCTION

By Jake Needham

When the folks at EspionageMagazine.com asked me to write the introduction to their first collection of short thriller fiction, I said this to them....

What? Are you nuts?

I don't know anything about short fiction, I told them. I really don't read short fiction, whether it's thriller fiction, crime fiction, or something else. I don't write short fiction, thriller, crime, or otherwise.

Anyway, the problem I have with short fiction in general is that it's...well, uh, short.

Real life is messy. It's filled with blind alleys and loose ends, and stories don't feel real to me unless those kinds of things are in there, too. Short fiction is too neat, too tidy for me. I figure you need a bit of space to tell a good story. The writer needs room for his story to meander around a little, just like real life does, and the reader needs room to explore those blind alleys and chase those loose ends. It's just that simple really. I've never thought you can tell stories that feel real without having the breadth and sweep of a full-length book to do it.

Look, I'm flattered you asked me, I told the EspionageMagazine.com folks, but you've got the wrong guy.

Just read the material we're putting in the anthology first, they said. Then make up your mind.

So I did. They sent me the novellas and the short stories that are included in this anthology and I read them and...Here I am.

Okay, I'm just going to say this once. So listen up.

Boy, was I wrong.

You have a real treat in store for you here, my friends. These guys tell great stories; stories that feel so real you'll be looking over your shoulder. They just do it in an extraordinarily economical way.

Before you dig into this banquet, however, bear with me for just a minute. I have a couple of reflections on the general subject of crime fiction that I think might contribute modestly to your enjoyment of the rich variety of stories that follow.

First, there's this. We all use the term crime fiction all the time – everybody does – but have you ever asked yourself just exactly what in the hell crime fiction actually is?

Walk into any bookstore these days, or search the category at an online bookstore like Amazon, and you'll find a gumbo ya-ya of books that don't seem to have all that much to do with each other. Just a few years ago, it was all pretty straightforward. Crime fiction was detective fiction. Simple as that. A detective sallied forth to solve a crime. He may have been a cop, or he may have been a private detective, but the path he followed to get to the bottom of whatever riddle he had been presented with was pretty much the same either way. And he followed that path heroically.

Raymond Chandler famously put it like this in an essay entitled 'The Simple Art of Murder:'

INTRODUCTION | iii

> *"Down these means streets a man must go who is not himself mean, who is neither tarnished nor afraid. The detective in this kind of story must be such a man. He is the hero; he is everything...If there were enough like him, the world would be a very safe place to live in. The story is this man's adventure in search of a hidden truth."*

These days, the crime fiction category is vast and wide-ranging. For example, Amazon calls it 'Mysteries, Thrillers, and Suspense,' and then within the category there is a feast of sub-categories: legal thrillers, medical thrillers, techno-thrillers, spy stories, historical mysteries, police procedurals, British sleuths, and – I swear I'm not making this up – even cat sleuths. There have been so many books published about cats that solve crimes that they get their own category on Amazon? Who knew?

If you can give me a clear and simple definition of crime fiction these days, you are far cleverer than I. The truth is I really haven't the first idea how to define crime fiction anymore.

It is perhaps an overly facile observation to say this, but in many ways the anarchy of stories and characters and categories that is now grouped loosely under the heading of crime fiction reflects the growing anarchy of our own senses of the cultures in which we live. We have, whether we intended to or not, become multi-racial, multi-cultural, multi-national, and even multi-sexual in ways I'm sure Raymond Chandler never imagined. And so has our crime fiction.

In Chandler's day, detectives were white, working-class males. All of them. Today, our protagonists are male, female, rich, poor, gay, straight, local, foreign, physically fit, physically handicapped, smart, dumb, vicious, gentle, altruistic, and venal. They are not always the hero; they are not always everything.

So am I saying that crime fiction these days is completely different from what it was just a few decades ago? No, I'm saying that mostly it just looks different, and that makes it harder to categorize explicitly.

What Raymond Chandler said is always found somewhere at the heart of good crime fiction, is still generally found at the heart of good crime fiction. Crime fiction is a story of a man's (or woman's, or cat's) adventure in search of a hidden truth.

Whether you're reading about Lee Child's Jack Reacher, or James Lee Burke's Dave Robicheaux, or Mike Connelly's Lt. Harry Bosch, or even Jake Needham's Inspector Samuel Tay, you are reading variations on a similar journey: the search for a hidden truth.

Three elements then, I suggest, are found in pretty much all crime fiction.

A search.

For something hidden.

Which is the truth.

Okay, that sounds simple enough, doesn't it? So, if that's the formula, shouldn't crime fiction be pretty easy to write?

I admire the stories in this anthology in particular because crime fiction is really difficult to write. Okay, let's stop mincing words and just put the point clearly. Good crime fiction is difficult to write. Average crime fiction is another matter altogether, which may be why there is so much of it around.

Permit me to refer you to Mr. Chandler again for guidance on the topic:

> *"The detective story, even in its most conventional form, is difficult to write well. Good specimens of the art are much rarer than good serious novels...It seems to me that the production of detective stories on so large a scale, and by writers whose immediate reward is small, would not be possible at all if the job took any talent. In that sense the raised eyebrow of the critic and the shoddy merchandising of the publisher are perfectly logical. The average detective story is probably no worse than the average novel, but you never see the average novel. It doesn't get published. The average detective story does."*

So what's wrong with so much crime fiction that causes it to fall short? That makes it, not bad, but...well, average.

Average crime fiction follows Chandler's formula. But, sadly, it doesn't do much of anything else.

Good crime fiction does do something else. Principally, I suggest, it transports you into a credible world in which you do not normally live, one that feels entirely real to you.

It ain't as easy as it looks, folks.

Some writers take an obvious shortcut. They use the world as they find it. You may never have been anywhere near the Cajun country of southern Louisiana, but read a few of James Lee Burke's Dave Robicheaux books and you'll be the next thing to a native. The back alleys of Los Angeles may be foreign territory to you, but read a few of Mike Connelly's Lt. Harry Bosch books and you can find your way around them without a map. And you may never have been anywhere near Singapore, but when writing about my

Inspector Tay novels, a reviewer in the Bangkok Post said that he always felt like he had just gotten off a plane from Singapore when he finished one.

Others writers make up the world they write about. Ed McBain, for example, set his long series of 87th Precinct police procedurals in a fictional city that seemed very much like New York. Someone asked McBain once why he didn't just use the real Manhattan and be done with it. And he said something like this: 'Because I didn't want assholes writing me letters telling me that I had put some building in the wrong place or that a character had turned left when he should have turned right.' I can identify with that, and I'll bet most writers who write about real places can.

Whether the 87th Precinct was a real place or not, it sure felt real, and the cops who worked there and the crooks they pursued seemed real, so we believed it was real. That was what made Ed McBain one of the great practitioners of the art of crime fiction. He made up his landscape, but it was so credible that he made us believe it.

And that was one of the principal reasons we enjoyed following McBain's characters so much...

As they searched.

For something hidden.

Which was the truth.

Some of us who write crime fiction have lived at least part of what we write about and thus we find the information we need to make our worlds credible right in our own life experiences. And sometimes yet we write about one man killing another, and we have to make that credible, too, in spite of the fact that we haven't had that specific experience. At least most of us haven't. There are a couple of crime fiction writers out there I'm not all that sure of. You know who you are...

You, Mr. or Ms. Reader, know what's real when you read it, and you know what isn't. Your Shit-O-Meter goes off at the slightest provocation. And it's the first goal of a good crime writer to make sure the damn thing never lets out a peep.

When a reader purchases a book, he makes a commitment to the writer. I'm not talking about the money the reader pays us for our work, for that is a relatively insignificant commitment in many cases these days. No, I'm talking about the time the reader commits to reading our work. Even a guy who shoplifts one of my books is still investing six or eight or ten hours of his time in my work, and that is a far more valuable thing than the two or three dollars I would have gotten in royalties if he had paid for the damned book like he should have.

I owe him something in return for the investment he is making in me.

What I owe him is a credible journey through a world or a time that he might not otherwise know.

While he searches.

For something hidden.

Which is the truth.

Okay, I hear you ask, so how do good crime writers, as opposed to average crime writers, pay off what they owe to the reader?

They do it by respecting their readers and fearing the buzz of their readers' shit detectors. Writers of good crime fiction know our readers are at least as intelligent as we are. This isn't a game in which the intelligent writer sets out to lead the simple reader through a world by the nose. In good crime fiction, reader and writer undertake the journey as partners.

We just want you to wish that the journey could go on forever.

The writers who have contributed to this anthology have delivered on their journeys in spades. You may invest your time with them and know you are about to receive a fair, even an excessive return on your investment.

In reading this analogy you are about to travel for the first time a road I recently traveled for the first time myself. And it was a hell of a trip.

Sadly, I can never travel it for the first time again, no matter how much I might wish I could.

But now you can.

I do envy you that.

-- Jake Needham

DEATH TOLL

HIATUS
By Stephen Leather

"We're clear on this, right? Nothing physical. No shoving, no pushing, no punching." Garry Dobbs looked into the eyes of his protégé. Jack Martin was two years younger than Dobbsy and a hell of a lot less smart, but beggars couldn't be choosers and Dobbsy had to make do with what was available. "You understand, Jacko? You absolutely can not get physical."

Jacko sighed. "How many times are you going to tell me?" he said. "I get it. They're old. We don't hurt them." He scratched the rash of old acne scars across his cheek. Jacko had the sort of face only a mother could love; a weak chin, a pig-like nose and the blank eyes of a teenager who had spent too many hours on his PlayStation.

"It's not about not hurting," said Dobbsy. "That's the thing. Most of them are so old you can bruise them just by blowing at them. If they fall over they break a hip, if you grab their wrist you can snap their arm. Most of them are confused, you just have to talk to them like they're simple and they'll do as they're told. If they do turn belligerent, there's nothing they can do, remember that. They can't force you to do anything and if you keep their phone away from them they can't phone for help. The cops take forever to answer nine-nine-nine calls anyway these days. And when they do answer it takes them forever to get anyone out."

Jacko rolled his eye. "Dobbsy, I'm not stupid. I've robbed houses before."

"This isn't robbing," said Dobbsy. "This is conning." He leaned over, popped the glove box open, and pulled out two laminated ID cards on blue lanyards. He gave one to Jacko and put the other around his neck. "This says we work for the council and we're police-approved. I made them myself and they look the dog's bollocks, but most of them are almost blind anyway. But if they look worried, you just smile and show them the ID and tell them we work for the council."

"And they believe it? It's as easy as that?"

"They're old, mate. This guy is over eighty. He's one step away from being in a home. The trick is just to keep smiling and tell them not to worry."

Jacko nodded. "Got it."

They were sitting in Dobbsy's black Golf GTI in a road lined with shabby terraced houses. There were three sorts of households – the elderly, families on benefits, and recently arrived immigrants. The house that Dobbsy was interested in was Number 27. There was only one occupant, a man in his eighties by the name of Duns. Duns rarely left the house. Twice a week he would walk slowly down the road to the Tesco Express store between a bookmakers and a charity shop, and would return half an hour later with a carrier bag full of food. He never went near an ATM and so Dobbsy assumed there was cash in the house. Old people didn't trust banks and preferred cash wherever possible. They tended to have jewellery, too. In one house he'd found a dozen sovereigns in a red velvet pouch tucked away in a sock drawer.

Dobbsy had just turned twenty years old. As a teenager he'd been a prolific burglar, and over a six year career had broken into more than a thousand houses. Two or three a week, on average. He'd been caught several times but only as a juvenile, and always got off with a caution.

It was when he turned twenty that Dobbsy had an epiphany. Instead of breaking into houses at random, usually chosen because a window had been left open or a door unlocked, he decided to choose his targets more carefully. And instead of

HIATUS

breaking in, he began to simply walk in through the front door. The idea had come to him when his mother had called in a locksmith to fit a peephole viewer and a security chain. Dobbsy had watched, fascinated, as the man had worked, and had asked a few questions. Later, as he lay on his bed staring up at the ceiling, he realised that old folk would probably jump at the chance of having the extra security fitted. The next day he'd gone around to a hardware store, bought himself a toolbox, drill and a selection of viewers and chains, and had started knocking on doors.

His original idea had been to charge the old folk a tenner for a peephole and a tenner for a chain, but it soon became obvious that it was going to be a struggle getting them to part with their money. But what he realised was that a simple knock on the door got him into the house. That was when he'd had his second brainwave. If he could find a partner and the two of them could get into the house, one of them could distract the occupant while the other could move through the house looking for cash and valuables.

He'd teamed up with an old school friend, Gordo, and together they'd honed the technique that had netted them thousands of pounds in just a few months. Dobbsy would do the talking, and give them the spiel about the council giving them free peepholes and security chains. Then Gordo would take the owner of the house into the kitchen to make a cup of tea. Dobbsy would then check the bedrooms and the sitting room, stealing whatever he could, then when he was done, he would make some excuse about not having the right tools and they would leave. It was clean and no one got hurt, and it was practically risk free. Most of the old folk they dealt with were so forgetful he figured that most of them would never know that they had been ripped off.

Cash was the best thing to find, obviously, and old people always seemed to have cash in their homes. Dobbsy didn't know if it was because they didn't trust banks or because they didn't know how to use credit cards, but either way they always had something tucked away, more often than not in their bedrooms. There was usually jewellery, too. The women usually had necklaces and rings hidden away, but so too did the men, probably left over from the days when they had wives. Dobbsy had also started taking an interest in antiques. Old people generally had old things in their homes, and while a lot of it was crap he did sometimes come across a Royal Doulton figurine or a Wedgewood pot that he could sell down the Portobello Road. He'd started reading up on antiques on the internet and always made a point of taking a closer look at what was on the mantelpiece and sideboard.

All had gone swimmingly until Gordo had gotten into an argument with a drunken Polish builder in a pub and received a pint glass in his face for his trouble. He wasn't able to leave his house, and if he did, Dobbsy reckoned he'd scare the pants off anyone who opened their door, so he needed a replacement.

The best he could find was Jacko, Gordo's cousin, who like Dobbsy had been a prolific burglar. Unlike Dobbsy, Jacko tended to forget things like gloves and escape routes and had been caught red-handed more than a dozen times. He'd been lucky enough to come up before a succession of well-meaning magistrates who had listened to his story of a broken home and an absent father and dyslexia and God knows what else, and decided that prison was absolutely the wrong place for him and that he'd be much better off sent on his way with a pat on the head and a plea for him to behave himself in future.

"I know this is your first time, Jacko, but there's no need to be nervous," said Dobbsy. "Just take it nice and slow."

"Piece of cake," said Jacko, rubbing his hands together.

"Let's do it," said Dobbsy. They climbed out of the GTI. The car was Dobbsy's pride and joy. The only reason he could afford it was because he lived with his mother and so didn't have to pay rent. He'd put on alloy wheels and souped-up the engine and had fitted a stereo that was so powerful that it vibrated the fillings in his teeth at full volume.

Dobbsy opened up the back of the car and took out a blue metal tool kit. He took out a door security chain in a plastic bag and gave it to Jacko.

They walked over to the house and Dobbsy pressed the doorbell.

"You sure he's in?" asked Jacko.

"They're always in," said Dobbsy. "They've got nowhere else to go." He pressed the doorbell again, longer this time. Dobbsy leaned forward and pressed his ear against the door. He heard a cough from inside. "He's coming," he said. "He walks with a stick. Takes him ages to get anywhere."

The door creaked open and a pair of watery eyes blinked at them. "Who is it?"

"Mr Duns?" asked Dobbsy.

The old man nodded.

Dobbsy smiled brightly. "We're from the council, Mr Duns." He held up his badge. "They've sent us to fit a peephole viewer so that you can see who's outside." He held up a plastic bag containing a peephole. "And we'll fit an extra strong chain so that no one can get in." He turned to look at Jacko, and Jacko held up the chain.

The door opened wider and the old man looked up at them suspiciously. "Who sent you?" he asked.

"The council," said Dobbsy patiently. "They are offering a free service to upgrade your security. It won't cost you a thing."

The old man's eyes narrowed. "Free?"

"Absolutely free," said Dobbsy. "There have been a few robberies in the area and the council wants senior citizens such as yourself to feel more secure. It'd make you feel better to know who was outside before you open the door, wouldn't it?"

"I suppose so, yes," said the man. He opened the door wider. "I suppose you'd better come in. But wipe your feet, mind. Those pikey bastards next door let their dogs shit all over the pavements."

"No problem, Mr Duns," said Dobbsy. He stepped over the threshold and wiped his feet on a mat. Jacko did the same. The old man ushered them into the hallway and closed the door behind them. Dobbsy wrinkled his nose in disgust. He hated the smell of old people's houses. Stale cabbage and sweat and piss, but at least this one didn't seem to be a smoker. The houses of smokers were the worst by far.

The walls had once been cream or maybe even white, but now they were the dirty yellow of an old sponge. The carpet was a red and black pattern that was so threadbare that there were patches of grey underfelt showing through. The ceiling was covered with a woodchip paper that was stained with black mould and peeling away at the corners. The hallway looked as if it hadn't been touched with a paintbrush for at least twenty years, maybe thirty.

"So, this won't take too long, Mr Duns," said Dobbsy, putting his toolbox on a side table. He looked expectantly at Jacko.

"I'm gasping for a cup of tea," said Jacko, on cue.

"Tea?" repeated the old man. He was almost bald, the scalp mottled with red scaly patches and dotted with irregular moles. His eyes were watery with large, oyster-like bags underneath them. His lips were pale and bloodless, and loose skin hung around his neck, giving him the look of a malnourished turkey. He was wearing baggy grey pants, a blue and white checked shirt and a tatty purple cardigan that had worn through at the elbows. On his feet were red slippers that were stained with years of sweat. At least Dobbsy hoped it was sweat - there were similar patches on the front of the man's trousers.

"Yeah, tea would be great, thanks," said Dobbsy. "Milk and two sugars. Thirsty work, this." He opened the toolbox and took out a drill.

Jacko put his hand on the old man's shoulder. "I'll help you in the kitchen," he said.

Dobbsy frowned and threw Jacko a warning glance. It was best not to touch them, not even slightly. They were so fragile, the old.

Jacko took his hand away. "The kitchen, yeah?" he said nodding encouragingly. "Let's go and make that tea, shall we."

"Tea?" repeated the old man. He was leaning on a wooden walking stick with a large rubber tip on the end.

"Yeah, tea," said Jacko. He mimed drinking from a cup. "Tea. Maybe a biscuit."

HIATUS

The old man shuffled along the threadbare carpet towards the kitchen. Dobbsy watched Jacko follow the old man to the kitchen and close the door. Jacko flashed Dobbsy a thumbs-up just before he disappeared from sight.

Dobbsy put down the peephole viewer, slipped on a pair of white latex gloves and tip-toed up the stairs, keeping close to the wall to minimise any squeaking from the old floorboards. The smell of urine was worse upstairs. There were three doors. One was open and Dobbsy saw a stained bath and a mildewed wall. He opened one of the other doors and stepped into what was obviously the old man's bedroom. There was a single bed with blankets and a grubby pillow. Dobbsy wrinkled his nose in disgust as the stench of body odour assailed his nostrils.

He went over to a wooden chest of drawers and pulled open the top drawer. On the left were yellowed pairs of underwear; on the right were balled-up socks, mainly grey. Dobbsy rifled through them. Nothing.

There were shirts in the second drawer and at the back, in a manila envelope, a handful of used banknotes. Dobbsy grinned as he rifled through the money. They were mainly twenty pound notes with a few tens and one five. Just under two hundred pounds in all. He shoved the money into his pocket and put the envelope back where he'd found it.

He struck gold when he opened the third drawer, literally. Under a pile of shirts he found a red velvet box, about six inches long and three inches wide. Inside, was a collection of rings, eighteen in all. Five were straightforward gold wedding rings worth at most a couple of hundred quid, but there were two sovereign rings and the rest were diamond engagement rings and dress rings with what looked like genuine rubies and sapphires. Dobbsy whistled softly. The diamond rings were worth thousands. No question about it. And the ruby and sapphire rings could be worth as much. He picked up one of the rings and held it up to the light from the streaked window. The diamond was the size of a pea and it sparkled like the real thing. Dobbsy's heart began to pound. It was a serious diamond, one of the biggest he'd ever seen.

He took the diamonds from the box and slid them into his jacket pocket, then put the box back under the shirts.

He was lifting up the mattress when he heard a dull thud downstairs, the sound of a body hitting the floor.

"Shit," he said, and let the mattress fall back into place. "I told you, Jacko, no bloody violence!" he shouted.

He hurried out of the room and ran down the stairs, two at a time.

"I'll bloody swing for you if you've hurt him," he shouted. He hurried into the kitchen. He saw a pair of legs at the side of the table. "You idiot!" he shouted. He took a step forward and then was then he noticed that the legs ended in a pair of expensive Nikes. "Jacko?"

He heard a noise behind him and turned just in time to see the old man walking towards him, his walking stick held high. Dobbsy opened his mouth to speak but before he could say anything the old man brought the stick crashing down on Dobbsy's head and everything went black.

When Dobbsy came around his head hurt like hell. Something was making breathing difficult and he realised that there was something soft in his mouth. He tried to spit it out but there was something keeping it there. He blinked and realised that although he was sitting up he couldn't move his arms and legs.

As his eyes came into focus he saw Jacko, sitting in a chair on the other side of the room. His arms and legs were bound to the chair with what looked like lengths of washing line and a tea towel tied around his mouth.

Jacko was awake and straining at his bonds. When he saw that Dobbsy had opened his eyes he tried to say something to him but the tea towel muffled any sounds he made.

HIATUS

"That's better, I was starting to think I'd topped you, and where would the fun be in that?" said a voice. Dobbsy looked to his right. The old man was sitting on the sofa. In front of him, on the coffee table, was a coiled up washing line and a large pair of scissors. Dobbsy looked down at his hands. His wrists were tied to the arms of the wooden chair. They were tied tightly and expertly with almost no movement, no matter how hard he strained.

"You went down like a sack of spuds," said the old man. He chuckled. "So did your mate, but him I had to hit twice."

Dobbsy strained at his bonds again but his arms and legs were tied fast.

"I'm good with knots," said the old man. "Had to ruin a perfectly good washing line, but I wasn't prepared for visitors." He took a deep breath and exhaled slowly, then grinned, showing a mouthful of decaying teeth. "I can't believe you lads are here. I don't really get any visitors any more. Well, I get a home help now and then but that's it, really."

Dobbsy stared at the coffee table. There was an untidy pile of banknotes there, the money he'd taken from the chest of drawers, and the collection of rings.

The old man rubbed his hands together. "This is so unexpected, you know? I have absolutely nothing planned. It's all off-the-cuff. Reminds me of my first time." He frowned. "How many years ago was that? A bloody lifetime ago, I can tell you. I was a different man back then. Fit as a butcher's dog, strong as an ox, I could have given the two of you a belting and wouldn't have needed a stick."

He laughed, but within seconds his frail body was wracked with coughs and he bent forward, patting his chest hard.

He gradually recovered his breath and looked at them with watery blue eyes. "Let me tell you boys, there's nothing good about getting old. Not one thing. Your bones ache, your bladder empties whenever it feels like it, you forget things. I can't tell you the number of times I've gone into the kitchen to get something and then forgotten what it is I wanted." He chuckled softly. "Yet I can remember my first like it was just yesterday. It's true what they say, you never forget your first."

He took a deep breath and exhaled slowly. "She was a prostitute, name of Caitlin. Only found out her real name after it was in the papers, though. Told me that her name was Vanessa. She was a hooker in Liverpool. She was what they called a half-caste back then, her dad was from Jamaica and her mum was a Scouser. Lovely colour she was, like coffee, with just a touch of milk. Strangled her in my car, with my bare hands."

He held up his hands and looked at them as if seeing them for the first time. The skin was almost translucent, revealing thick blue veins, and the nails were yellowed and gnarled. "Couldn't do that these days, lads. Not with my arthritis. Can barely open a tin of beans now." He smiled ruefully and there was a faraway look in his eyes. "But back then, I was a right fighter, I'd take anyone on. I boxed a bit, in the army. National Service. We all did it back then. The war was over but we still got called up. Did me a power of good, I can tell you. You lads missed out on that. You'd have enjoyed it. They teach you how to drive and how to fire a rifle, you get to hang out with a bunch of mates." He looked over at them. "Some of the best times of my life, back then." He frowned. "What was I talking about?" His frown deepened. "I keep forgetting. I hate that."

He pounded his hand against his forehead. "Caitlin, that's right. The Scouse hooker. My first. Did her with my bare hands, I did. Did her and then took her to a railway line and threw her down the embankment. Disorganised, that's that they call that on CSI and whatnot. I was a disorganised killer." He grinned. "But I got organised, soon enough. You learn from your mistakes, you know? The more you do something, the better you get. And I was bloody good, lads. I was the best."

He laughed but the laugh turned into another coughing fit and he banged himself on his chest with his fist. "How many do you think I killed, lads? How many?"

He looked at them expectantly as if they could answer, but all they could do was grunt fearfully.

HIATUS

He shrugged, not caring whether they answered or not. "Twenty-seven," he said slowly, as if relishing the number. "Nineteen women and eight men. Twelve teenagers. I prefer teenagers, but I tried to vary it." He chuckled again. "What, you don't believe me? It's as true as I'm sitting here. Twenty-seven. And I never got caught. Never even came close. I can prove it to you." He pushed himself up off the sofa with a grunt, then stood for a few seconds as he fought to steady his breath. "Have to be careful when I get up," he said. "I get dizzy. I've fallen over a few times and I'm lucky not to have broken a hip. You don't want to go breaking a hip, lads, not with the way the NHS is these days. You have to wait a year to see a surgeon and then they give you that E. coli bug and kill you. Nurses don't even wash their hands." He reached for his walking stick and hobbled over to an old wooden sideboard.

He propped the stick against the sideboard and used both his hands to fumble open a drawer. He reached inside and pulled out a bulky photograph album that was bound in what looked like green leather. He shuffled slowly back to the sofa and sat down carefully. He placed the album on the coffee table and gently caressed the cover with both hands.

"I never screwed them, the women. It wasn't about sex. It was never about sex. It was about power. And control." He sighed and then arched his back and shuddered as the memories flooded back. He looked back at the album, opened it and flicked through the pages. Dobbsy could see that it was full of cuttings from newspapers and magazines. As the old man flicked through the pages, words jumped out at Dobbsy. MURDER. KILLER. VICTIM.

"I started off disorganised," said Duns. "Even now I don't know why I killed Caitlin. I think it was always in me, because nothing she said or did set me off. I just looked at her and knew that I wanted to kill her and so I did." He held up his arthritic hands. "With these." He chuckled. "It was only when she was dead that I realised I'd have to get rid of the body, I mean, I had a dead hooker in my car. What was I supposed to do with her?

How stupid was that? I was so bloody lucky that the cops didn't catch me. I didn't worry about forensics or fingerprints or anything, I just drove to a railway line and tipped her over. I didn't even take a souvenir."

He flicked back through the album and tapped a page, a cutting from the News Of The World. "That's her picture. She was pretty plain, it has to be said. She was a big girl, too. With a thick neck. It took all my strength to kill her. And it took her three minutes to die, maybe four." He flexed his fingers as if reliving the experience. "But I learned a lot from Caitlin. I guess you always learn a lot from your first."

He chuckled softly. "I spent the week after I killed her in a state of terror. I was sure the cops were going to find me. Every time the doorbell rang or the phone rang I thought it was them. I couldn't sleep, I couldn't eat, I couldn't think about anything other than being banged-up for life. Then, bit-by-bit, I began to realise that they hadn't a clue. Literally. It was the randomness of it, you see. In ninety-percent of murders, the victim knows the killer. All the cops do is to look for a relative, a colleague or a neighbour. It's box-ticking, and there's nothing the cops like better than ticking boxes. But if the killer is a total stranger, then they have to work and they don't like that. If it's random and if there are no witnesses and no forensic evidence, then it's almost impossible for them to find the killer."

He grinned slyly. "Once I'd realised that, I knew what I had to do. I had to keep moving. Because if you keep moving and choose your victims at random there's almost no way they can catch you." He swallowed and rubbed his throat. "I'm parched. All this talking. You know, you two are the first people I've spoke to in weeks. No one wants to talk to you when you're old, you know that? Even in the Post Office. You talk to them but they look right through you as if you're not there. I was a good-looking sod when I was your age; I was fighting birds off with a stick. I could pick and choose." He grimaced. "Now it's like I don't exist. It's like I'm not a human being anymore. I'm an embarrassment, a reminder of what lies in store for them. For everyone." He shook his head sadly, then stood up and reached for his stick. "I'm going to make myself a cup of tea. Now, don't you boys go anywhere."

He shuffled out of the room, muttering to himself. Dobbsy struggled with his bonds but the washing line left him very little room for movement. He tried rocking from side to side but the chair was heavy and barely budged. After a few minutes he was exhausted and he looked over at Jacko, gasping for breath.

Jacko's face was bathed in sweat and his eyes were wide and fearful. He tried to say something to Dobbsy but the gag muffled it to a series of grunts.

Dobbsy shook his head, trying to let Jacko know that he couldn't make out what he was saying. Tears began to run down Jacko's face. Dobbsy tried to scream but whatever the old man had stuffed in his mouth meant he couldn't do more than groan. He tried pulling at his arms again but no matter how hard he strained, the bonds held fast. He slumped in the chair, panting.

Eventually the old man returned, holding a blue and white striped mug in his left hand and his walking stick in the right. He walked slowly over to the table, carefully put down the mug and stick, and then sat down. "Now where was I?" he said. He looked at the two boys in turn as if he expected them to answer. "Oh yes, keep moving. I had to keep moving. And changing. That's the important thing. You boys watch television, don't you? Of course you do. That's all you lads do these days, isn't it? You watch TV and you play video games. Because there's nothing else, right? No bloody jobs, not any more. Not for the likes of you. So you watch all those detective shows? CSI? Criminal Minds? Silent Witness? You know what they always talk about?" He nodded expectantly.

Dobbsy looked over at Jacko. The old man was crazy, no doubt about it. Tears were streaming down Jacko's face and his head was bobbing up and down.

"Profiles," said the old man. "It's all about profiles. That's how they catch serial killers. They look at the victims and they look at the way the killer kills them and they build up a profile.

Like the Yorkshire Ripper. He killed hookers in Leeds. Or that Fred West. He killed young girls. Once the cops work out the profile it helps them narrow down the list of suspects. That was my epiphany. If I kept it random, I'd never fit a profile." He chuckled. "It was easy as that. I preferred to kill young women; I mean that's only natural, isn't it? You want them pretty and you want them young. But I killed men. And middle-aged women. And pensioners. And I did it in different ways. I liked to use my hands, I always preferred it to be up close and personal, but sometimes I'd use a knife. Or a hammer. Sometimes I used a tie and once I used a dog's lead. And I moved around. I never killed in the same city twice. That was my golden rule. Once I'd killed I'd move to another city. I was a chef. Well, that's what they call it nowadays. Back then I was a cook. A cook can always get work. You turn up in a town, any town, and you can get a job the next day. So that's what I did. I moved to a town, got a place to live, got a job, and wait for the urge."

He sipped his tea. "That's what it is, an urge. And the urge gets stronger and stronger until you can't resist it. The longest I ever went was three years. I had a girlfriend then and I guess that's why, but eventually the urge got the better of me. I didn't kill the girlfriend, of course. I killed a traffic warden. A black guy. Killed him with a hammer. Killed him and disposed of the body and left town."

He reached out to the collection of rings and pulled out a gold band. "This was his," said Duns. "He had a wife and six kids. Six, can you believe that? That's just stupid in this day and age. Even back then." He looked at the ring and shuddered and Dobbsy instinctively knew that the old man was reliving the killing.

After a few seconds Duns put the ring down. "I know that was risky, taking souvenirs. That's another way that serial killers get caught. If anyone found those rings then I'd be done for. But you need something to remind you of what you did. The cuttings aren't enough. And memories fade. But when you can hold something that was physically there when you did it, then all the memories flood back. The sounds, the smells, the feelings." He shuddered again.

Duns took another sip of tea, then put down the mug and slowly turned the pages of the album. He found a newspaper cutting from The Sun. TRAFFIC WARDEN KNIFED. The old man tapped the cutting. "I stabbed him in the neck and stayed to watch him die. I didn't bother trying to hide the body, he was walking down an alley in Birmingham and I came up behind him. One cut, across the throat, that's all it took. He gurgled for almost a minute before he bled out. If I hold that ring and close my eyes I can still hear the sound. Like a babbling brook."

Dobbsy strained at the washing line bonds and rocked from side to side, but even as he struggled he knew that he was wasting his time.

"I was an equal opportunity serial killer," the old man continued. "That comes down to the profile. I did two black men, and three black women. I did a Pakistani and a Chinese girl. I made sure that the cops wouldn't think that I had a type. In fact I did. I preferred young women and I preferred blondes. But I couldn't let them know that."

"The last one I killed was fifteen years ago," said the old man. He opened his eyes. "It was a girl. A shop assistant in Cardiff. I had a van. A rental. I did a Ted Bundy, put my arm in a sling and asked her to help me lift a table into the van. Tied her up and took her to a cottage I'd rented. Miles from anywhere it was. I spent three days with her. Three wonderful days. Then I strangled her with my bare hands." He held up his gnarled hands and smiled ruefully. "Couldn't do it now, of course. But back then… there's no feeling like it, boys. To put your hands around a soft, warm throat and to squeeze the life out of a girl, to watch as the eyes glaze over and the body goes still. Sarah, her name was."

He turned over the pages until he found the cutting he was looking for, and he tapped it. It was from the South Wales Echo. He held it up so that they could see a photograph of a smiling blonde girl, a sprinkling of freckles across her upturned nose. "She was lovely, was Sarah. She even said that she loved me. She didn't, of course, she was just saying that because she thought it might stop me killing her. Silly cow." He chuckled throatily.

"I cut her up in the bathroom. That's always the best way. You cut the body up into manageable bits and then you dispose of them in places where they'll never be found. Burying them is best, but you have to bury them deep. There's a knack to cutting up a body, you know that? You don't just hack away. You cut the tendons at the joints and pop the joints out. The knees, the elbows, the shoulders, the hips. That gives you eight manageable pieces right there. Then you work the spine out of the skull and the head pops off. It literally pops off. Sounds like a balloon bursting. Then all you have to worry about is the torso and there's no way around it, the torso is messy. But at the end of the day you can get any body into two small suitcases. Toss them into the boot of a car, and Bob's your uncle."

He put the album back onto the coffee table and sat looking at the photograph of Sarah. "She was a student. Studying economics. Her parents spent years looking for her. Every anniversary they go to the papers. They do that computer stuff to show what she'd look like today. But she's not getting any older. She's buried out in the Black Mountains. Buried deep."

He sighed and closed the album. It made a dull thudding sound, like a coffin lid falling into place. "Why did I stop, is that what you're thinking?" He looked at Dobbsy and Jacko in turn, nodding slowly as if they were replying.

"I got old, boys. I got slow. I lost my strength. There comes a point when you can't strangle with your bare hands and you don't have the strength to tip a body into a car boot." He grimaced. "They took my licence away four years ago. And who ever heard of a serial killer using public transport? Can't be done. I had to stop. What is it they call it? A hiatus. That's it. I'm on hiatus." He laughed without mirth. "That's why I'm so glad that you two lads popped around. I always tried to tell myself that eventually I'd get back into the saddle. But I never did. It's no fun getting old, boys." He grinned and then cackled. "Mind you, it's better than the alternative, isn't it?"

HIATUS

He scratched his bald head and frowned. "Now, where's my kit?" he muttered. He stood up, scratched his head again, and left the room.

Dobbsy and Jacko strained at their bonds but the knots held them fast.

After a few minutes, Duns returned holding a black plastic roll. He sat down, took a couple of deep breaths to steady himself, then opened the roll to reveal a dozen knives of all shapes and sizes. "This was my play kit," he said. His eyes sparkled as he stared at the knives. "I put this together after my tenth. A hooker in Durham. I knifed her but she bled out so quickly that it took the fun out of it. I used a kitchen knife, you see. It was too big. Went straight through a major artery and she was dead in seconds. I realised then that I was a professional and that, like all professionals, I needed to use the right tools."

He pulled out a knife with a serrated edge, studied it and then put it back. "Too much blood," he muttered to himself. "Better to start small."

He looked over at the two boys. "You need your strength, of course, to be a killer. You have to be able to overpower your victim and control them. And the older you get, the weaker your muscles become." He shrugged. "It's just the way it is. And you shrink. Did you know that? I'm three inches shorter than I was when I was in my prime. Everything shrinks, except your ears. They keep growing, even after you're dead. An undertaker told me that once."

He sighed. "You know, I was thinking of ending it myself. A small nick in the jugular, that's all that it would take. But you boys, you've given me a reason to live. Really. I can't thank you enough for that."

He took out a scalpel and smiled at it as if it were an old friend. He ran the blade slowly across his thumb and then jumped as it pierced the skin. Blood blossomed over his thumb and he put it to his mouth and sucked on it like a feeding baby. He held up his injured thumb so that they could see it. "Look at that. That's as sharp as a blade gets."

He stood up slowly and steadied himself. "Right, let's get started. You can scream all you want, I enjoy it so much more when you scream. And beg." He smiled. "And just so you know, it's going to hurt you a lot more than it hurts me." He chuckled at his own joke. "That was my catchphrase, towards the end. That's what I always said just before I started torturing them." He laughed again, and then shuddered. "I just want you two lads to know how much this means to me, you coming around like this. You've made an old man very happy."

He licked his lips and walked towards Dobbsy, swishing the scalpel back and forth, a hungry look in his cold, blue eyes.

HETMAN: DONETSK CALLING
By Alex Shaw

Kyiv, Ukraine

Brian Webb swayed as he hailed a taxi. It was the early hours of the morning and he'd been drinking since that evening. The heat of the day had long since given way to the chill of the night. Webb shivered in his short-sleeved shirt and cargo shorts.

Within seconds a battered, yellow *Daewoo, Nubira*, pulled into the curb. The driver lowered the front passenger window and then, with a price agreed-upon, Webb climbed into the back. It was four a.m. as they sped along the all but deserted city streets. Even by his standards this had been a late night, Webb chuckled to himself. Life was good. He had a great life in *Kyiv*, a great wife and a great daughter. What more could he want? He let his eyelids drop as the taxi moved from tarmac to cobbles and headed downhill toward the *Dnipro River*. The vibration made his stomach wobble and his head nod.

Webb had arrived in Ukraine in October 1997 with only four words of Russian, *Da, Niet, Babushka,* and *Vodka*, and had somehow managed not only to survive, but to thrive. Not passing for a local with his thick Yorkshire accent, but being accepted as one by his neighbours, he would be sad to be leaving his adopted home.

He opened his eyes as the taxi crossed the river, and he wound down the window slightly, breathing in the river-cooled air. His eyes met those of the driver, who quickly looked away. The man seemed to be in no mood to talk. The taxi continued on across the bridge, through Hydropark and then onto *Levo Berezna* – Kyiv's left bank, when it abruptly pulled in at the side of the road.

Webb sat forward and looked around. It wasn't his street. The driver quickly got out and walked away. Slowed by alcohol, Webb remained seated for several seconds before he realised that something was wrong. He hauled his bulk out of the car and leant against the door. As Webb stared at the driver, the man looked back, and then broke into a run. Webb heard footsteps behind and turned around. It was then that he saw them, illuminated in the eerie glow of the streetlights. A group of four large men was heading directly for him. Webb watched, mesmerised, for a moment before his eyes focused on the baseball bats two of them were carrying.

The nearest figure pointed at him, and then the group broke into a run. Webb felt his pulse quicken. He was defenceless. He looked down and saw that the keys to the taxi were still in the ignition. Without giving it a second thought he clambered into the driver's seat, took the hand brake off, and spun the taxi away from the curb. He heard shouts and then a loud crack as something hit the rear of the taxi. Webb's heart started to beat raggedly; it felt as though it was trying to escape from his chest. He forced the Daewoo to accelerate away, and squinted to focus on the road ahead. He was now sweating, his hands wet on the wheel. He chanced a look back and saw that there were lights behind him now, following him. What was happening, why was he being chased? Webb had no idea.

He shot through a set of traffic lights, narrowly missing a large tanker. He knew the roads now, he wasn't too far from home but he couldn't lead them there. The road swung in and out of focus as the alcohol refused to leave his system. Webb was heavy on the controls, and the car jerked as he downshifted to negotiate a bend. He clipped a parked car with his wing mirror, the glass shattering as it was ripped off. The chase lights he now saw belonged to a large BMW and were getting closer. His breathing became heavier. Thoughts raced through his mind; who were they…what did they want…? He reached the highway that bisected the *Harkivskiy Massif* district and saw, lit-up by the neon lights of the *Billa Supermarket* signage, a *Lada, Samara*, with militia markings. Webb aimed for it. As he slowed and drew near he saw that it was empty. Webb banged his fist on the wheel in frustration and was about to curse when there was a loud crack and something pinged off the Daewoo. He ducked. He had never heard gunfire before but instantly realised that was what the noise had been.

Whoever was chasing him had started to shoot! He floored the accelerator. The Daewoo jerked forward, cresting the curb and across the car-park, before bouncing over the grass verge and back onto the tarmac. A grating noise started to come from the front suspension as Webb thrashed the car back up the gears. He saw a gap in the central reservation, snapped the steering wheel to the left and crossed to the other side of the road, changing direction. He urged the taxi to go faster; he had to get away. The Daewoo started to vibrate angrily as it reached the 100k mark. He wiped the sweat from his brow. There were a few more cars about now as he continued along the main road back towards the river. He looked in the rear-view mirror but couldn't see anyone following him. He let out a deep breath and relaxed slightly as the adrenalin started to leave his system.

It was now almost five a.m. and a wave of tiredness rolled over him. His eyes closed…the Daewoo violently shook and bucked. Webb's eyes snapped open. He had driven off the road. Too late to avoid the bus stop, Webb folded his arms in front of his face. His head hit hard and he blacked out.

Webb tried to understand where he was as the world swum back into focus. He slithered out of the crumpled car. His eyes stung. He wiped them with his hands and saw blood now covering his palms. Pulling a handkerchief out of his pocket, he dabbed at his eyes again. Webb looked back and saw that the passenger side of the car had been concertinaed, taking the brunt of the impact. He was lucky to be alive. It was a Saturday morning, and the pavement was still mostly empty as he tried to walk. His left ankle gave way, and he all but fell. He hobbled from the scene of the accident, still not knowing what to do. On the other side of the road he saw a large dark blue BMW saloon stop. Two men got out and started to run across the road, dodging the light traffic whilst the car moved off again looking for somewhere to cross. Webb took a deep breath, put his head down and tried to run.

He was fifty-six, overweight and drunk…and the pain in his foot was excruciating, but he managed to move. He loped away from the road and toward the nearest block of flats. Reaching the monolithic high rise, he clambered up the five steps to the entrance hall and went straight out of the other side. He was in a courtyard created by four apartment blocks facing each other. In the middle there was a small children's play area. He bumped past the slide and into the entrance hall of the next block. The building was very much like his. He called the lift, was surprised to see it worked, and sent it to the top floor as he ducked around the side of the lift-shaft and hid in the shadows by the entrance to the maintenance room. He hunched over, panting. All was quiet apart from the sound of his chest heaving. He vomited as waves of pain roared through his body. He couldn't go home; he couldn't go to the militia. He had no other choice; there was only one person who could help, one man he knew who would not let him down. He pulled out his old Nokia and called Aidan Snow.

Worthing, United Kingdom.

Aidan Snow slowed his pace as he felt his Blackberry vibrate in his zip pocket. He retrieved the device and saw that it was an incoming call from one of his closest friends; a friend, however, he had not seen for too long. Snow answered the call and started to walk.

"Brian Webb, how are you?"

"Aidan, is that you?"

"Er, yes. Don't tell me you're pissed already? What time is it in Kyiv, eight a.m.?"

Webb's voice was rushed and his breathing laboured. "Aidan, I need your help, I don't know what to do – they are threatening me and the family."

Snow stopped and placed his right foot on a bench to stretch his hamstrings. "Brian, take a breath and tell me what's happening?"

"Aidan, I've got to keep moving they've found me..." Webb stopped talking abruptly and Snow could hear raised voices at the other end, and banging.

"Brian. Brian, are you still there?"

"Aidan, can you come to Kyiv? Can you get here quickly? I need you to help..."

"Brian...Brian!"

As Snow looked out to sea he could hear Brian speaking to someone, then he heard a yell and what sounded like a crashing sound. Suddenly a deep voice came on the phone and asked in Russian, "Who is this?"

Snow replied in English. "Is Brian there?"

The voice switched to heavily accented English. "Yes." The line went dead.

Snow redialled and the call went to voicemail, Brian's voicemail. "Brian, call me when you can." Snow looked up Brian's home number, hoped it hadn't changed and dialled. He let it ring for a minute before disconnecting. Snow frowned; he could count his number of true friends on one hand and Brian was one of them. Brian now owned a chain of English language bookshops in Kyiv, but it had been before this that Snow had met him. They had both been teaching at the same international school and Snow was the 'new boy.' Brian had taken Snow under his wing. The Yorkshireman was twenty years Snow's senior but the age gap had not made a jot of difference especially, to Brian's pretty wife Katya who was younger than Snow. He had never heard the happy Yorkshireman speak like that before. Still carrying the guilt of failing to save a friend years before, Snow had vowed never to let it happen again. Snow dialed his boss's number.

"Patchem" a voice said after four rings.

"It's Aidan, sorry for calling you this early on a Saturday."

Jack Patchem, Snow's controller at the Secret Intelligence Service (SIS) also sounded out of breath. "Not at all. Okay, I'm listening."

"Jack, I need to take a few days off, some of that holiday time I'm owed."

"You are asking for a holiday?"

"No something's come up, a personal matter."

On the golf course, Patchem raised his eyebrows. "Anything that I should know about?"

"No. I just need to help a friend out."

"So from the timing of this call I expect you need it immediately? Yes?"

"Yes."

"Go, but make sure you can get back if I need you."

"Thanks." Snow ended the call and then tried both of Brian's numbers again.

Snow put his Blackberry back into his zip pocket and ran the remaining mile home along the promenade. Back indoors, he quickly purchased a ticket online for the next flight to Kyiv, which on this occasion happened to be with Ukraine International Airlines, before taking a quick shower. Dressed in khaki combats, dark blue polo shirt and a pair of UK Gear PT1000s; he collected his grab-bag before leaving the house and rapidly driving to Gatwick.

Gatwick Airport, United Kingdom

Ukraine International Airlines flight 502 would not get Snow to Kyiv until late afternoon, but was the earliest available. Snow had been forced to pay a premium for a business class seat, but money was not on his mind. What was bothering him was Brian Webb and what may or may not have happened to him. He again tried both of Brian's phone numbers but to no avail. He'd spent the three hours he'd had to wait until his flight boarded snoozing in the business lounge, and reading the latest Stephen Leather

Spider Shepherd thriller. Now as they took off, he found himself sitting next to a businessman in a tight-fitting suit. After the pre-flight drinks were served, Snow's neighbour, who'd ordered a double Scotch, introduced himself.

"Cheers! Donald Bass, Don to my friends."

Snow tried not to let his amusement at the man's name show. "Aidan Snow."

"Nice to meet you. I know it's a cliché but business or pleasure?"

"Personal."

"Not internet dating? I've heard the women there are quite tasty!"

"They are, but I'm just going to help a friend. I used to live there."

"I've never been. I'm meeting my Ukrainian business partner. He owns a few bars but now wants to open a fish-and-chip shop." Bass handed Snow a business card. "Yep, that's my shop, *Bass' Plaice*. Do you think the locals will understand the pun, you know, my name being a type of fish. and 'fish's fish'?"

Snow shrugged. It was a daft name. "Does it matter?"

Bass shook his head. "Not to me, I'm now selling the franchise internationally."

"I think it will do well."

"Do you mind if I pick your brain?"

"No." Snow was glad of the distraction.

"Is it Kiev or Kyiv? Look this newspaper is *The Kyiv Post* but my guidebook says *Kiev*."

Snow remembered when 'The Kyiv Post' was 'The Kiev Post' but did not want to confuse issues. "Kiev is a translation from Russian but 'Kyiv' is from the Ukrainian."

"Oh. So what should I try to speak?"

"You can use either in Kyiv but Ukrainian is the official language."

Bass pointed at the paper. "But this report says that they have passed a law granting Russian second-language status."

"In the East the majority of the population is of Russian descent, so they prefer to speak Russian. And because the President is from the East he wants Russian to be used more. It's his first language."

"So it's a bit like Wales then? In Cardiff they speak English but go north and it's all *Yaki-da*?"

"Yes."

"I get you. It mentions here, *Bandits from Donetsk*. Are there a lot of mafia types in Kyiv? Should I be worried?"

"I lived there for a few years and never saw any trouble," Snow lied, but then his experience of Ukraine had not been usual. "In the early nineties they had problems of course but that all got worked out. Kyiv is very safe; the new President has brought his cronies in from the East. But as a foreign businessman, they'll welcome you. At the end of the day people are people, regardless of where they are from or what language they speak."

"That's true. So what are the women like?"

"Most of them have two legs."

Bass started to laugh noisily as the cabin crew delivered their safety demonstration and then readied themselves for take-off. As soon as the plane levelled out, Bass ordered another double scotch and before long, fell asleep. Snow tried to doze again but his mind was too troubled.

Levo Berezna, Kyiv, Ukraine

Snow paid the taxi driver and climbed the stairs to the entrance of Brian Webb's apartment block. As usual the Soviet-era building was grimy and smelt vaguely of rubbish. Snow pressed the lift button, hoping that it worked.

Brian had once joked that he lived in a penthouse. His flat may well have been on the eighteenth floor but it was certainly no penthouse. With a jolt the lift doors opened, and Snow was jerkily taken to the top floor. As the doors closed Snow turned left and found the correct flat. He pressed the bell, which sounded like a strange kind of Chinese bird, and waited. The door remained closed. He listened, heard nothing, and then rang again.

There were noises from inside, and then it was suddenly pulled open. Snow could not help but smile at the vision of Katya dripping wet, clad in nothing but a bath towel. He still had no clue how Brian had pulled her.

"Aidan!" Her frown turned to a smile, and she stepped forward and hugged him.

"Katya." He dropped his holdall. He could feel her curves through the thin towel and had to remind himself that, although she was gorgeous, she was his friend's wife.

She moved away and looked up at him. "You look good. Come in."

"Thanks, so do you."

She smiled mischievously, and as she turned, he caught a flash of her bum as the towel rose up. Snow closed the door and followed her into the lounge. She sat and lit a cigarette.

"Is Brian here?" Snow thought he already knew the answer but had to ask.

Katya exhaled angrily. "No, he's bloody not."

In any other circumstance Snow would have laughed at Katya's use of language, clearly influenced by her husband. "Do you know where he is?"

She shrugged. "He was meant to pick us up from the central railway station this morning. We had to drag our bags to the taxi rank." She noticed Snow was frowning. "We went to *Yalta* for a week, Vika and me. You remember Vika?"

Snow nodded. She had big breasts, and Brian had a nickname for her, which Snow wouldn't repeat. "So he wasn't with you and he didn't turn up at the station?"

"Yes. Aidan, what's wrong, what are you doing here? I haven't seen you since after..."

"Arnaud was killed? It's okay; it's been four years. Look, Brian called me this morning and said he was in trouble, I've never heard him speak like that."

Katya now seemed more concerned than angry. "He's not come home some nights when he's been out drinking. Euro 2012 was awful; he met up with a group of England fans and Michael Jones, well, you know Michael. I just thought that he'd done the same. I thought you were him at the door. Do you think something has happened to him?"

"That's what I'm going to find out."

"You are a good friend, Aidan, for coming here."

They were both startled by the doorbell. Katya looked at Snow. He nodded and made for the door. He looked through the peephole and saw two men in uniform. He sensed something was not quite right; he put the chain on and opened the door.

"Hello, can I help you?"

The two officers reminded Snow of Laurel and Hardy, and looked a little confused by being faced by a foreigner. The nearer and much thinner of the two spoke. "Is Webb, Katya at home?" he asked in Russian before adding in English, "Please."

Snow continued to play the dumb foreign visitor. He did not want to let on that he spoke Russian fluently. "You want Katya, *da*?"

"*Da*."

"Okay." Snow called back into the flat, "Katya, the police are here and want to speak to you. I don't understand, as I don't speak Ukrainian." He was telling the truth, Russian was different enough.

Katya looked at Snow, eyebrows raised but made no comment. She had pulled on a long t-shirt dress. "*Tak?*" 'Yes' - she asked in Ukrainian.

Stan Laurel persisted with Russian and said, "Can we come in?"

"What is this about?" Katya too now used Russian.

"Your husband," Oliver Hardy stated.

"Come in."

Snow stepped aside as the two uniformed men entered the flat. They all went into the lounge. Katya took up her previous seat and lit a new cigarette.

"Who is this?" Oliver Hardy the older, more senior officer asked as he tilted his head towards Snow.

"A family friend. Now what is this about?"

"Your husband has been taken to our station for questioning." It was Stan Laurel, the younger officer again.

"About what?"

The older officer took over, and Snow wondered if this was an attempt at *good-cop bad-cop*. "He has been identified as being at the scene of a very serious incident. We need you to tell us where he was yesterday."

"What kind of incident?"

"I am afraid that until we have investigated further, I cannot tell you any more."

"What kind of answer is that?" Katya's face flashed with anger. "I demand you tell me why you are holding him!"

"It really would be in your own best interests to answer the question." The younger officer smiled, as did Snow.

"Where was he yesterday?"

"He was here."

"With you?"

"No."

Oliver Hardy looked confused. "Where were you?"

"Yalta."

"So how do you know he was here?"

"I called him."

He nodded and pointed to the house phone. "On that number?"

"Yes, I mean, no. I called his mobile."

"And he said he was here?"

"Yes." She could feel herself starting to redden.

"So how do you know he was really here?"

Snow cut in, still using English. "Anyone for tea, or coffee or perhaps *Sto Gram* of vodka?"

"Ask him to be quiet, please," the older officer asked Katya.

"Do it yourself."

He didn't. Stan Laurel pointed at Snow. "Mister, quiet please."

Snow smiled, the officer now sounded more like a young, homosexual *Borat*. "Oh, sorry."

"So how do you know he was here or not?" the older officer persisted.

Katya did not reply straight away but let the smoke flow out of her mouth. "Have you informed the British Embassy that you have arrested my husband?"

"He has not been arrested."

"So he is free to leave?"

"No."

"I don't understand."

The older officer abruptly stood. "It is difficult. He is being questioned."

Katya stood and stabbed her finger in the man's direction. "I demand you let him go."

The officer's face changed, and Snow sensed that violence might be on his mind. "You are in no position to make any demands! In fact I may have to arrest you for obstructing a police investigation."

"Please just answer our questions," the younger officer pleaded.

Snow stood and readied himself for a physical confrontation. "So how many was that for tea? Milk and sugar?"

"Shut up!" the older officer spat in Russian. "Now, tell me do you know where your husband was yesterday?"

"He said he was here."

Oliver Hardy seemed to relax and looked at his colleague and nodded. "That is all for now, but we will need to come back if we have any more questions. Your husband's situation is serious."

"When can I see him?"

"We will let you know." Both militia officers headed for the door. Snow gladly let them out.

Katya shook her head in despair and lit another cigarette. "I mean what the fuck? What is happening? What is this all about? Aidan, do you understand anything?"

Snow put his arms around her. "Look, you and I both know that Brian is harmless, he's a lover not a fighter."

Katya snorted. "He's not a lover either."

Snow ignored the insinuation. "At least we now know where he is. I'll go to the Embassy. I have contacts there, and if they aren't going to charge him, I'll get him out."

Katya started to cry. "Thank you, Aidan. I'm scared. Can you stay here with me?"

Snow looked down at her. "I've got to see a few people, but yes, afterwards I'll come back and stay here. Get a pen and write down my number, just in case."

"Okay." She smiled and moved away.

Snow had a thought. Brian and Katya's daughter was nowhere to be seen. "Where's Ana?"

"Summer camp." Katya replied as she returned from the kitchen clutching a pen and a Post-it note.

Snow scribbled down his number. After they had finished there was a moment of silence. Katya spoke first. "Aidan, I'm scared."

"I know. It's a scary thing to happen, but wait here. Don't open the door or speak to anyone. I'll be back as soon as I can. Call me if you get worried or if anyone unexpected turns up. Okay?"

"Okay."

Snow kissed her on the forehead and left the flat.

Volodymyrska Street, Kyiv

Alistair Vickers enjoyed relaxing in the bath. He had a CD of *Bruch's Violin Concerto No. 1 in G minor* playing as he luxuriated with a very expensive glass of Ukrainian cognac. It was early Saturday evening; and for once he had decided to cocoon himself from the world and its worries; his phone was off, and he had no intention of answering the door. He found nowadays that he generally preferred his own company in his down time. Running with the *Kyiv Hash House Harriers,* or going to the ex-pat hangouts was fun, but more and more it left him feeling empty. If he had been asked years ago where he would have seen himself at the age of forty-five, he would have said living in suburbia or some such foreign equivalent with a wife and two-point-four children, yet here he was, single and inebriated, sitting in a bath.

Vickers smiled. He mustn't allow himself to get depressed; that had been a side effect of the painkillers he had become addicted to after being attacked by a Belarusian assassin. No he must just relax and stop trying to explain his unbelievable lightness of being. He half-smiled. Life was good; his life was good.

Alistair Vickers was the SIS intelligence officer responsible for Ukraine. He closed his eyes but reminded himself that he mustn't fall asleep in the tub, lest he become a second Whitney Houston.

He snapped his eyes open. The bath water was cold, the CD had ended, and there was a ringing at his front door. He dragged his tired body out of the bath, pulled on a dark satin robe, and made for the door. He peered through the spy-hole and couldn't believe who he was looking at.

Snow removed his finger from the bell as the door opened. He shook his head; for the second time that day he was being greeted by someone in an advanced state of undress. "Alistair, you needn't have bothered getting dolled-up for me."

"Very droll. Come in."

Without being bid to do so, Snow made for the kitchen and started to make himself a coffee. "I thought you would know I was here already?"

"On a work day maybe, but my phone is off, and so is my computer. So, to what do I owe this unexpected pleasure?"

"Brian Webb is being held by the police."

Vickers sat at the kitchen table. "What for?"

Snow shrugged. "I don't know; the militia wouldn't say."

"And how do you know this?"

"Coffee?"

"No I'm fine."

Snow added boiling water to his cup and stirred. "I was at his flat when the militia came to question Katya." Snow sat and explained the events of the day thus far.

Vickers nodded. "If they haven't charged him, they have to let him go, *habeas corpus* and all that, unless the militia has reason to believe it's related to terrorism."

"The only things Brian terrorises are the local bars."

Vickers nodded at Snow's truism. Brian Webb was the biggest ex-pat boozer, possibly in the whole of Ukraine. His marriage to Katya had initially seemed to steady him somewhat. "You want me to go to the militia station and petition for his release, or at least get a clarification of his charges?"

"Alistair, you are not just a pretty face."

Vickers shook his head. "Fine. Let me get a suit on, and then you can tell me which regional station he's in."

"Thanks, I owe you one."

"It's my job, just get me a bottle of the good stuff and we'll be even."

As Vickers left the room to dress, Snow went onto the balcony and looked at the street below. He missed Kyiv, he missed his old life, but most of all he missed the friendships. For tuppence ha'penny he'd quit the SIS and teach again. He'd happily swap his licence to kill for a contract to teach.

"Let's go." Vickers looked imposing in a dark blue, Savile Row suit, bespoke brogues and an 'old boy' public school tie.

Snow nodded his approval. "You scrub-up well for a dustman."

"Aidan, as always I appreciate your honest feedback." He tossed Snow the keys to his diplomatic Land Rover Defender. "You drive, I've had a few."

Berezniki Rayon, Kyiv

Snow parked the Rover in front of the *Berezniki Rayon* militia station and Vickers got out. They had decided that Snow would stay with the car; him potentially being seen by the same two officers who had questioned Katya earlier would raise questions. Snow opened a can of *burn* energy drink and observed the lives passing by.

Vickers entered the militia station and was greeted by the desk officer berating an elderly woman. She was pleading with him to let her son go, as he was innocent, but the officer would have none of it. In an angry voice, and using no uncertain terms, he told her to get lost. She left, talking to herself. The desk officer looked up from his papers and was surprised, to say the least, to see Vickers standing in front of him. His mouth creased up a little as he asked, "Can I help?"

"Yes." Vickers answered in Ukrainian. Like Snow he was a fluent Russian speaker, and unlike Snow, he had also started to learn the real language of the country he lived in, Ukrainian. "My name is Alistair Vickers. I am the Commercial Attaché at the British Embassy and I believe you are holding a British citizen without the due authority."

The militia officer's mouth dropped open and he struggled for words. This was the third Englishman he had met in the last twelve hours, but unlike Webb and the annoying one at Webb's apartment this one had some authority. The officer started to panic. "Wha...What is the name of this Englishman?"

"Brian Webb."

The official swallowed. "I see." He stared at his computer and wished it would engulf him. "He was here but he has now been transferred."

"What?" Vickers started to ham-it-up. "Has Mr. Webb been charged with anything?"

Again the official looked, too hard, at his computer screen. "No. Not yet but he is being questioned in relation to a serious incident."

"Which is?"

"I'm sorry I can't say."

When Snow had approached Vickers earlier, Vickers had thought this all to be a commotion over nothing. A drunken episode perhaps that had done no real harm, but now he was starting to feel that something indeed was not as it should be. "So correct me if I am wrong. Mr. Webb is being held, but not here, for something that you say he may have been involved with, but that same something, you cannot confirm to me the nature of. Correct?"

The officer paused, confused. "Yes, that is so."

"So where is he now?"

The officer again checked his screen. "He is under the authority of Captain Budt."

"Now we are getting somewhere. Where is Captain Budt?"

"In transit with the prisoner."

"But Mr. Webb has not been charged."

"But sexual assault is a serious matter."

"So are you confirming to me that Mr. Brian Webb is being accused of sexual assault?"

The militia officer had been forced into a corner and had made a mistake. "No, not at this time, but perhaps."

"So where is Mr. Webb in transit to?"

"I am sorry, I cannot say."

"What is your name, officer?"

"*Brovchenko, Yuri.*"

"Well, Officer Brovchenko, first thing on Monday morning, if Mr. Webb does not reappear, or is not released, I shall be lodging a complaint with the head of the city militia and the Ministry of Internal Affairs. Am I making myself understood, Yuri?"

Brovchenko nodded. "Yes."

"Good. Goodbye."

Snow watched Vickers leave the militia station and was irked to see he was alone. Vickers climbed into the Land Rover, the look on his face showed confusion. Snow asked, "Where's Brian?"

"That's the thing, they won't tell me."

"What? I don't get it."

"Drive and I'll explain."

Snow shook his head after Vickers repeated the conversation and said, "Have you ever heard of this happening before?"

"Never. That is what's so strange. He is guaranteed access to a representative from the Embassy, yet we weren't informed, and now he has been moved without being charged." Vickers massaged the bridge of his nose between his thumb and forefinger. He had the start of a headache. "There's nothing more I can do until Monday morning. Where are you staying?"

"At Brian's flat with Katya."

Vickers removed his hand from his face and looked at Snow. "Isn't she that sexy one with the..."

"Yes and she is also my friend's wife."

"Good, just as long as you remember."

Snow rolled his eyes. "Who do you take me for – Mitch Turney?"

"No." Vickers laughed. Their mutual friend had a well-deserved reputation as a womaniser. "Are you going to give him a call?"

"I should, and Michael Jones. They may have been with Webb yesterday."

The two SIS operatives arrived back at Vickers' apartment building. Unlike Webb's 1980's monstrosity on the city's left bank, this building had architectural worth and character. All its occupants were expatriates. Snow turned off the engine and handed Vickers the keys. "So I'll call you first thing on Monday?"

"Agreed."

"Thanks."

They got out of the car.

"Aidan, if he is implicated in sexual assault, then you know we both have to distance ourselves from him, don't you?"

"I know, but he's not."

"I just know of him, but you know him, so I'll bow to your better judgement."

Vickers waved as he entered his building.

Khreshatik Street, Kyiv

Snow headed for Kyiv's main shopping street, *Khreshatik*, and his meeting with Michael Jones. Jones had been only too happy to get away from his wife, Inna, and catch-up with his old drinking partner. As Snow walked, he suddenly realised that he had not eaten since lunch on the aeroplane some hours before, or indeed had much to drink. The temperature was still in the high twenties; a whole fifteen degrees higher than it had been in Worthing. Snow used the underpass to cross from one side of the wide street to the other and then entered the large McDonalds that stood on top of the Metro station. It had been Jones' choice of meeting place. Even after years in Ukraine, the Welshman remained fussy about what he ate unless he'd cooked it himself. The eatery was fairly busy with a few families, but mostly twenty- and thirty-somethings chatting and flirting or taking advantage of the free Wi-Fi.

A figure waved from a large, semi-circular seat. Snow couldn't help but smile at seeing his old friend. Michael Jones had not changed a bit. With his craggy features and dark blonde hair he looked like the drinking man's Gordon Ramsey.

"Aidan, *hokay?*" The Welshman's accent caused a couple of diners to stare.

Snow adopted a Welsh accent. "Hallo Meester Jones, how are you?"

"Eh, not bad," Jones beamed. "Just look at the crumpet in here!"

They sat and Snow laughed out loud. Jones had never been subtle. "It's good to see you Michael."

"You too. It's been far too long. You teaching again?"

Jones knew of Snow's military past, that he had been a member of the SAS, and, of course, the events that had led to the death of their mutual friend Arnaud. Jones did not, however, know that since then Snow had been recruited into the Secret Intelligence Service.

Snow decided to stick with his legend. "I'm teaching at a private school near Knightsbridge."

"Full of Arabs, I bet."

"Not politically correct, but correct."

Jones raised his eyebrows and the tone of his voice to express mock outrage. "Politically incorrect? Politically incorrect! As a native Welsh speaker, I'm an ethnic minority myself!"

It was good to see his friend again, but he had to move things on.

But Michael sensed Snow becoming serious. "So what's all this about Brian?"

"He called me this morning asking for help, I got here to find he's being held by the police for sexual assault."

"Brian? Sexual assault? GBH – grievous beer harm, I could envisage, but sexual assault?" Jones' Welsh intonation rose at the end.

"Only that's not all." Snow then explained the visit to the militia station.

"So where is he?"

Snow shrugged. "They won't say, just that he is in the custody of an officer named Budt."

"It's the bandits from *Donetsk*, mark my words."

"When was the last time you saw him?"

"Yesterday. We started off in the Dockers Pub – you know the new name for 'The Cowboy Bar' and then onto Arena."

"And nothing happened?"

Jones shook his head. "Mitch was with us, but he went home with a tart from his office. Inna ordered me to come home, and the last I saw of Brian, he was getting into a taxi."

"What time was this?"

Jones frowned. "Dunno, maybe three-ish? You know how it is."

Snow nodded. In his day, the drinking sessions usually ended in the small hours. "Is Mitch around?"

"No, he flew back to the US this morning to see his kids and ex-wife."

Snow felt his stomach rumble and stole a fry from Jones' tray. "None of this makes sense."

"Correction, none of it would make sense in the UK. Here it makes perfect sense; someone is after a *Vziatka*."

"A bribe?" Something clicked in Snow's mind and things became a little clearer.

"For sure. Look at the time I got stopped without my passport back in the days when you needed a visa. Even though I had a photocopy on me, they wanted $100. The next day they came to the flat and saw Inna. She told them to piss off because she knew their boss."

"I hope you're right, Michael. But we still have to find out where he is." Snow felt his Blackberry vibrate. He retrieved it from his pocket and looked at the number displayed. It was Brian's flat. He accepted the call. "Katya?"

"Aidan, the militia came back – I pretended not to be in. They were banging the door."

"I'm on my way."

Her voice almost broke as she asked, "Is Brian with you?"

"No. I'm sorry; I'll explain when I see you." He cut the connection and looked at Jones. "Gotta go."

Snow stood at the side of the road and stretched his arm out. A beat-up Volkswagen saloon immediately swung in from the early evening traffic and came to an abrupt stop in front of him. As was common practice, it wasn't a legitimate taxi, but a *Kyivite* taking the chance to make bit extra. Snow gave the driver the address, and in return the driver stated an inflated price. Snow was in no mood to haggle, agreed to the price and jumped in. Twenty minutes later, he was outside Webb's building; he called Katya again and let her know that he was on his way up. Two minutes after that she opened the door.

"Are you okay?" He asked.

She nodded and looked over his shoulder expectantly. "Where's Brian?"

"I don't know. The militia have moved him. Let's get inside."

She shut the door and bolted it. "Where is my husband?"

"I don't know. They wouldn't say but my friend at the Embassy has threatened to make an official complaint if Brian is not released or charged by Monday."

Katya folded her arms, and prepared herself for the worst. "What are they going to charge him with?"

"Let's sit down first."

"Bollocks, Aidan just tell me. Please."

"Sexual assault."

Katya backed away into the kitchen and raised her hand to her mouth, stifling a laugh. Snow couldn't tell if it was nerves or if she actually found it funny. "He can barely assault me."

"Tell me what happened here, with the militia?"

"The same two officers came back. They rang the bell, and when I didn't answer, said they knew I was in. They then banged on the door for a few minutes and said that I couldn't help Brian if I didn't let them in. Aidan, I thought they were going to break the door down."

"I doubt that they would have done that. You did the right thing."

"Are you hungry?"

Snow was, but didn't want to make her cook. "If you're going to eat then I will."

"Stop being so bloody English." Katya pointed at a chair. "Sit. Eat. And take your shoes off."

Snow looked down, first at his trainers and then at a bowl of *borscht* that had been awaiting his arrival. "Thanks, and sorry."

She sat opposite him and held her hands together tightly. "Aidan, I'm scared."

"Katya, I think I know why they have Brian, well, sort of."

"I don't understand. What do you mean?"

"We both know that Brian wouldn't sexually assault anyone, so what are they holding him for? A bribe. Think about it. He's got his own company, Okay, he lives here, but I know he's worth a bit. Or at least he used to be."

"What's wrong with my flat?"

"It's very nice."

"Aidan, I know it's shit so don't try and put spaghetti on my ears." She pushed a plastic pot towards him. "*Smetana?*"

"Thanks." Snow ladled the sour cream into his soup. "So someone has been watching and has decided that Brian needs to pay to operate here."

"Then they have chosen the wrong person. Brian has never once paid for a Krisha, and he won't start now."

Snow ate his soup and thought in silence. The Krisha Katya referred to was the roof, the protection offered by one mafia gang against attacks or threats by others, and in some cases, protection against the militia and tax police. "Well this is the most logical answer, unless of course it's a misunderstanding or a case of mistaken identity."

"Or he's guilty." Katya managed a smile. "Which he's not. So what can we do now?"

"We have until Monday for official channels to do anything, but I think that we'll be contacted before that with a demand."

Katya frowned and shook her head. "Doesn't this mean he's been kidnapped?"

Snow hadn't thought about it like that. "That's one way of looking at it." He finished his borscht, and pushed the plate away.

"More?"

"No, I'm full."

Katya stood, collected her cigarettes and moved onto the balcony. Snow washed his plate and spoon in the sink then joined her. The view of the city was quite something and worth more than the flat itself. It was one of only a few flats in the complex that still retained an unobstructed sightline to the river and the distant city beyond. As the summer evening gently lost its light, the air seemed to glow with both the heat of the day and the myriad of windows reflecting it.

"Screw me."

"What?"

"Aidan, I want you to screw me." She reached for his belt.

"Katya stop." He placed his hands over hers.

"Don't you want to?"
"How can I answer that?"
"Don't you fancy me?"
"Of course I do, I always have."
"But?"
"You are the wife of one of my closest friends."
"Just because I want to have sex with you does not mean that I don't love Brian. And besides he'll never know."
"But I will." He looked into her eyes; she raised her eyebrow suggestively. "No. I'm sorry and believe me I'm regretting turning you down already."
"You really are a knight in shining armour coming to the rescue?"
"Yes, and my lance is staying locked up."
She laughed and pulled her hands away. "Tart."
"What?"
"I have some tart, would you like some?" Before Snow could answer the doorbell rang, and then there was the sound of heavy banging. "It's them."
"Okay, talk to them through the peep-hole, I'll stand by your side. Then we'll decide what to do. Agreed?"
"Agreed."
They moved towards the front door as the ringing and banging continued, now joined by the sound of, "Militia, open the door."
"What do you want?" Katya asked.
"Open the door. We have some questions that you need to answer. It will help your husband." Oliver Hardy's voice was slurred. "You surely don't want us to conduct our business on the doorstep? Do you want your neighbours to know what your husband had done?"
Snow touched Katya's arm. "Let them in. I'll wait behind the door in the kitchen. I'll be ready if you need me."
"But Aidan, they may hurt me."
"If they do, I'll kill them."
Katya looked at Snow and saw on his face an expression she hadn't seen before. "Okay."

Outside the officer shouted again, "Come one now Madam Webb, let us in so we can discuss the criminal activity of your husband."

She took a deep breath and opened the door. "Come in."

Oliver Hardy leered at her and walked directly into the lounge whilst Stan Laurel removed his cap and smiled weakly. They both sat on the settee. Katya remained standing, arms folded.

"What kind of hospitality is this? You have not offered us a drink!" the older officer barked. Katya could tell he'd been drinking. Snow could hear it in his voice, too, and knew it would make him volatile but slow. "Even your homosexual American friend who was here earlier offered me tea."

"He was English and he has manners."

"I am sure. So, Officer Brovchenko, explain to Madam Webb here the situation."

Stan Laurel swallowed hard and readied himself. "We received a report from a young lady who stated that your husband made unwarranted sexual advances to her last night. When she told him to stop he attempted to..." Brovchenko started to blush.

"Go on," goaded Hardy.

"Your husband grabbed the woman and tried to have sex with her against a wall."

Katya burst out laughing. "With his bad knee? My husband is very overweight and almost fifty-six. Let me tell you that his days of athletic fucking are long gone!"

"I think you should watch your language."

"And I think you should bring my husband to me and stop being a disgrace to your uniform! And another thing, try speaking Ukrainian, both of you!"

Hardy fought to restrain himself. "Enough! You will listen to Officer Brovchenko, or things will only get worse!"

"Please go ahead, I like fairy tales."

Brovchenko frowned. This was not going as planned. "There is no doubt from the evidence that your husband is guilty and he would be found as such by any judge. But there may be something we can do, to help."

From his hiding place Snow was praying that Katya would not provoke them anymore. All she really had to do was to listen. And that gave Snow an idea. He switched on the audio record function on his Blackberry, carefully reached around the kitchen door and placed it on the floor in the lounge.

Brovchenko looked at his colleague. "*Officer Klyuyvets*, shall I...?"

Klyuyvets held up his hand. "What my young friend is attempting to say is that the lady, the innocent victim of your husband's unprovoked attack, is willing to drop all charges, withdraw her sworn statement for financial compensation. You understand she is a student from a good family, and any publicity, while she is blameless, would tarnish her reputation."

"How much?" Katya asked.

"I believe that she would accept seventy-five thousand dollars."

"And what guarantee do I have that this goes no further?"

Klyuyvets put his hand to his heart in mock surprise. "My word, our word, Officer Brovchenko and I."

"And if we pay eighty thousand can my husband fuck her?"

Snow sighed. Katya was playing with fire.

Klyuyvets pulled himself to his feet. "Do you think this is some kind of a joke? This is a serious matter."

"It would be best for your husband and his business interests if you were to pay," added Brovchenko.

There was a ringing. Snow cursed silently. It was his Blackberry. Katya moved to collect it.

"Is someone else here?" Klyuyvets snapped.

Snow decided the time for playing hide and seek was over and stepped into the lounge.

"You again!"

"I think you should tell Mrs. Webb where her husband is before I force it out of you."

Klyuyvets almost fell over. "He speaks Russian and insults two officers of the law!"

Snow took a step forward. "Where is Brian Webb?"

"Hold out your hands, I will cuff you and take you to him. You are under arrest for attempting to assault two militia officers."

Brovchenko started to unclip his cuffs. "Please give me your wrists."

"Because your own are limp?"

Brovchenko frowned; the true meaning of the idiom did not translate from English to Russian. "No, I need to put handcuffs on you."

Klyuyvets lunged at Snow, swinging his arm. Snow adjusted his stance and stepped aside. The fat man's face contorted with rage, and he reached for his baton. Without hesitation Snow grabbed the officer's arm, turned his wrist and, using a pressure hold, pinned him to the floor. Klyuyvets grunted and struggled. Brovchenko gawped and then reached for his pistol. Snow sprang up and with one hand, pushed the trigger arm sideways whilst the other landed a punch on his jaw. The thin officer stumbled backwards and then collapsed. His head hit the floor with a heavy thud, rendering him unconscious. Snow turned to the older man who was now on his knees.

"You piece of shit!" Klyuyvets swung his baton at Snow, who stepped out of the way and kicked the officer in the head, which snapped back, rendering him too, unconscious.

"Aidan, what have you done?" Katya put her hands on her head.

He ignored Katya's question and checked both men were still breathing and that their skulls were not fractured before securing them with their own cuffs. "At least we now know what they wanted. Check their ID."

Still in a mild state of shock she did as she was told. "Ah, that's why they refused to speak Ukrainian." She pointed to a driving licence. "They are from Donetsk."

"Makes sense, new faces come in and want their share of the cake."

Katya nodded and started to rant. "Since that goat became President he's been replacing everyone with his own people. My friend's an estate agent, and she says that most of the companies renovating flats are from the East, especially the *Donbas* region. On the roads there are more and more cars with number plates starting with 'AN' – Donetsk, and can you believe this, even the supermarkets are using Eastern Ukrainian suppliers! The country is going down the toilet!"

Snow knew all of this, but did not interrupt her. She needed to talk, to vent - it would help lessen her shock. Most of the Russian-speaking population of Ukraine wanted closer ties with Russia now that their man had become President, and the last vestige of the Orange Revolution had been swept away. Party men from the East had come to the capital and started what was at first called a quiet coup. Now, however, more and more noise was being made as they continued to gain control of public and private bodies.

Katya continued. "That's why we are going to move. I've been offered a job in London. My bank's re-launching its Eastern European venture capital unit. They want me to be part of the team dealing with Ukraine and Russia."

"So you'll be speaking Russian and dealing with the Bandits from Donetsk."

"Oh shit." Her focus turned again to the two recumbent officers. "Oh shit, Aidan, what have you done?"

"I saw red, I hate bullies." Snow realised he had made a mistake, but it had felt good to slap the two men silly.

"But they'll be missed; we'll get arrested!"

Snow looked at his phone. "Maybe not, we've got some leverage. Tell me about your neighbours?"

"But why..."

"Please."

She frowned. "That side," she pointed to the left, "is owned by an old woman. She never speaks to me. She's half-deaf, keeps herself to herself."

"So she probably wouldn't have heard anything."

"And the flat across from us is owned by an alcoholic."

"A friend of Brian's?"

"Ha ha. No. He's very loud when he's pissed."

"So we can assume that if anyone did hear anything, they may think it was the bloke across the hall?"

"Okay, I get it. But what happens when the militia come looking for them?"

"Hopefully, we won't need to keep hold of them for that long."

"Aidan, I don't like any of this. This is my home, and now I've got two bound-up policemen in the middle of my lounge."

"Then we'll move them."

"Great. Where to?"

"The bathroom."

"I thought you meant somewhere else? Somewhere outside."

"Can you get me your ironing board, duct tape and any spare belts of Brian's?"

Katya cast him an odd look. "Have you been reading Fifty Shades of Grey?"

"Just do it."

Whilst Katya moved into the bedroom to look for belts, Snow dragged the diminutive Officer Brovchenko into the bathroom, where he removed the man's shoes. Katya showed him where the ironing board was, and Snow placed it under the still comatose officer. The man's shackled arms were behind him and underneath the board. Katya handed him two belts. Snow nodded in approval. Made for a man with a huge waist, they easily went around the thin officer twice and secured him to the board. Katya looked on, none the wiser, whilst Snow searched the bathroom.

"Is this your facecloth?" he asked her.

"Yes but it needs to be washed."

"All the better. Katya. I need you to go and sit in the lounge and keep watch over Mr. Angry."

"What are you going to do?"

"You don't want to see what I'm going to do."

"Who are you Aidan, I mean really?"

"A friend. Now go into the lounge."

Snow removed his polo-shirt then manoeuvred Brovchenko so that the board was leaning against the bath like a see-saw. The board creaked slightly; it wouldn't hold for long but was all he had available. He then lowered the end with the officer's head into the bath before turning on the shower.

The icy cold water splashed onto the officer's face; his feet began to tap and his eyes shot open. As the water travelled into his mouth and up his nose he started to splutter and choke. Snow pushed down on the board and the man's head came clear of the water. He coughed and then fought for air. Water-boarding was an extreme measure, but Snow was in a hurry. He still, however, hoped that he would not have to take it too far. Snow started his questioning without wasting any more time. "Where is Brian Webb?"

"I don't know...let me go." Brovchenko spluttered.

Snow placed the wet facecloth over the man's face and then let his head drop down again into the shower. This time the material clung to his face, making it more difficult for air to get into his nostrils and mouth. Brovchenko felt as though he was drowning. He pulled with his arms and tried to kick with his feet as his panic increased. It was at this point that he emptied his bladder. Snow pulled him up again and removed the towel.

"Where is Brian Webb?"

"You can't do this to me I'm a serving militia officer! You'll be thrown in jail!"

Snow slowly draped the facecloth once more on the young officer's face, and as he did so the man started to talk, the words muffled. Snow removed the cloth. "Where is Webb?"

"I've got a Krisha! I'm protected by..." His words were cut short by the facecloth once more.

Snow held him under longer this time before snapping him upright. He wasn't sure how long the homemade device would last so he had to increase the risk. "Now tell me, where is Webb?"

Gasping for air Brovchenko replied, "He's at a house in *Petropavlivska Borschagivka*."

"Not a militia station?"

"No."

"Where exactly? What's the address?"

"It's in Meer Street...26. Yes, Meer 26. Now please let me go."

Meer, the Russian for *peace*. The fact that Brian was being held at a private house and not an official address confirmed to him without a doubt that this was all a ruse. "Who provides your Krisha?"

Officer Brovchenko became wide-eyed as he realised the full cost of his error. "No, I can't!"

Snow slapped him in the face with his open palm, replaced the facecloth and dunked his face again. This time he held him for as long as he dared before tipping him back up. It took thirty seconds for Brovchenko to recover enough to be able to speak. "*Ruslan Imyets*." The name meant nothing to Snow, and Brovchenko noticed this fact with shock. "Ruslan Imyets is a *Verhovna Rada Deputy* with the Party of Regions for Donbas."

Snow nodded, satisfied that he'd got all he needed. "Officer Brovchenko, were you responsible for the abduction of Brian Webb?"

Brovchenko saw a way out. "No. There were others involved."

Snow nodded, the man had taken the bait. "Your group has made a serious error in kidnapping Mr. Webb and attempting to blackmail his wife. Now I understand that, perhaps, you are naïve enough to have been caught up in this, possibly coerced into becoming part of this criminal group."

"Yes that's what happened."

"So in that case I can offer you a deal."

For the second time that evening Snow was asked, "Who are you?"

"I am the person who, if he wished, could drown you here like a rat, but I'm giving you the chance of a clean break."

Obolon Rayon, Kyiv

An irritating buzzing awoke the Ukrainian from his much-needed sleep. He picked up his mobile and looked at the screen. The number was withheld. The average person may have ignored the call or let it go to voicemail, but *Vitaly Blazhevich* was not an average person and his number was anything but public. The Ukrainian Intelligence Service (SBU), anti-corruption and organised crime operative pressed the accept button. "Allo?" His voice was thick from sleep and his mind still dulled, but this instantly changed when he heard the English voice at the other end. "Aidan, where are you?"

"Left bank."

"Kyiv's left bank?"

"I'm not in Paris, if that's what you mean."

Blazhevich sat up, looked at his clock and shook his head. It was just after midnight, he'd been in bed for forty minutes. His wife groaned next to him, and he wisely decided to leave the room to continue the call. The last time Blazhevich and Snow had worked together, they had prevented a terrorist attack. "Okay, so I guess it's important?"

"Important and personal."

"Let me have it." Blazhevich padded to the kitchen, poured a glass of water, and then walked out onto his balcony. A new high-rise development in Kyiv's *Obolon district*, it too had a river view. He sat on a plastic chair as Snow recounted the day's events.

"Well?" Snow asked.

"Aidan, you have an uncanny knack of walking into things. There is an ongoing investigation into Deputy Imyets. If we can implicate him in this, then I am sure even *Dudka* would be happy."

"How is the old man?" Snow had a soft spot for the elderly SBU Director.

"Grumpy."

Both men chuckled.

"So when can I expect you?"

"I'll be there in half an hour," Blazhevich replied.

Levo Berezna, Kyiv

Officers Brovchenko and Klyuyvets were both gagged. Brovchenko stank of his own urine whilst Klyuyvets stank of alcohol and fear. Snow had taken great pleasure in informing the senior officer that their operation was blown and that they were now the ones in trouble. Neither of the militia officers knew quite what to expect, but when Vitaly Blazhevich arrived, it certainly had not been the SBU. Both policemen watched in shock as the newcomer identified himself to Webb's wife as a member of the SBU's Main Directorate for Combating Corruption and Organized Crime—and then joked with the Englishman. They felt their hearts sink even more when the Englishman produced a recording of their attempts at extortion. Although inadmissible, as all audio recordings were in Ukrainian courts, it could be leaked to the press and posted on the internet. In short, unless they co-operated fully, they either faced lengthy jail sentences, or ran the risk of being 'taken care of' by their own group.

"I've checked the address you gave me. I thought it sounded familiar, and as you would say it has come up trumps."

"How?"

"It is the address of Ruslan Imyets' new Kyiv *dacha*. If that is indeed where Mr. Webb is being held, then I cannot see how Deputy Imyets can deny his own involvement."

Katya had been sitting in silence and starring at the two militia officers. She was one to hold a grudge, and whilst Snow had been wondering if his interrogation technique had been too much, she had told him it had been too little. Brovchenko had of course been the weaker of the two officers, but that pig Klyuyvets had deserved to be drowned. She looked across at Blazhevich, a man who she had not met before but who seemed to be very friendly with Snow, and asked, "When do we go and get Brian?"

"I shall have to ask my Director, but there are two possible scenarios that come to mind. The first is that we get a warrant to search the address – but this will tip-off Imyets. The second is that we wait until Vickers has gone through his official channels. This is of course on the provision that Mr. Webb is not released."

"What about the third option?"

Blazhevich fixed Snow with a hard stare. "I know that it hasn't stopped you before, but you are not here in an official capacity, remember? We have an ongoing investigation which we must not jeopardise."

"So," Katya asked again, "when do we go and get Brian?"

Snow sipped his coffee as Katya moved around the kitchen making breakfast. During the night an SBU team had arrived to take Laurel and Hardy into custody. Snow and Katya had been left alone. They had shared the same bed but she had not made any more advances toward him, and he was glad that his resolve had not been tested further. She was a beautiful woman, doubtless a great mother, and propositions aside, a good wife. Inside he felt a pang of jealousy for the normal life that he couldn't have.

"Are you staring at my bum?"

Snow was. "Yes, but I was thinking about something else."

"Charming. Here's your omelette."

"Thanks." He waited for her to sit and then ate in silence before speaking again. "Look, I know what Vitaly said about his department's investigation, but the longer Brian is held the higher the risk is that he may get hurt."

"I agree."

"So I'm going to check out the house myself."

"Aidan, you are not Rambo, and besides, didn't Vitaly say they had an observation post set up nearby?"

"Katya, I can't just sit here and do nothing. Vitaly is good at his job. His boss, Director Dudka, is a living legend. But the SBU is a state apparatus and as such by definition ponderous and prone to leaks."

There was silence as Snow ate. Katya broke it. "Aidan, you really are a good friend. I feel bad that Brian and I weren't here for you when your friend Arnaud was killed."

Snow shrugged. "Thanks, but you were both in *Odessa* at the time, trying to make a go of it."

"And look where it got us, four years later."

"I still think it's a nice flat."

"I still think you are at times too English."

The bell at the front door chirped.

"That'll be Vitaly." Snow answered the door and Blazhevich entered.

"So I've spoken to Dudka."

"How is he?"

"Even though you are the reason I had to get him out of bed, he is happy you are not yet dead, Aidan. He asks that you call Vickers and tell him to hold off with his complaint. He says that we must preserve the investigation until we have positive proof that Brian Webb is at the house. And then he says we can, by all means, storm the place."

"That sounds like Dudka."

Katya glanced at Snow then at Blazhevich. "So can't you just take a photograph of Brian through a window?"

"Yes, if he is near or passes by a window."

"Oh." She frowned.

"So apart from *eyes-on* I'm at a loss," Blazhevich admitted.

"Get me inside," Snow said.

"How?"

"You said it was Deputy Imyets' new dacha?"

"Yes."

"Well is it new or did someone live there before?"

"I'll find out."

"Good. If there was a previous owner, then I become their drunken, ex-pat friend who's come over for a drink."

Blazhevich looked at Snow with a strange expression. "You don't just think out of the box, you dispense with it."

"Is that a compliment?"

"An observation."

"Hm, boxing clever."

Petropavlivska Borschagivka Village, Kyiv Oblast

The observation post was in a partly built church almost opposite the target building. Snow had passed the church many times over the years, as his American pal Mitch Turney lived a few streets along. A two-man SBU team had kept a vigil on the target overnight and were happy to be relieved by Blazhevich and Snow. Blazhevich had found out that the house was nine years old and the last person to live in it had been a German by the name of Eric. Snow laughed at this, but Blazhevich did not see the humour. After discussing it with Dudka, who now was at his own dacha away from the Ukrainian capital city, Snow's plan had been officially agreed upon. Snow would approach the house, feigning inebriation, and see what he could find out. In Snow's mind he would either catch a glimpse of Brian, or he wouldn't. Either way he saw no risk, at least this is what he had told his friends in the SBU. Snow, however, had other ideas as to what may happen.

Whilst they waited until a reasonable hour for Snow to make his approach, Blazhevich and Snow reviewed the surveillance tapes of the day before. When they reached ten a.m., a lumbering, overweight figure could be seen being taken into the house, but unfortunately his face had been pointing away from the camera. Snow was sure it was Brian, but Blazhevich shrugged, he didn't know him.

"Time to go." Snow checked his watch. It was almost midday. Blazhevich nodded. "No heroics, just see what you can see."

HETMAN: DONETSK CALLING

Snow smiled. "I'm not a hero."

He shuffled away from the window to the back of the church and opened a bottle of beer. He took a swig and poured the rest into his hand and rubbed it over his face, letting some run onto his day-old polo-shirt. He then picked up two bottles of whisky and left the church by the rear exit. He walked into the woods behind, turned right and found a path; it brought him back to the street but farther up the road and out of direct line-of-sight of the target address. He walked with the gait of someone who clearly had been drinking. As he rounded a bend he saw the house and immediately crossed the road, heading directly towards it. The house faced the road and had a two-meter-high brick wall surrounding it. There were no signs of exterior security except for the large ornate metal gate that acted as an entrance. The house itself was three-storeys tall and was built of red brick. In comparison to the other overtly ornate or ugly houses surrounding it, the target seemed quite tastefully done. Snow rang the doorbell then stared into the small camera he now saw mounted slightly above him.

He waited, and then a voice asked in Russian, "What do you want?"

Snow started to prepare his Oscar acceptance speech. "Eric you wanker! I'm back in town and I've brought two friends!" Snow held up the bottles to the camera. "Come on you German Gay-Lord, open the door and let's get drinking!"

There was a hiss of static before a voice answered in faltering English, "Eric no here. You go."

Snow needed to get into the house; he'd see nothing otherwise. "Eric open the door and stop being a poof! Come on, my two friends here are getting impatient!"

There was a slight buzzing sound and a click. The gate opened and Snow stepped inside. It was closed behind him by a large figure in a black t-shirt and Gorad patterned combat trousers. He glared at Snow then pointed to the front door. Snow surreptitiously looked around. He was standing in a large paved courtyard. The house was directly ahead; to the left was a slope, which led down to the underground garage. Past this he could see a lush, green lawn. Directly to his right was a fountain and small, dacha-style out-house. The front door opened and two uniformed militia officers greeted him.

Snow smiled. "Is Eric having a party?"

"Who you are?" the first asked in English. Snow realised it was the same voice he had heard on the telephone the day before.

"I'm a friend of Eric. Who are you?" Snow replied, and placed his bottles on the step.

"My name is *Officer Kopylenko*, and you are very drunk."

Snow raised his arms smiling. "Guilty as charged!"

Kopylenko pointed at him. "Tell me please, what is your name?"

Snow gave his own name; he had no reason to lie. "Aidan Snow. Nice to meet you."

"Can I see your passport, Mr. Snow?"

"I'm sorry; I don't have it with me."

"Hm, I see. In that case I am very sorry but I shall have to issue you with a fine."

Snow pointed at the bottles. "Is there not something else I could give you?"

"We will take those too, but you must pay a fine."

"Fine, that's fine!" Snow started to laugh and retrieved a wad of notes from his pocket. As he did so he made sure that it slipped through his fingers and fell on the ground. He noticed Kopylenko eye-up the bundle of bills greedily. Snow shakily retrieved the money and smiled. "Now officer, how much do I need to give you? Will $100 be enough?" As Snow held out the notes he looked around. "Where is Eric?"

"I told you Eric is not here. This is the wrong house. Give me all your money and you can go."

Snow made a decision, double or nothing. "Where is Eric? Are you robbing him?" He tried to push past the two men but the second officer grabbed his arm. Snow half-heartedly punched him in the face before shouting, "Eric I'm on my way!" The officer loosened his grip and Snow burst into the house, only to be pushed to the floor a moment later. Several heavy kicks connected with Snow's torso, and as he was dragged to his feet, a fist hit him in the side of the head causing him to see stars.

Kopylenko spoke again. "You have assaulted a militia officer. We now must arrest you and keep you here until you are processed."

"Let me go. I'm a British citizen!" Snow protested.

Kopylenko spoke to the second officer in Russian. "Take him away and put him with the other English idiot."

Snow let his feet drag and his head loll forward as the officer moved him down a flight of stairs, then pushed him into another room. The heavy door was locked behind him. Snow rubbed his head and looked around. It was a wine cellar but empty apart from the racks. There was a narrow, barred window to one side at head height, which let in the only source of light. Through it, he could see a flowerbed.

"Bloody Hell! Aidan, you found me!"

Snow noticed a large, dishevelled figure sitting on a patio chair. "Hello, Brian."

Webb smiled. "How the heck did you get here?"

"Connections."

"Aidan, thanks a million for coming."

Snow held his forefinger to his mouth, then moved back to the door and listened. He could hear nothing through it. He nodded at Webb. "Tell me what happened?"

"I was out with Mitch and Michael having a few – you know how it is, and then got a taxi home. The driver stopped the car, I thought he needed a piss, but then he just legged it. Then when I got out to see where the heck he was going, some blokes came at me. I thought it was a bloody team of hit-men! Aidan, I was that tanked-up that I just got back in the taxi and drove off. I tried to lose them but crashed into a sodding bus shelter, shook me up, I can tell you." Webb lifted his grey fringe to show his blooded forehead. "I kept moving until I couldn't go any farther. Then I called you."

"And they grabbed you."

"Yep. I was that blotto and shagged out that I couldn't do anything to stop them. They slapped me around a bit for good measure."

One against four was bad enough odds for anyone, but an overweight drunk pushing sixty had no chance. "The militia came to see Katya."

"How is she? Is she Okay?" Webb's face showed real concern.

"She's fine. She told the Militia to go screw themselves. They said that unless she paid them seventy-five-thousand they were going to charge you with sexual assault."

Webb burst out laughing. "On whom, me-self?"

"They say you grabbed a woman and tried to shag her up against a wall."

"If only." Webb stood, hobbled towards Snow and hugged him. "Thanks again for coming, I knew you would."

"What are friends for? Brian don't worry, I've spoken to the SBU. They are building a case against the bloke these goons report to."

"So who you are working for now, MI6?"

"It's called the Secret Intelligence Service nowadays, but yes."

"Does your watch become a power boat?"

Snow found another chair and sat. "You really can be a silly sod, do you know that?"

Webb nodded. "So the SBU are investigating Katya's ex-husband?"

"Her 'ex' is a politician?"

"No, he's the militia thug running this situation, Pavel Kopylenko."

Snow frowned. "He's Ana's father?"

"Yes. He's the reason I'm here."

"I don't understand."

"Aidan. Katya's been offered a great job in London. But as Ana is underage we need her father's written consent for her to leave the country."

"Which I assume he had refused?"

"You assume right. So, Katya and I have had to start legal proceedings to attempt to get a court ruling, stating that we can take Ana to the UK."

"And he's trying to stop this?"

"That's why I called you, Aidan. Katya doesn't know about this, but first he went after my business and now he's going after me. Shit, if I get framed for sexual assault, no judge in their right mind will grant me custody over him for Ana." Webb put his head in his hands and it was several seconds before he spoke again. "I'm her dad, not him".

"What exactly has Kopylenko said to you?"

"He never said anything about sexual assault, the crafty bastard; I thought it was all about my joy-ride in the taxi. He said on Monday they are going to present me and their evidence to the judge. Kopylenko said unless they receive payment from Katya, the judge would have no option but to find me guilty. So who's this politician bloke the SBU are after?"

"The owner of this house, Ruslan Imyets."

Webb rolled his eyes and let out a humourless laugh. "Imyets, the Verhovna Rada Deputy? I should be honoured."

"You know him?"

"I've heard of him, he's in pharmaceuticals, before that he was a militia officer. The channel TVi ran a story on him, very nearly putting itself out of business. He's one of the most aggressive bandits from Donetsk, one of the President's own Donbas business buddies. In the last two years, Imyets has won more tenders than anyone else, and he's used some very unsavoury means to secure them. Heck, if Kopylenko's working for Imyets, he's got some serious Krisha!"

Snow thought for a moment. "What's the connection between Kopylenko and Imyets?"

"Kopylenko is a militia officer from Donetsk. Apart from that I don't know."

"Have you ever had any dealings with Imyets?"

"No, we don't move in quite the same circles."

Snow stretched out and felt his ribs. He'd just have a few bruises. "You know, I don't think Imyets knows anything about this. No offence Brian, but why would he bother with you?"

"I agree. I just sell books, not even mucky ones. I could murder a drink." Webb raised his arms and gestured around the room. "Ironic, eh, they put me in an empty wine cellar."

Blazhevich checked his watch again. What was taking Snow so long? He cursed. But he knew the Englishman too well; he'd improvised. There was a buzzing next to him and he picked up Snow's Blackberry, which the SIS operative had intentionally left behind. "Hello, Alistair."

"Vitaly, this means Snow is with you?"

"He was, but now he's checking out the address where we believe Webb is being held. I've got an eyeball on the location."

"Which militia station are they in?"

"They are not. It's a private house belonging to Ruslan Imyets. They are holding him hostage."

"So the kidnappers are militia officers in the pocket of Ruslan Imyets?"

"Correct, which is why Dudka wanted you to back off."

"Understood." Vickers was annoyed it was all happening without him. "So what is Aidan doing?"

"He is inside looking for Brian. We had a plan; Aidan's a drunk ex-pat looking up an old friend."

"I see. So now they've got two hostages?"

"It looks that way."

"So the plan is working, Vitaly?"

Blazhevich shook his head. Both Vickers and Snow always thought they knew best, even though they had very different approaches. "Yes. If it was not the correct location they would have sent Aidan packing, but if we assume they are holding him, then all we do is wait until he is moved."

In his flat, Vickers sipped his tea. "So what would the SBU like me to do?"

"We need to get something on Imyets. The SBU cannot go in unless there is evidence of his involvement that'll hold up in court; otherwise our entire investigation will be blown. I can watch but I can't act."

"OK. I'll wait until Monday lunchtime and then if we don't have Webb or Snow, I'll go ahead with my official complaint."

"You think Aidan will wait until then?"

"No. Where are you?"

Blazhevich decided there was no point in keeping the location a secret from his SIS contact. "Petropavlivska Borschagivka, I'm in the unfinished church."

Vickers knew the place; it had become somewhat of a landmark. Commissioned by a Kyiv businessman twelve years before and never completed; its large bell lay outside, still wrapped in its protective cover. The bell had proved too heavy and too sacred for anyone to run off with. "I'm here if you need me."

"Thanks." Blazhevich ended the call. There was movement at the front door. Through the telephoto lens of the camera he saw two militia officers in shirtsleeves smoking and grinning. One held a bottle of whisky and took a swig before handing it to the other. Blazhevich muttered to himself as he took some more pictures. "Come on, Aidan."

The cellar door opened and Kopylenko entered, followed by another officer. The second officer spoke quietly into Kopylenko's ear. Kopylenko sneered and said, "Captain Budt would like to know how your head is, Brian?"

"Tell him that his mother should be proud that he hits like a girl."

Snow sighed; Brian and Katya were both graduates of the same charm school.

Kopylenko frowned. "I will tell him it is serious. But a more serious matter is you, Mr. Snow. You were not looking for Eric at all, were you? No, you came here because Brian called you. I have his phone and have also checked with immigration. So I have a question for you Mr Snow, who are you?"

"Why ask questions, just shoot him," Budt stated in Russian, as he removed his sidearm from its holster, holding it by his side.

Had he underestimated the men, would they try to kill him? Snow readied himself for action as he spoke. "I am Brian's friend. He asked me to come, and here I am."

Kopylenko scratched his chin. "Now I believe what you are saying, but that leaves us with a problem. You have assaulted a police officer. This is something that I cannot ignore, so here is the deal. You will pay Captain Budt compensation of fifteen thousand dollars and me another fifteen thousand dollars, and once you have paid us, I will personally drive you back to the airport."

"And what about Brian?"

"He must see the judge; his offence carries a much higher penalty."

"Why can't you just let it go, man?" Webb stood, arms out at his sides and palms upwards trying to placate the policeman. "I am not the reason Katya left you. We both love Ana; we should be working this out together."

Kopylenko's face contorted with rage, and he pointed angrily at Webb. "Because of you my daughter will not talk to me! I am her father! You have stolen her from me, from her grandparents, and now you want to take her away forever!"

"Think of her future, man."

"You have no future! Her future is here with me!" Kopylenko took a step forward. "Don't you understand? Now I can offer her the best. The best! I have power; I have respect. I am no longer a simple officer from Donetsk."

"No, you are a puppet."

Kopylenko struggled to control his anger, but now spoke in Russian to his colleague. "Take them outside to the van. We shall move them to the woods and finish this."

Snow started to move but stopped when the Glock was aimed at his forehead. At point blank range he had no chance of avoiding a round. There was a tense silence, which was broken by the Nokia ringtone.

Kopylenko pulled his phone from his pocket. "*Da? Suka!*" He swore. "Ruslan Fedorovich is early. Move them quickly."

Budt nodded. "Okay."

Kopylenko left the room. Budt smiled, the Glock still trained at Snow's head. He now spoke in English, the accent all but incomprehensible. "Move now, up step. You one, you two. Now."

"Do what he says, Brian," Snow said in an even tone.

Blazhevich had watched the owner return home in his dark green Bentley, Continental GT. A long-legged brunette had been in the passenger seat. The woman was not Imyets' wife. Blazhevich was getting more and more concerned for both Snow and his SBU investigation. He retrieved his mobile and started to dial Dudka's number but then he saw a three-car convoy approach the house. The lead and the last vehicle were matte black Mercedes, G Wagons, most definitely AMG versions and most probably armour plated. The middle car was a piano-black Maybach, 57S. There was something familiar about the convoy, and Blazhevich frowned as he tried to remember who favoured that particular set-up.

The large gates opened once more and all three cars entered the courtyard. A bodyguard from each of the G Wagons alighted, only then did a third man step out of the front of the Maybach and open the passenger door. A tall white-haired figure dressed immaculately in a slate grey suit stepped out.

"*Valeriy Ivanovich Varchenko,*" Blazhevich said to himself quietly as if not quite believing his own eyes. What was he doing here? Varchenko was a former KGB General and had been awarded the title, Hero of the Soviet Union. As Director Dudka's boss back in the days of the USSR, he had remained one of the man's oldest friends. He was a member of the elite group nicknamed, *Nedotorkany* - 'the untouchables;' oligarchs who played both sides of the law and as such were above it. They were friendly with presidents and bandits alike. Blazhevich had met Varchenko, and he didn't like him much. Whilst Blazhevich tried to make sense of what he was seeing, the men moved into the house.

In the study Imyets had poured himself a large cognac and was swirling it around in the bulbous glass after listening to Kopylenko explain his presence. "Do you take me for a complete fool, Pavel? Do you not think that I am aware of the petty racketeering that you and your men engage in under my protection?"

"No, Ruslan Fedorovich."

"I make allowances for your little indiscretions. I've even allowed you to go after this Englishman, because I am a father, I have a heart, and because in the past you have served me well. But now you bring him here, to my house? You bring your dirty laundry here to be cleaned?"

"I intended no offence, Ruslan Fedorovich. I am sorry."

Imyets downed the cognac, then clicked his fingers before speaking. The brunette woman re-filled his glass. "Do you not see what you have done? You have signed their death warrant."

"But they have seen nothing…"

Imyets screamed, "Shut up! I cannot take that risk. I cannot let them leave this place. Do you not understand what I have here?"

Kopylenko had no idea what Imyets was talking about; to him it was just a house, but his pride was such that he would not let on. "I am sorry…."

"Is that all you have to say? Pavel I trusted you, I offered you a real chance. Did I not bring you and your men to Kyiv with me?"

It was a rhetorical question but Kopylenko answered. "Yes you did."

Imyets drank some more then rolled his head from side to side. He had made a decision. He had no choice. "Pavel, you are sorry and I am truly sorry also. If only it had not ended like this."

Kopylenko was confused but realised that his life was in danger. "Ruslan Fedorovich, please…"

"Bring in the Englishmen," Imyets ordered. The brunette nodded crossed to the door and several seconds later reappeared with Budt, Webb and Snow. Imyets switched to English and pointed at Webb. "You are the husband of his wife?"

"Er, yes." Webb frowned.

"Who are you?" Imyets now pointed at Snow with his glass.

"His friend."

Imyets nodded, placed his glass on his desk, then opened a drawer. From this he produced an Uzi sub machine gun. "Say hello to my little friend!"

Snow's eye widened, Webb started to shake and the woman screamed. Imyets roared with laughter. "Do you really think that I would use this, in here, with all this hand crafted oak? No, even though it would make much less mess than an M203. So the question is, what happens next?"

Snow held eye contact with the politician. "Your men open the door and we go home."

Imyets shook his head. "No. It cannot happen. Pavel has made a mistake and I am sorry that all of you will pay."

Budt stepped forward and placed his Glock against Kopylenko's temple. Imyets picked up his glass and drank again. Snow and Webb stood motionless.

"No, Officer Budt, do not do it here. You may ruin the rug. Just hit him."

Before Kopylenko could make any protest, his former underling whacked him in the temple with the Glock, and he instantly fell limp to the floor.

"Take him away. I shall call you with further instructions."

"Yes sir." Budt leant down and scooped Kopylenko up and over his shoulder.

"Now back to the Englishmen." Imyets sipped.

The doors to the study burst open to reveal Valeriy Varchenko. "You keep me waiting, Imyets?"

Imyets smiled and raised his arms. "Business calls, General. I am sorry but I have just been attending to a small problem."

Varchenko strode across the room then abruptly stopped when he saw Snow. "What is happening here?"

"These two men broke into my house. As you can see, the militia has made an arrest. I believe that they may have stolen some of my papers."

Varchenko fixed Imyets with an icy stare. "You will let these men go. They are under my protection."

"But General, they are under my roof."

"Yes and they are under my Krisha!"

Imyets looked confused. Even he dared not contradict Varchenko, a man who the President respected highly. "Then that is what I shall do, Valeriy Ivanovich."

"Good." Varchenko turned to Snow. "Go home, Aidan."

Snow nodded, and grabbing Webb's arm hustled him out of the room.

Varchenko returned his gaze to Imyets. "Now, are you going to insult me further by making an old man stand and not provide him with a drink?"

"Of course not, please." Imyets gestured to a large leather armchair.

"Thank you." Varchenko sat and the brunette brought him a glass of cognac. "Now, a toast before we move onto more serious matters. *Za nas, za vas, e za Donbas!*"

To us, to them and to Donbas. Imyets approved of Varchenko's words.

Snow guided Webb into the hall and out of the front door. As he did, several large men in dark suits looked on impassively. Imyets' own men, however, did not look pleased.

"Are you Okay to walk?" Snow asked his friend as he helped him down the steps to the courtyard.

"I may be fat, bloodied, and nursing a hangover, but I am not a pensioner."

When they reached the gate it was opened for them. They stepped outside and it immediately shut. Snow breathed out a sign of relief. Webb slapped him on the back. "You did it Aidan, you got me out. But why did they let us go?"

"General Varchenko, I helped him once."

"You're a very helpful bloke, aren't you, Aidan?"

Snow chuckled. "Come on, we've got to move. This way, towards the woods."

"You want to take me on a teddy bear's picnic?"

"Silly sod."

Blazhevich waited in a car around the corner by a path that led from the woods. Snow climbed into the front of the Passat, telling Webb to get into the back.

As they moved off, Blazhevich passed a can of beer to Webb. "You look like you need a drink."

"You must be my guardian angel." Webb pulled back the ring-pull and gulped down the Obolon.

After Snow had handled the introductions he said to Blazhevich, "I don't understand why Varchenko was there."

"Neither do I, Aidan. I have no idea why, but you are lucky that he was." Blazhevich was also struggling to understand what all of this meant for his ongoing investigation.

Snow thought back to the last time he had met Varchenko. It had been four years before and Snow had prevented a paramilitary group from relieving Varchenko's bank of ten million dollars. Snow had been injured in the assault and Varchenko had visited him in hospital to give his thanks.

"Here, call your wife." Blazhevich handed Webb a mobile phone.

"Thanks, I'll just finish me can first or she'll smell the beer."

Snow looked at Blazhevich. "Did you see where they took Kopylenko?"

"Who?"

Snow explained, while Webb spoke to Katya.

"I saw a militia van leave a few minutes before you appeared. It was going deeper into the village," Blazhevich said.

Webb reached forward, handed the phone back to Blazhevich, and then quickly grabbed Snow's head. He kissed him on the cheek. "That's from Katya."

"I won't ask if I get one." Blazhevich kept his eyes on the road as they headed back towards the city centre.

Snow wiped his cheek with his hand in mock disgust. "We need to go after Kopylenko. Imyets means to get rid of him."

Webb shrugged. "He is Ana's father after all, even though he is a knob-head."

Blazhevich would have used a stronger term. "There is also the small issue of kidnapping, but I agree, we need all the intel we can get on Imyets. I'll get the boys back at HQ to ask Officers Brovchenko and Klyuyvets if they have any idea where Kopylenko may have been taken."

"Please do more than ask."

"Aidan, we are not going to water-board them."

"Pull over," Webb pointed. "There's an *Apteka* there and I feel like me skull's splitting open."

The Passat left the *Zhytomyrska Highway* and glided into the bus station that served long-distance travellers. All three men got out. The car was not parked in an official bay, but its SBU number plate would avoid any fine or complaint.

"Can the SBU lend me some cash?"

"Here." Blazhevich handed Webb a two hundred *Hryvnia note*. He then shook his head and gave Snow one too. He retrieved his phone and stepped away to call HQ.

Webb gestured at a stall selling draft beer, snacks and water. "Get the drinks in, lad, I'll be back in a mo."

Snow ordered two cans of *burn*, a couple of nuts bars and a half-litre of *Lvivski beer* from the overly attractive girl, and then sat on the long, green, wooden bench seat that was affixed to the front of the concrete building. As he drank the energy drink and munched the chocolate, he saw Blazhevich gesticulating into his phone, and then to his right he heard raised voices. He glanced over. A thin drunk was waving his arms at a chubby woman who also appeared the worse for wear. She told him 'where to go' and stormed off, her tight jeans barely concealing her large buttocks. The drunk caught Snow's gaze and raised his plastic beer glass. Snow looked the other way, but the man was not dissuaded and shuffled over.

"Where are you going?" the man asked in Ukrainian.

Snow looked up. "Nowhere."

The drunk laughed and tapped his chest. "Sergey."

"Sasha." Snow gave a false name; Aidan would mark him out as a foreigner.

Sergey swayed and then sat. "That woman you saw me with, she is a professional. You understand?"

"Yes."

"Sasha, did you like her? I could call her back. A real professional." He laughed and spilt some of his beer on his dirty jeans.

"He is a professional too." Snow pointed to Blazhevich who was walking towards them.

"Whatever you like you like." Sergey seemed puzzled and moved away.

"I think we'll have an address soon." Blazhevich stated as he sat.

"How soon?"

"Ten minutes perhaps. Where is Webb?"

Snow was suddenly worried but then relaxed as he saw the Yorkshireman nearing them, carrying a plastic shopping bag.

Webb pointed at the beer. "Is that for me?"

Blazhevich looked him up and down. "You really need to get some medical attention."

Webb dropped down heavily next to them. "I'm gonna start now." He retrieved a bottle from the bag. "Dr. Vodka."

"I'm serious, Brian."

"So am I." Webb reached into his bag again and produced two packets of pills. He then proceeded to pop three ibuprofen and two *paracetamol* tablets. These he washed down with the vodka straight from the bottle. "Ah, that's better."

"How is the ankle?" Snow asked.

Webb held up his leg. "No ballet for a bit, but I'll be Okay. To be honest, I think it's just a hangover. I'll soon drink it off."

The three men were silent as they watched a coach arrive and a stream of travellers walk in front on them. It was a stiflingly hot Sunday afternoon, and Snow did not envy anyone travelling without air conditioning.

Blazhevich answered his phone. "Tak?" A smile spread across his face. "*Dobre*." He hung up. "The boys have worked their magic; apparently Brovchenko was very concerned that we may torture him."

"What a drip."

Blazhevich cast Snow a stern look. "So as I was about to say, we have an address. There is a full tactical package in my boot, if you are interested?"

Snow stood. "Let's do it."

Stoyanka Village, Kyiv Oblast

The part of *Stoyanka Village* where the target was being held was nicknamed *Cuba* by the locals. Blazhevich did not know why. It was only three kilometres farther along the Zhytomyrska highway than Imyets' house. It had originally consisted of a handful of dachas on a large plane surrounded by a border of high trees. Over the past fifteen years, however, an ever-growing number of three- and four-storey houses had been built with new and dubious money. Half-built houses and pegged-out plots littered much of the remaining grassland.

The address that Officer Brovchenko had given-up was one of the original Soviet-era single-storey houses that had not yet been engulfed by new developments. It was on the edge of the village and faced the trees. A twenty-five minute drive from Kyiv's centre, with militia lights flashing, Kopylenko's men had used the house for nefarious purposes.

Blazhevich parked his Passat on the main road a quarter of a kilometre away from the target, next to a second SBU vehicle. As ordered, Webb stayed in the car and finished the remains of the chocolate and vodka. The SBU officer, who was already at the scene, shook hands with Blazhevich and then Snow before spreading a map across the bonnet of his Mazda.

"This is the target. As you can see it is on the edge of the village with one access road here. We can, however, gain access via the copse here."

Blazhevich asked his fellow operative, "How many men are inside, Roman?"

"Victor and I have observed two men in the garden and other shadows inside. But we cannot confirm the number of hostiles."

"Victor has a visual now?"

Roman nodded. "He is in the trees directly opposite the dacha."

Blazhevich turned to Snow. "So Aidan, you have been better trained than us in hostage rescue techniques. What would the SAS do?"

"Go in, hard and fast and use the element of surprise. Roman, do you have schematics?"

"No. But it is a single storey building."

Without intel, planning and time, any assault would have an element of Heath Robinson about it. "Okay. Here is my idea. We simultaneously throw flash-bangs in windows at the front and rear, but we go in through the rear. We clear each room and grab Kopylenko. They are militia officers not terrorists, they do not expect to be attacked."

"Agreed, but as they are not terrorists we are not shooting to kill. Roman, you and Victor will go to the front of the house and Aidan and I will take the rear. Fire warning shots, engage only if fired upon."

Snow smiled humourlessly. Not engaging an enemy was a recipe for disaster but Blazhevich was right, it would be senseless to kill members of the militia, however corrupt they may or may not be.

"Suit up," Blazhevich commanded.

Blazhevich and Snow changed into digital camo overalls, and all three men put on ballistic vests with SBU stencilled on the back in thick white letters. Snow fastened a couple of stun grenades into his webbing and checked the Glock 22 he had retrieved from the tactical package.

Blazhevich took Snow to one side. "You do know that you are not actually officially here?"

"Yes, and thank you." He respected the risk Blazhevich had taken in including him in the assault.

Blazhevich nodded. "Let's rock."

Snow supressed a laugh, Blazhevich had been watching too many Hollywood movies.

Silently they worked their way into the treeline as the late afternoon sun started to fade. Roman collected Victor and they skirted the target until they were concealed in the shadows opposite the front of the building caused by a half-built house.

Blazhevich spoke to them via his throat mic once he and Snow were at the rear. "In position. Counting down. Three…Two…One...Go…Go…Go!"

As one, Snow and Blazhevich hurled flash-bangs at the windows. Both men covered their ears and closed their eyes. The stun grenades shattered the glass and sailed inside before exploding with a deafening roar and a disorientating flash of white light. Milliseconds later Snow and Blazhevich climbed through the shattered glass, weapons up in a tactical stance. A woman, naked from the waist up, screamed and moved away from a man, who caught like a rabbit in headlights sat frozen on a sofa with an erection protruding like a weapon from his underpants. Snow pistol-whipped him to the floor and moved further into the house. A doorway led to a narrow hallway and two more doors. Blazhevich and Snow took a door each. Blazhevich's room was empty, but Snow's contained the target.

In the middle of the room Kopylenko sat, bound to a wooden chair.

"You?" Captain Budt charged at Snow, but the SIS operative was too fast. As Budt swung his fist, Snow stepped outside the punch and simultaneously pushed down the arm with his own left forearm as he struck Budt's jaw with his hand still holding the Glock. Budt dropped, but Snow kicked him in the stomach for good measure. Snow searched the room in wide arcs and acquired a second target, another uniformed officer. The man instantly raised his arms. Snow took one step forward and kicked him in the groin, then as the man doubled-up, struck him on the back of the head with his Glock.

"Clear," Snow shouted as he stood and stared at Kopylenko.

"W...why?" The face of the militia officer from Donetsk registered incomprehension.

Snow crouched in front of him. "You are Ana's father. Regardless of what I personally think about you, I am not going to let a little girl I love lose a parent."

"Th...thank you."

"Thank me, and thank Brian."

Volodymyrska Street, Kyiv

Blazhevich shook Vickers' hand as the diplomat let him into the flat. Both men moved to the lounge where Snow was sitting with a cup of coffee, watching an infomercial for a vibrating foot massager.

"I see you are reacquainting yourself with Ukrainian television, Aidan?"

Snow smiled. "This is one of those channels that Alistair pays extra for."

"I do not." Vickers folded his arms.

Blazhevich smirked. "So I've come to give you an update."

Vickers grabbed the TV remote and switched the screen off. "Have a seat."

Blazhevich took an armchair whilst Snow made room for his host. It was eleven a.m. on Monday, and Snow had spent the night at Vickers' flat, giving Brian and Katya space to catch-up.

"Of the six men that we have in custody, four have thus far provided us with intelligence regarding the activities of Deputy Imyets," Blazhevich said.

"Do you have enough to bring formal charges?" Vickers asked.

"That is not an easy question to answer. We have the testimony of men who claim to take orders from Imyets, but they are serving members of the militia. I have agents looking into their claims, and until we find anything concrete, it is still their word against his."

"What about Kopylenko?" Snow asked.

"He acted under his own authority when he abducted Brian and held you."

"But Imyets ordered us done away with," Snow said.

"True, but again, it is his word and the word of those present against yours. In the West, perhaps things are easier and the rule of law prevails, but I am afraid that in Ukraine, Krisha is everything. Imyets is protected by the President who in turn owns the prosecutor's office. So unless we have a smoking-gun and someone who will testify that they saw Imyets pull the trigger, we are pissing into the wind."

"And of course, Vitaly, if you share these same thoughts with the wrong people, you may yourself be arrested for slandering the President."

"You are right Alistair; our new laws get sillier and sillier every day."

"So what is to be done?" Snow now asked.

"The prisoners we have will be prosecuted on corruption charges unless they can come up with verifiable evidence against Imyets. The investigation will continue; however, I am sure Imyets will wash his hands of those men we have."

"What about Varchenko?"

Blazhevich let out a sigh. "Dudka has made it clear that the SBU is to not investigate or put any surveillance on Varchenko. This again makes me wonder what the General is doing with Imyets." Secretly Blazhevich also wondered if Dudka was holding back information from him, but this was not something he wished to discuss with anyone.

"Vitaly, I'm sorry if I messed up your investigation."

"Aidan, you didn't mess it up. Shook it up perhaps, and perhaps we shall see if anything falls. So now that you have saved Webb, what next?"

"Drinks."

Podil District, Kyiv

The small tented bar in Kyiv's *Podil district* was a favourite of Michael Jones. He let out a trail of smoke from his cigarette as he lazily stared at the cleavage of their waitress. "Great place, eh Aidan? Great place."

"Yep." Snow drank hungrily from his half-litre beer glass. It was his first of the day, and he had some catching up to do.

Jones' eyes followed the woman as she returned to the bar. "What more could you ask for? Great beer, great tits."

"Michael." Katya wagged her finger at the Welshman. "What would Ina say?"

"Oh, she would agree. She also likes tits."

Snow snorted into his beer. He had been away, yet nothing had changed. His friends were still the same, and even though many bars had been renamed, Kyiv was still Kyiv.

Webb raised his glass. "I would just like to say a toast to friendship, for without it, we are all truly buggered!"

Katya nudged him in the belly. Snow and Michael both raised their glasses. "Buggered."

"Your friend Vitaly spoke to me today," Webb stated, matter of fact. "He says that Kopylenko is now being very co-operative and wants to grant us permission to take Ana to the UK."

"That's good news."

"True, but in return he wants me not to give evidence against him."

Snow raised his eyebrows. "So what are you going to do, Brian?"

"He is going to give evidence, and then when they put that idiot away, a judge will of course let us take Ana to England." Katya crossed her arms.

Webb sipped his beer before winking at Snow. "That is what I am of course going to do."

Snow felt his Blackberry vibrate. It was a message from Patchem. He'd have to fly home in the morning, but tonight he was home. Snow switched off his phone and ordered another round of drinks.

THE ASSASSIN'S MISTRESS
By J. H. Bográn

"Come with me if you want to live." The man stretched out his hand, his voice almost inaudible over the constant blowing of the mountain wind.

Chantal gripped the edge of the cliff for dear life. Her hands were going numb, both the cold and effort taking their toll. Her black gloves were covered by the falling snowflakes. She looked up at him and saw her frightened reflection in his goggles. He wore an electric blue cap, but a ponytail of flaming red hair dangled toward her as he leaned forward.

The way he spoke caught her attention. She had heard that phrase before. She felt silly trying to place it when her life was in peril.

"Hey! Take my hand!"

Mon Dieu, I can't hold on. I'm going to die! Chantal felt her fingers opening against her will. She slightly shook her head. "I can't."

She slipped off and screamed as she dropped, though after a couple of inches she stopped with a jolt. He had a grip of iron. Her wrist hurt but she would not complain about it.

"Don't pull or I'll slide over the edge," he said. "It's very slippery here."

She looked up again, and saw him flat on his belly, reaching with both hands. The man, her savior, let her hang there for what she thought an eternity, but had to be only a few seconds as he worked the situation through. He moved her to one side, then the other. Each swing, she rose higher and higher, until she took advantage of her momentum and threw out her leg. The heavy ski boot grabbed on the edge. He changed position and began pulling. She heaved too with all her might, not wanting to depend solely on his strength.

She reached the top and together, like entangled lovers, they rolled away from the cliff's edge.

They ended up lying face up, side by side and out of breath. Relief washed over her and she felt like shouting. She wanted to do snow angels right then and there.

"*Merci*," she said after a minute.

"You're welcome. You ski very well, but you lost it on that last jump."

"*Oui*, I know. The second I touched ground the left ski broke. Lucky for me you were close by. I'm Chantal." She put out her hand.

"Robert Prescott." He shook her hand.

One year later Robert I. Prescott sat in a half-filled movie theater in Los Angeles. They were playing back-to-back Kill Bill 1 and 2. He was not there to watch the movie though.

A black wig covered his flaming red mane. The damned thing itched, but was necessary. He had followed his mark, a businessman. There was nothing more he needed to know about his would-be victim. He did not care about motives or reasoning, only about his payment. The target sat with his secretary, a secret lover, in the row in front of him, toward the center. On the way in, Robert saw them buy a large coke. This far into the movie, he was certain the liquid would give him the opportunity he needed.

Sure enough, about half way through, just as The Bride was ending her training in Japan, the lady got up and walked out, presumably to visit the restroom. The room filled with the movie's soundtrack. *The Flight of the Bumble Bee* by Nikolai Rimsky-Korsakov was a thunderous classical piece that reached popular gold status in the '60s as TV's *Green Hornet* theme.

Just as she disappeared out the door, Robert stood up and moved toward his mark. The man was engrossed in the movie. Robert pulled out his .22 handgun, a silencer already in place.

Without even breaking stride, he passed behind the victim, put the business end of the firearm against the man's nape, and saw him go rigid then limp as he pulled the trigger. The small thud was drowned by the movie's score.

One hour later he sat comfortably at the writing desk in his hotel room. He was barefoot, making fists with his feet on the carpet as he typed an encrypted email to the person who had contracted him. The message was simple: Mission accomplished.

He sat back and took a sip from his short tumbler. He enjoyed his Gold Label scotch served neat. He pictured the lover's scream at finding the businessman dead upon her return from the john. Now it was time to relax and enjoy his hard-earned money.

The laptop beeped, signaling the arrival of a new email. He turned his attention to the screen.

Yes, it was a new business offer. He read the first part of the profile. This time it was a woman. He knew some hit men refused to do women. He thought it a ridiculous notion, as he had no such aversion. Women, men, he didn't care. Well, that was not correct. He did draw the line at children.

The target's place of residence was in France. Robert liked that. It'd give him a chance to visit Chantal. Back at the lodge after saving her life on that cliff in the Alps, she'd shown him her gratitude. After several passionate nights, they decided they wanted to continue seeing each other. During the following year, he dropped by Paris where she lived, and had meetings, always in the best hotels. Once they'd enjoyed a midweek getaway in Palma de Majorca.

He knew Chantal was a made-up name, but she bluntly refused to tell her real one. One night, alone and drunk, he'd searched her name on the internet. Chantal was old French for 'stony place.' At first, he felt dubious of the coincidence, as his own pseudonyms were always a play on gravestone words.

Robert I. Prescott stood for R.I.P, rest in peace. He sometimes used Peter Graves. His job was sending people to the grave, so he saw his name choices as fitting. Of course, he could not use The Grim Reaper, but alas, he had plenty of other options.

He knew he should have confronted her and learned her real name, but that could end up in him having to get rid of her. He simply enjoyed her company very much. In bed she was fiery and romantic. She had a fetish for candles, especially the aromatic kind. He often wondered if she traveled with them in her bag or bought them on-site. Robert felt aroused just thinking of her.

Not the time and place, he thought. He shook his head to clear the thoughts and continued reading his potential new assignment: the woman was married to an Austrian industrialist named Karl Kelhmann. Her name though, Marthe, was French. In his experience, a man only got rid of his spouse when she had cheated or when it was beneficial, money-wise – perhaps for the insurance – or if she was just too expensive to divorce.

The last part of the email was a special request: it must look like a suicide, and must be done within ten days, and in such a way that the man she loved would suffer most. That told him it was probably a love affair. People after the money wanted an accident to collect double indemnity.

He clicked the attachment containing the target's picture. His heart stopped when he recognized the face on the screen.

THE ASSASSIN'S MISTRESS

Chantal's pulse quickened. It always did when she was about to meet her *sauveur*. It was getting more and more difficult to find good excuses to give to her husband. She knew she had to stop at some point, but she could not bring herself to do it. She liked her lover far better than her husband, both in bed and out. Robert would never hurt her, she felt sure, while the man whose last name she carried certainly would.

Taking great risks, Chantal escaped her gilded prison on the outskirts of Paris for a romantic rendezvous with Robert. That first night in Switzerland had sparked a fire in her heart. His trim, taut body, the way his red hair fell over his shoulders, the freckles she could only see up close. Although she'd spent more nights with him, she often thought of that first night.

This morning she'd received his email, thrilled knowing they would be together tonight. She used the untraceable, prepaid cell phone she had bought to call the hotel they loved. Their room had a wonderful view of the Notre Dame Cathedral. Expensive, but worth every Euro.

She arrived at the hotel and entered the lobby but did not stop at the front desk. The keycard was already in her purse. She reached the bank of elevators, and whistled to the tunes on the lift's music while feeling like a silly schoolgirl enjoying a first crush. When she opened the door of the penthouse, the first thing she noticed was the fragrance of fresh flowers. She turned to find an exquisite bouquet arranged with a rainbow of flowers in white, yellow, orange and even a few deep red roses.
"Hello, Chantal."
"*Mon cheri!*"
She rushed to him, but before she could embrace him, he put up his hand. "Or should I call you Marthe?"

She stopped dead in her tracks. Oh no! He'd found out her real name! She had to think fast; she did not want to end it with him yet. "To you, I will always be Chantal." She smiled.

He stood with his back straight, his arms folded across his chest. "Do you want to know how I know that name?"

She nodded.

He lowered his hand. Until that moment, she hadn't noticed the firearm in his right hand. "Mr. Kelhmann hired me to kill you."

Chantal gasped, and her heart raced, though not from excitement this time. Fear. Fear that she had fallen into a trap.

He moved towards the Louis XVII chair and sat down. He placed his hands on the armrests, still gripping the gun in his hand. He tilted his head. "Sit down." She did not move.

"Sit down!" his voice boomed.

She obeyed and sat opposite him.

Tears rolled down her cheeks, and when she spoke they tasted salty. "Are…are you going to kill me?"

Very slowly he shook his head. "First, I want to know."

"Will you do the same for me?"

He arched an eyebrow, and then nodded.

She recounted her story: her humble family in the farms outside of the great City of Light, how she met her future husband during her senior year of college. He'd swept her off her feet. He was older, a consummate industrialist, and she could not help feeling he was making a transaction more than a marriage. The pre-nuptial agreement should have been the first sign, but she ignored it. After the first year, his manipulative manner had gotten the best of her. She became a piece of furniture to be displayed at business dinners with his partners, a prize. Then one night she had not prepared the dish he had specifically requested for dinner.

That was the first time he'd hit her. She tried to leave but he said he'd kill her and she believed him. A few years passed by, and she found him in bed with another woman. After receiving a cracked rib for catching him before he was done, she escaped for a few days to the Alps. Her trips now allowed him to sleep around and kept her safe from another blow. On one such trip she'd met Robert.

"You know the rest," she concluded.
"Was I the first?"
"*Oui*. I wonder how he found out."
"A picture of you came with the dossier. I recognized the façade of our hotel in Majorca." He held out the printed photo to her.
"That's probably why he wants to kill me now."
She looked at him expectantly. He did not speak for a minute. "Your turn," she prompted.
He smiled that wicked smile of his. But instead of arousing her like before, this time it had a chilling effect. She realized she'd never seen this side of him before. He stood up, paced the room as he explained his walk in life, his early years in the northern part of England, the teasing over his red hair. Then the military training that changed his life and gave him the skills he used now.
"These days I rent my skills to eliminate problems."
He had a way with words. Like most British nationals he liked to fence around the subject, unlike Americans who would rush to cut to the chase.
"And he hired you to kill me."
"Not directly. It is a complicated arrangement with some layers for both the customer and my protection. Let's just say I received a contract to take you out."
"Do you sleep with all of your victims?"
"No." He paused, and then added as an afterthought, "I took the contract last week." His tone was defensive.
"You took the contract?" She arched her eyebrow.

"If I don't do this within a few days, the contract goes to somebody else. I took the job to ensure I had time to reach you first."

"What now?"

"If I don't kill you, somebody else will." His tone was grave.

A tense silence fell around them. Her initial fear had turned to resignation. If she was to die, what better way to go than at the hands of a consummate professional whom she also happened to love? "Do you remember the first thing you ever said to me?"

"Grab my hand?"

"No." She paused. "You said: 'Come with me if you want to live.' That was a line from the movie *The Terminator*."

He shrugged. He did not see the connection.

"It caught my attention. Life is ironic, you see. It turns out you are a terminator sent out to kill me."

"I am not from the future," he said somberly.

"No, *mon cheri*." He still did not understand. She spelled it out. "You are not, but I want you to be a part of my future."

He looked straight at her. Would he kill her right after her declaration? The tension was palpable. The blue eyes looked like cold steel. Chantal found them impossible to read.

"*Je suis désolée*," she said.

"I'm sorry, too. *Je suis désolé*. If you love me, then I will solve our problem."

"How?" She could not see a way out of their dilemma.

"The way I know best."

Robert waited for his mark in the study. The place reeked of money: the thick carpet, the wood-paneled bookcases covering opposing walls. Of the other two walls, one had the door in the center, the other a large window thick enough to be bulletproof. A wood desk, heavy enough to push the carpet down, stood on one side; a high-back chair of genuine dark brown leather behind it. The room in general looked very clean. No dust on the books or the ornaments. All the bottles in the bar held different levels of alcohol, and all the labels were facing the front. The one with clear vodka was the lowest.

Entering the house had been easy. Chantal – or rather, Marthe – had given him an access code. Not hers, but the one used by one of the servants. His white latex gloves gave him confidence that he would leave no fingerprints while he snooped around.

He checked the bottom left drawer in the desk and found what he was looking for. The Germans built amazing firearms. The Luger P08 was an antique dating back to before WWII but looked well taken care of. He checked the mechanism and it worked as the first day. The clip contained eight rounds of 9mm ballpoint ammo. Good. One would get the job done. He swiveled the chair to face the window, noting in his faint reflection the difference his wig and sunglasses made on him. He could not see anything in the dark outside.

The door opened. The carpet muffled the footsteps. Still, he felt the presence. He calculated and swiveled back, gun in hand, just in time to see the man one step from the desk. Karl Kelhmann looked startled in his immaculate tailored dark blue suit. The white linen shirt and silver gray tie completed the ensemble. He looked like a bank president.

"Who are you? What are you doing here?" He spoke in quick German.

"You do not need to know the answer to the first question. The second, however, concerns you very much," Robert replied in English.

A frown appeared, and proved he understood every word. The Austrian passed a hand through his perfectly combed blond hair. "I will pay you double if you kill whoever sent you."

There it was – the unfailing dangling carrot. Awfully tempting. Robert had heard it almost every time a target had a chance to speak before the end. He shook his head.

"You will not hurt your wife anymore." The words escaped his mouth before he could stop. It was the first time he had given a name away. Second, if he counted Chantal, he corrected himself.

"So this is about that cheating whore! That woman has never been content with one man." The man put up three fingers, "Triple! I'll pay you three times what you are getting from her." This time, the last word was tinged with fear.

"I'm afraid you're out of luck with your math."

"What?"

"Three times zero equals zero." Robert removed his wig and glasses. "This one is on the house."

"It's you!" Kehlmann made a move, but Robert was ready. Kehlmann began to laugh, "In the photo!"

In his left hand Robert held a device that appeared to be a fountain pen to the casual eye, but in reality it held a needle and a potent tranquilizer. He stuck the man's arm. The serum was instantaneous, and the man's laughter stopped, eyes widened in surprise at the prick. He then dropped to one knee and tumbled to his right. He remained conscious, his eyes open, but unable to move, yet something of an eerie smile remained on his lips.

Placing the Luger on the desk, Robert delivered a second injection through the scalp to corroborate the ruse. Robert heaved the man onto the chair. He pushed the man's feet under the desk, assuming a normal seated position. Robert took the man's right hand and closed it around the firearm, then pointed to the temple. A gentle squeeze and the projectile blew a hole in the man's head, exiting with bits of brain, bone and hair on the opposite side.

"Till death do you part!"

Worried that the housekeeping staff may come due to the noise, Robert pulled out an envelope from his jacket breast pocket. The emblem on the upper left corner was from a tight-lipped and money hungry medical laboratory; the contents carried the name of Karl Kelhmann. The report showed the industrialist had been tested for HIV. The results were positive, as was now the case.

THE ASSASSIN'S MISTRESS

Robert walked into the hotel room. He had changed clothes on the way and he was now wearing a cream-colored suit. He removed his jacket and threw it on the bed. He still felt the rush of adrenaline from his kill. He looked around and saw the bathroom door partially closed, light coming from inside, with a faint sound of water running.

He sniffed. Aromatic oil. Vanilla was Chantal's favorite when they made love in the bath, and black cherry when they maneuvered on the bed. Robert could not believe she would want to do it right after having her husband killed. Even with the adrenaline rush, he didn't feel like making love to the newly widowed. Not yet anyway.

Robert wondered about the future. Now that Chantal was free, he may go calling to her house – through the front door for a change. The thought amused him, as it would be the first time he would return to a place where he'd operated.

Approaching the bathroom, he caught the essence of black cherry. Some other time he'd be out of his clothes already, but now he stayed fully dressed. As he reached the door, his footfalls made splashing sounds. He looked down to find the carpet soaked, water flowing from beneath the door. His pulse accelerated.

"No, no, no," he begged before he pushed the door open.

The image was bizarre, Chantal lying still, inside the bathtub. Her right arm hung over the edge, blood trickling from her wrist onto the flooded floor.

He rushed in, and knelt beside her. Not even a feeble pulse in her arm. She'd been dead for a while. Tears trickled down his cheeks.

"It can't be," he moaned.

He looked around. A meter from the bathtub lay the creased photo of Chantal he'd been sent. It was soaked. The words in

French on the back of it were barely readable. It said *"Je suis désolé."* I am sorry.

He grew furious, seeing through the misspelling and now the wet smile of her photo, fighting back the recollection of his contract, tears welling-up in his eyes unable to obscure the new awareness of the merest reflection of him taking the photo of her in the window behind her.

BEST SERVED COLD
By Stephen Edger

When the doorbell rings before five a.m. most people's reaction is fear or panic; after all, who in his right mind is awake at that unnatural hour, let alone ringing other people's doorbells?

Tom Manning noticed the time on the bedside clock, and the fog of confusion thickened as he peeked out of the curtains and saw intermittent blue lights down below. The two police squad cars, one on the drive and one pulled up on the kerb, were unexpected.

Tom was one of life's losers: he considered himself a smart individual although he lacked the wisdom to back up this claim. As a teenager he had spent several hours in the company of the police, though he had escaped with no more than a rap on the knuckles. He believed they had wasted their own time, pulling him in for sharing his art on the wall of the local Asian newsagent's. It's not like he was the only one who did it; the building was littered with tags. It just happened to be him scrawling when they'd arrived. It was his father's fists that had pulled him back onto the straight and narrow. Tom hadn't cried when his father passed away.

Tom turned to his wife to tell her to go see what they wanted, but there was just a space where her body should have been. As he tried to focus on whether she had even come up to bed the night before, the headache forming behind his eyes prevented him remembering: he wondered where she might be at this odd time.

Mrs. Becky Manning worked as a computer programmer in town; she was a busybody, never happy unless she had something to worry about. She occasionally slept in the spare room, to avoid his snoring, or would sit up late at night on her laptop typing an urgent email to a colleague. Being an understanding, yet foolish husband, he had bought her a set of earplugs for her birthday, but couldn't understand why he had never seen her use them.

The doorbell rang a second time. Fearing that the noise might wake his children, Tom slipped a t-shirt over his shoulders and headed downstairs. He poked his head into the spare room on his way, but his wife wasn't there either. Flipping on the porch light, he unlocked the door and opened it.

"Yes?"

"Good morning, sir," replied the large frame standing before him wearing one of those yellow, high-visibility vests. "Are you Thomas Manning?"

"Yes," he replied, unable to stifle a yawn.

"Mr. Thomas William Manning?"

"Yes," he repeated, a little louder this time, grimacing as the ache in his head worsened.

"We need you to come down to the station with us, to answer a few questions."

"What about?"

The officer ignored the question and advised he would escort Tom upstairs while he dressed. Lacking the will to argue, Tom turned and ascended the stairs once more, with the officer in close pursuit. The other two remained downstairs in the living room, although Tom was not sure what they were doing until much later.

He perched on the end of the bed, and picking up the clothes on the floor that had clearly been discarded the night before, he dressed. He heard a little voice say, "Daddy?"

Standing, Tom saw his eldest son, Ethan stood in the doorway in his pajamas, one hand rubbing at his eyes.

"Go back to bed," he snapped.

The boy let out a yawn, nodded and headed back to the room he shared with his five-year-old brother.

"Kids, huh?" Tom gestured at the officer.

"Err, yes," he replied, sounding less confident. "Is there a neighbour or a relative who can come in and watch them?"

Before Tom could answer, he saw that the other male officer was now standing in the doorway.

"Did you find it?" the first officer said to him, and in return received a quick nod. "There are kids, here," he added.

"My wife is around somewhere," Tom offered. "She'll watch them while we sort this out."

A knock at the front door caught their attention.

"That'll be her now," Tom supposed, and then observed the questioning look the first officer shot his colleague.

"It's a neighbour," called up the female officer, suggesting she had opened the door.

"Good," shouted the first officer in response. "She can watch the children."

Unsure that he was happy for the police to be organising his child-care requirements, Tom pushed between them and glanced down the stairs to see whom the neighbour in question was.

"Is everything okay, Tom?" asked the neighbour, an interfering old busybody whom Tom despised.

"Yes it's fine, Margaret," he reassured her. "Just some kind of mix up..."

"I saw the lights," she interrupted, "and thought I would see if I could help."

Thought you would come and get the latest gossip! he wanted to shout but resisted the urge and settled for, "It's all fine, thanks for dropping by."

"Right," said the first officer, "We'll leave WPC Murray to wait until we can get a relative to look after the children. Are you ready to go?"

Still unsure where his wife had got to, he headed downstairs and was escorted to the rear of the car on the driveway.

Sitting on the back seat of the Astra, he was reminded of the feelings of fear that first time he had been arrested. Now, he hadn't been placed under arrest or read his rights, but he was sure there was more going on than they were telling him. He watched out of the window as they drove along the Northam Bridge, in the direction of the Police Headquarters building in the Milbrook area of Southampton.

As they arrived at the station, he again asked what this was all about and whether they could give him something for his worsening headache. It felt like he was badly hung-over, but he was certain he had not had that much to drink the previous night. Both questions were ignored and he was led to an interview room. Two men in suits were already in the room and identified themselves as local C.I.D. They told Tom to sit on one of the chairs at the far side of the table, while they sat down opposite.

The detectives introduced themselves and asked Tom to confirm his name, address, place of work and date of birth. They then proceeded to ask him questions about his whereabouts and activities the previous evening. Paranoid about what they believed he had done, Tom was sketchy with the detail he provided. It didn't help that the fog in his memory had still not lifted.

"I don't know who you think I am, but you've made a terrible mistake," he declared. "Tell me what is going on!"

"Tom, do you mind if I call you Tom?" Detective Kyle Davies asked. "I'm sorry we woke you so early, but we're investigating a pretty serious incident and are hoping you might be able to help us with it. I appreciate that we've not said much so far but perhaps this will shed some light on what is going on."

Detective Capshaw moved an iPad forward and switched it on. The screen loaded up, and Tom saw that the browser page was connected to YouTube, and he suddenly had an idea about why he had been pulled in.

"Look, if this is about me downloading music illegally, was it really necessary to get me out of bed so early in the morning? I admit I've downloaded songs and movies that I've not paid for, but surely that doesn't warrant you holding me? It's just a breach of copyright for Christ's sake!"

The detectives didn't answer and instead loaded up a video, indicating for him to watch. He watched the video buffer, and eventually an image of an underground car park appeared. A car pulled into view and it became apparent it was some kind of CCTV footage.

The car was a dark-coloured estate vehicle, not dissimilar to Tom's own Volvo. A date in the bottom corner of the video indicated it was captured the night before. The digits of the licence plate were not visible as the image was too grainy. The vehicle remained parked in the same space, not moving. Eventually, they watched the passenger door of the vehicle open and a woman resembling Tom's wife, Becky, emerge and run off-screen. This was followed by the driver's door opening and a man leaping from the vehicle, following the woman off screen.

"What is...." Tom began, but was quickly shushed by Davies.

After a minute, the man and woman returned to the screen. They appeared to be arguing. Several hand gesticulations suggested that the argument was getting heated. The man then knocked her to the floor.

The woman clambered to her feet and wagged a finger at the man, who promptly struck her again and then as she fell, climbed on top of her. The grainy image and angle of the footage made it seem like the man was throttling her. He remained on top of her for a couple of minutes before he stood and hoisted her limp body into the boot of the car. A moment later the car drove away. The video clip ended. The detectives stared at Tom, demanding a response.

Tom eyed the detectives nervously; could it be that they thought he was the man in the video assaulting the woman?

"It's not me in that video if that's what you think," he eventually said to break the silence.

"Really Tom? It certainly looks like you; same build, dark hair. What car do you drive?"

Tom didn't like the angle Davies was following.

"A black Volvo estate."

"Like the one in the video?" Davies fired-off, without pausing for breath.

"Well, yes…I suppose so, but that wasn't my car and it wasn't me!"

"I disagree, Tom. I think it is you in the video, striking your wife, and then placing her body in the boot."

"What? Why? I would never hit my wife."

"No? So you didn't cause the broken nose she was admitted to hospital for last May?"

Tom knew exactly what they were referring to.

"No I did not," he replied evenly. "Her nose broke when one of my children inadvertently head-butted her. We explained that at the time."

"Oh, I know you did, Tom. I've read the notes on the medical report. It says your boy, Ethan is it, leapt forward and his head caught your wife square in the face."

"Exactly!"

"Well I suppose these things can happen…." Davies trailed off.

"I didn't hit her then and I am not the man in that video hitting whoever that woman is…I mean, Jesus, that woman isn't even my wife."

"Oh, isn't she? You sure?"

"Of course I'm sure! I know my own wife!"

"The woman in the video does resemble your wife though, doesn't she?"

"Well…yes…I can see why you would think that…but it can't be her…she was with me."

"And where were you last night, Tom? Did you go to town? Maybe out for a few drinks?"

Tom rubbed his temples, his memory of the previous evening still hazy.

"We went out for dinner at a local pub. Check my credit card receipts if you don't believe me," Tom said, as confidently as he was able.

"We have done, Tom, don't worry about that," Davies replied menacingly, and then added, "Tom, you can tell me the truth, you know? It'll be better for everyone involved in the long run. Come on, it was you wasn't it? You went to the car park with your wife for…I don't know, whatever reason. You got into an argument, she ran from the car, you chased her, you argued some more and then you struck her. Maybe you didn't mean to kill her, but things got out of control and she stopped breathing."

Tom's mind tried to process everything that Davies had said but two words stuck out above all others: kill her.

"I haven't killed my wife," he said, half-laughing. "Becky isn't dead!"

"Isn't she, Tom? Where is she then?"

"Well, she's at home…she's…" Tom couldn't finish the sentence.

"Tom, we found the body; she is with the pathologist now. Tom, we know what happened."

"Body? What body? My wife…was with me last night…Becky is alive…you've got the wrong man…you've…"

Davies placed an A4 sized photograph on the table in front of him. It was an image of a gold neck chain, with a small crucifix on it.

"Do you recognise the item in the photograph, Tom? Does it look familiar?"

A single tear rolled down Tom's cheek as he looked at the photograph.

"Where did you find this?" he asked, quieter now.

"So you recognise the item?"

"Yes, I do. It looks like something I gave Becky on our second wedding anniversary. I didn't think she liked it. Where did you find it?"

"We removed this item from the scorched remains of a body discovered near the docks late last night. We believe the body is female…we believe the body is that of your wife, Becky."

"No, it can't be," Tom replied pushing the photograph away, more tears welling in his eyes. "She's not dead, she's…at home…she's…."

"Tom, there was what appeared to be an empty handbag found near the body. Hidden in a small pocket in the bag, we discovered a donor card with your wife's details on it, Tom. There is every reason for us to suspect that the body is Becky's."

Tom could not stop the tears from falling, unable to quite believe what he was being told.

"I'm sorry, Tom," Davies empathised. "Do you want to tell me what happened?"

"It can't be her," Tom sobbed.

Davies arrested Tom and read him his rights, strongly encouraging him to seek legal counsel. Although Tom pleaded his innocence, he was led to the custody suite where his details were logged by the custody sergeant, and the few bits of change in his pockets were confiscated. He was invited to rest in a cell while the on-call duty solicitor was called for. Tom spent the half-hour before she arrived, rationalising what he could remember from the previous evening; he could remember arriving home from work, Becky had been there, giving the boys their supper, she had suggested they go out for dinner and so they had called a babysitter and gone to a local pub. She had said she didn't mind him having a drink, but she wouldn't, as she had a headache. His next memory was of the police arriving. No matter how hard he tried, he simply could not account for the hours between arriving at the pub and waking up this morning.

The duty solicitor was called Ruth, and she looked old enough to be his mother, but was actually only a couple of years older than him. They talked at length, her questioning his actions and attempting to establish an alibi. He told her what he knew. She confirmed that the police had found a body, believed to be Becky, and they had other evidence they were preparing to present when the interviews resumed under caution.

She asked if Tom had taken any drugs or medication recently, whether he was prone to blackouts or whether he had suffered memory loss through alcohol before. He answered no on all counts. She asked if he could have accidentally ingested one of Becky's sleeping pills but he said it was unlikely as he wasn't sure where she stored them.

Ruth showed no empathy towards Tom, but did promise to make sure that the police followed their procedures in the interview and that she would guide him on points of the law. Tom felt grateful to have someone with him.

The interviews resumed.

"Tom," Davies began, "let me tell you what we know happened last night, to see if it jogs your memory at all. Just after ten, somebody posted footage, taken from the Podium car park here in Southampton, to YouTube with the comment, 'Thank God the bitch is dead.' Within an hour, thousands had viewed and posted comments about the video, which appeared to show a man throttling a woman to death, before driving off. The video was removed slightly after, and the footage passed to the police. The poster's IP address was traced to Southampton and we were asked to investigate the accuracy of the footage. When we deduced the footage was from the Podium car park, we reviewed the CCTV footage of the car park and found the same clip. We were also able to capture the car's registration number from the security barrier. Believe it or not, the address of the vehicle's owner matched the address of the I.P. Can you guess whose address that was?"

Tom remained silent.

"You said you took your wife out to dinner but cannot remember what happened afterwards. Does that not strike you as odd, Tom? Are you prone to forgetting what you have done and where you have been?"

Tom shook his head.

"For the purposes of the tape, Mr. Manning is shaking his head. So, Tom, you went for dinner and then, maybe, you started arguing. You pulled into the car park to finish the argument. Things got out of hand and you hit her. She falls, maybe bangs her head, you try to resuscitate her, but she is dead. Then what? You panic. You didn't mean to kill your wife and you worry that people won't understand, so you dump the body. You think setting fire to it will cover up your actions. You go home to rest and to relieve the babysitter, with a plan to flee the country the next day. Any of this sound true?"

"I've told you," Tom said evenly, "I didn't kill my wife. You've got the wrong man!"

"Who's the right man then?"

"I don't know! Someone made up to look like me."

"And why go to that trouble, Tom, revenge? Do you have enemies that would do this to you?"

"I don't know…I don't have enemies…I get along all right."

"Except when you drink and forget."

"It's not like that…."

Davies ignored the statement and continued, "Maybe it wasn't an accident. Eh, Tom? Maybe you planned to drive her to that car park all along. Maybe she kept talking at you and it got too much. You knocked her to the floor and then throttled her to death. Is that how it went? You dumped the body by the docks and went home to start a new life with your children. Is that what happened?"

"No!" sobbed Tom. "I wouldn't…I couldn't…I love her…I loved her."

"So why don't you tell me what happened last night, Tom?" Davies replied, raising his voice. "If you really went out for dinner, who paid?"

"I don't know," he wailed.

"Well it certainly wasn't you, Tom. We checked your debit and credit cards: no transactions or withdrawals last night. We checked Becky's too: same result. If you went out to a pub, who paid, Tom? Why is there no record of it?"

"I don't know."

"What was your car doing in the Podium car park at nine o'clock, Tom? It is your car in the video. It's your registration number."

"I don't know."

"Who uploaded the video from your laptop at your address, if it wasn't you? Did a friend do it?"

"I don't know!"

"Who ordered three tickets to Columbia on your credit card yesterday morning Tom? What's in Columbia, Tom? Did you think you could hide out there with your boys? Did you think nobody would look for you?"

"What? I didn't...I haven't booked any..."

"Whose is the body we found at the docks, Tom? Wearing your wife's jewellery? Matching her height, build and hair colour?"

"I don't know. It can't be Becky!"

"No? No, Tom? If it's not Becky, where is she now? She's not at your house with your children. So where is she? Where is she, Tom?"

Capshaw touched Davies' arm to warn him to calm down.

"I don't know, I don't know, I don't know," Tom sobbed.

"What will happen to my boys?" Tom asked Ruth when he was returned to his cell an hour later.

"Standard practice is: they will be put in the care of a relative and if one is unavailable they will be put into the charge of the state."

"You mean social services?"

"Yes. But your sister-in-law has come forward and offered to look after them."

"My sister-in-law?" Tom asked quizzically.

Tom had not met his sister-in-law before. He had only become aware that Becky had a sister a year ago when she had received a letter from Spain. Becky told him that they had not spoken in years following an argument, which is why her sister had not attended their wedding. The letter was a carefully worded apology, asking for forgiveness and urging Becky to come and visit her in *Malaga*. Tom had encouraged her to go but had claimed he could not get the time off work. The sisters had been corresponding monthly ever since but this was the first time that he was aware Laura had come back to England.

"Can I see her?" Tom asked, not sure he was comfortable with a virtual stranger taking custody of his children.

"I'm afraid not, Tom," Ruth frowned. "Under the circumstances, it just wouldn't be appropriate, and it certainly wouldn't be fair on you or on her."

"Will she move into my house? Do I need to give her any money? Will I get to see my children?"

"No, no. She is renting a property in the New Forest somewhere. She will take them there. You don't need to worry about giving her any money at this time, in fact, she's actually quite well off from what I've been told, so your boys will be well looked after."

"Really?"

"Oh, yes. From what D.S. Davies told me, she has a luxury apartment on the *Costa Del Sol* and a healthy balance in her bank account."

"But what if she changes her mind and takes them back to Spain? I might never see them again," Tom questioned.

"I'm sure that won't happen, Tom. Why would she?"

"Wait a minute, how does Davies know how much money she's got?"

"Oh, she was just here, dropping off identification to prove she is who she says she is. I think she had to present her passport, bank statements, proof of address, that kind of thing. That reminds me, there is a consent form you will need to sign to confirm you're happy for her to take custody."

As if on cue, Davies appeared at the entrance to the cell with papers in hand.

"Has your solicitor explained why I'm here?" he asked and received a solemn nod.

"Good, well, here is the consent form I need you to sign. I also need you to verify that the woman on this page is your sister-in-law."

Tom took the form and the photocopy of the passport. Although he had not met Laura, he could immediately spot the resemblance to Becky: the hair was blonder and shorter than Becky's and this woman had glasses, whereas Becky wore contacts. If he hadn't known better, he would have sworn it was Becky's twin.

"I guess that's her," said Tom honestly, passing the documents back over.

"If it's any consolation, Tom, she seems very nice and seemed really keen to take care of the boys. Once your wife's life insurance pays out, they will be well looked after."

Tom paused. "Life insurance?" he asked. "Becky didn't have life insurance."

"Oh she did, Tom. You took it out last year apparently. Your boys are named as beneficiaries. Maybe you were having a sixth sense that something would happen to her when you signed for the policy. Who knows?"

As Tom closed his eyes that night and tried to sleep, he couldn't help but feel he had been set-up to take the fall for a crime that he could hardly believe had occurred—his wife—murdered! Whilst Becky and he had had turbulence in their

STEPHEN EDGER

marriage, he loved her, and he couldn't imagine who could hate him so much to do this to her and put him in this position.

GOODBYE MARIA, SORRY
By Howard Manson

Danny Lane woke up lying next to his housekeeper, big brown eyes intent upon him. Her open mouth registered just a hint of shock punctuated with a small sliver of sunlight stuck between her teeth. He did not immediately recognize her, but her bare shoulder inspired him to check out the rest of her as a starting point, and, not being an aggressive man, Danny startled with modesty at her half-naked condition, returning his eyes quickly to hers. In the two years since his wife had died, he'd not been intimate enough with a woman to share a cup of coffee, so this was unique.

With his new housekeeper on the floor—having been referred to him by the new neighbors, and this was just the third time she'd been here—Danny became fearful and began to imagine how she could have seduced him into such a compromising situation. She was staring at him. She had beautiful eyes. She had straight deep brown almost black hair tousled about; the kind of alluring bed-head look men would go to war to keep to themselves. He took a chance; "Hi?"

Danny sat up, taking in the room around him: his couch and two chairs, a round coffee table centered on an area rug on his wood floor, a spilled coke can, coffee table knick-knacks spread across the floor. He didn't remember making a mess. Her shirt lay ripped and thrown toward the wall to the left of his front door.

HOWARD MANSON

He stood quickly to pick it up; looking around more he found her bra on the kitchen floor. Maria hadn't moved and did not turn to thank him as he dropped her clothes over her bare chest. He peered over slowly to look more closely at her very pretty but unmoving face. A sound a of car door slamming outside his house lifted him straight up, then to the blinds to peek out between the wooden slats.

Matt Bransford, 6'4", 210 pounds, an indefatigable glad-hander, walked up the path toward the door. Bransford could have been a Secret Service type, navy suit, white shirt, red tie, a crisp and clean character that did not belong in this neighborhood, a tract of thousand-square-foot cracker boxes built in the 'forties for the aircraft workers at the Douglas plant, then becoming the Boeing plant, then shutting down almost entirely. This guy didn't belong in Long Beach; he should be in RPV in a real house, not hunkered down here among iron workers, longshoremen and, in Danny's case, contractors and construction workers on this seen-better-days street.

Danny looked at Maria's back, the smooth and undulating plane of her twenty-six year-old back. He listened through the door to Matt's whistling approach, bewildered as to why a twenty-six year-old woman was topless and lying dead on the living room floor of a fifty year-old man's house?

Matt knocked. Danny cracked the door

"Hey, Danny. You having a great day, too? I'm here to pick up Maria." Perfect smile, perfect teeth.

"Ah, she's not here." He'd put his cheek and eye right up to the crack in the door.

"I'm supposed to pick her up at three to take her home."

"Ah, I don't know what to tell you. She's not here. She left!"

"That's so strange. You don't think she's coming back; should I wait around for a few minutes? You don't suppose she got a ride from someone, do you?"

GOODBYE MARIA, SORRY

"You know…I don't know. I wouldn't wait around. If she shows up, I'll send her over." Danny nodded toward Matt's house across the street, and two over to the right.

Danny leaned over Maria's face, turned her head side to side. She was warm, no rigor yet. He rolled her head to a side, seeing bruises on her neck, oblong shapes that had apparently come from his fingers. He rolled her head to the other side to see similar marks. He changed his body position and fitted his hands around her neck, first one hand then two, thumbs separated, thumbs interlocked. He was shaking, perspiring. He'd only touched one dead person before, and that had been his wife, who'd died of cancer. Danny didn't know Maria at all, and he'd certainly never felt malice toward her.

'Goodbye Maria. Sorry,' he thought. He ran to the back door but stopped. He ran to the front window to check on Matt. The car was gone. Danny ran toward the back door, then the bedroom, then back to the kitchen without accomplishing anything. He needed a minute to think before they broke down the door to take him away. He grabbed his keys off the counter as he ran to the back door. He stopped, ran back to the counter to get his wallet and ATM card. He just needed a minute to think. He stopped at the back door then ran back to the hall closet to get a light jacket.

Five or six blocks, past a low-income apartment complex, past a park populated by two soccer games and a group of Filipino stick-fighters, he jogged across the market parking to the bank at the far end of the lot, where he withdrew cash from the machine. He walked away across the lot, incoherent with fear and confusion. If he could get somewhere quiet, somewhere he couldn't be found, he could think this through. He would undoubtedly have to turn himself in, but he'd at least like to have any idea what was going on before getting the third degree.

At the edge of the lot, a woman was putting bags in her car, leaning back from the open door, pulling down her dress, reaching back for a bag that ripped open spilling its contents. Danny stooped to pick up a can and other items that rolled his way. She thanked him politely. A police car drove past on the street alongside the parking lot. Danny turned away from the street asking the woman, "Do you think you could give me a ride?"

She gave him a nervous look and hustled to get into her car quickly, dropping her keys, trying to get them in the ignition. He glanced at his clothes; he wasn't covered in blood or anything. He'd shaved yesterday, haircut about a month ago. He looked like a guy who worked. He didn't look like a psycho killer.

He tapped on her driver's side window. She turned to him with a startled look on her face. He said, "I need a ride; can you give me a ride?" She shook her head no as she tried to start the car, but dropped her keys again. Danny held up his money. "I could pay you." She ignored him, having significant trouble getting the key in the ignition. Danny walked away. When the police car see-sawed over the lip of the driveway into the lot, Danny hustled around to the passenger door, opened it just as the woman seemed to be fumbling to lock the doors from her door console. He sat down, lowering his face away from the police car.

The woman didn't scream or run or try to fight, but she was recoiled against her door, mouth open in fear. Her keys were on the floor under her bare legs. Danny reached down as she tried to climb away. He put the key in the ignition, started the car, and asked her to drive off please, soon, now, anywhere would do.

She drove nervously south on Atlantic, a run-down, under developed shopping street without one interesting store among them and traffic lights every two hundred feet. "Where am I supposed to go?"

"I don't care. Go where you were going. I'll get out somewhere."

GOODBYE MARIA, SORRY

The woman looked fearfully at him, not sure what to do. Danny was aware of this but offered no help, assuming if he didn't tell her what to do, he couldn't be charged with carjacking along with murder.

"What about my husband and kids? They're waiting for me."

Danny looked at her more closely, took a flier on intuition. "You don't have a husband and kids. Look, I'm sorry; I just need to get away. I'm not going to hurt you, but don't lie." She stared at him again with her mouth open. "Watch the road," he said.

"Why would you say I'm not married?" she asked but her attention was focused several blocks down the street on a police cruiser coming toward them. She rolled down her window, rested her elbow on the door, tapped her fingers too casually.

Danny was looking out his window. "I don't know. I guess things. Keep your hand still when the policeman drives by, please."

"What?" She looked around, feigning her discovery of the passing car. Her arm was out the window, her hand out of sight. "What…does that mean…guess things?"

"I'm good at guessing things."

"You mean like a fortune teller or a detective?" Her hand was dancing around out of sight, then moving up to the window, then down in random, agitated motions. "Is that what you do for a living?"

"Me? I'm a contractor. I remodel kitchens and fix stuff."

"And you guess things about that, like how much something will cost?" She'd begun to drive erratically weaving from lane to lane. Danny reached over, spilling her purse, to grab the wheel.

"Don't do that."

She drove with one hand now, leaning down to pick up her belongings, shove them back in the bag. The car began jerking side to side. Danny grabbed the wheel again, admonishing her to sit up and drive. He shoveled the items in the bag with an open hand, then put the bag back where it had been behind the shift lever on the low console between them. A plastic business card case got his attention, so picking it out of the bag, he removed

HOWARD MANSON

one of the cards. "Carol Ann Peters, MD, MSW, FAPA. You're a doctor!"

"Um, sort of."

"A shrink."

"A psychiatrist."

Danny laughed without the least humor. "Now that's funny. Well doc, I certainly am having one crazy day."

"I can tell."

"Yeah, I bet you can…." Danny caught the flash of light in the side-view mirror, leaned up to see it fully, turned around to see the police car signaling her to pull over. Danny sat back in his seat, head back, angry, frustrated, confused. He looked at Carol seriously. "I asked you not to do that. All I wanted was a ride away and a little time to figure this out." He looked at her business card once again before dropping it. "Thanks, Carol. Thanks a lot." Danny got out of the car, hands out to his sides at shoulder height, and stood there while the police figured out what they were doing.

Danny sat in an uncomfortable wooden chair in a stark interrogation room, discolored acoustic tile above a thin wood chair-rail and gray painted plaster walls. Detective Seminski sat directly in front of him, desk to the right, and two-way mirror to the left, door behind him. Seminski was brutish looking, a huge guy, wrinkled white shirt, tie undone, sleeves rolled up, badge on the side of his belt. The man leaned forward with his forearms on his spread knees.

"Tell me again about the woman."

"I told you. I just wanted a ride…somewhere away. I needed time to think."

"The other woman."

"Maria? Well, I told you, she was just there, half-naked. I guess I strangled her. I have no idea."

"What do you remember before waking up next to Maria?"

GOODBYE MARIA, SORRY

"Nothing."
"What time did you wake up this morning?"
"I don't know…six."
"Did you eat breakfast?"
"Coffee."
"Did you go to work?"
"I haven't really wanted to work since my wife died, so, no."
"Tell me what you did."
"I read news on the internet. I ate late…."
"And…?"
"What?"
"Something about Maria?"
"I don't know."
"How long did you read?"
"Three, four hours."
"Then?"
"I told you, I ate."
"What did you eat?"
"You know…I don't know. Cheese, lunchmeat, crackers. I drank a coke…."
"Then what?"
"I don't know! The coke or the food, probably the coke."
"What?"
"The coke. I'll bet it was drugged. I either went crazy and killed the girl, or…."
"Or what?"
"Or I didn't kill her. Someone drugged me, then came into my house, killed Maria and left me there…or…."
"Or…?"
"She wasn't there this morning."
"So you're telling me someone came into your house that you haven't been out of in days, drugged your soda, killed a woman who wasn't there, then took her clothes off somehow causing you to think you killed her; you run out of the house to think about this and carjack a woman telling her to let you out wherever she's going. Is that pretty much what happened?"

"It's the only thing that makes any sense."

Behind the two-way mirror in a small dark room with a barren desk to one side, two detectives and a uniformed officer stood with Dr. Carol Peters between them. "This is the man who forced you into your car with him?"

"Yes, that's him."

"Did he say anything to you at the time about this other woman?"

"No. He was very distracted, rambling. But nothing about another woman." She stopped talking as Danny's interviewer began another round of questions. They listened, looking at each other occasionally.

"Who can do things like that? Aliens?"

"I'm not crazy. I haven't said anything crazy to you."

"Then who do you think is responsible?"

"How should I know…wait…there is only one group that could pull this off, really."

"Who is that?"

"The CIA."

"So the CIA framed you with a naked woman?"

"It has to be."

"Why would the CIA want to frame you, Mr. Lane?" Seminski studied Danny's face intently, watching him give the question serious consideration.

"They're trying to make me to work for them."

The men standing next to Dr. Peters were chuckling as Seminski's voice came over the small speaker, "Mr. Lane, what would you say if I told you that we went to your house, that there was no woman on the floor, no mess, no spilled coke can?"

"What do you mean?"

"Detectives went to your house with a search warrant, searched the premises and found nothing."

"But I…You know what…you know, that makes sense now that you think about it. They wouldn't really kill someone for this. Right? I mean, they could send in a cleaning crew if they did, or use an operative as an actor, there are drugs that will simulate death down to near zero pulse and respiration. That makes even more sense. It has to be them."

"Who?"

"The organization."

"Who is that?"

"I've already told you. The CIA. Now that I think about it, you should be talking to the neighbors, not me."

"This guy's a whacko!"

"I'm sorry, Dr. Peters. This guy's crazy as a loon. You don't need to stay for any of this. He's completely wound up."

Doctor Peters stepped up to the glass to watch Danny more closely. The second detective asked, "You ever seen anything like this, Doctor?"

"I have," she said turning to face the men. "And he's not crazy, as you put it."

"You mean he's faking this?"

"No. Most mental health issues are impossible to fake."

"So if he's not faking, he's crazy."

"He's not crazy."

Danny was spitting as he shouted out to Seminski, "Go see Matt across the street, blue house. Ask him where Maria is."

"Cuff up, Lane." The deputy lowered the door on the tray slot as Danny backed up, hands together through the slot. "You have a visitor." He was escorted through the halls to a small room to the side of the main visitation rooms, ordered to step into a four by five room and back up to the closed door to be un-cuffed. Danny stepped up to the narrow counter, sat looking through the thick glass between him at Dr. Peters, as she pointed to the black phone to his right.

"Hello, Mr. Lane. How are you getting along in there?"

"What are…fine…what are you doing here?"

"I came to see you; see how you were doing. What happened at the arraignment today?"

"They put it off 'til tomorrow."

"Why?"

"Why? I don't know. Probably looking for more things to charge me with, no bail things; I don't know. How did you get in here? I wouldn't think they'd let a victim come to visit the alleged carjacker."

"I'm not pressing charges, Mr. Lane. I was behind the mirror for a few minutes while the detectives were talking to you. I don't think you're crazy, and I don't get the idea you're a murderer either. I came to offer to help you."

"Help me?"

"Can you tell me what Matt and Maria look like?" Dr. Peters made a few notes as Danny sketched out Matt's dynamic good looks and iron jaw and Maria's exotic mystique, both as out of place in the neighborhood as name tags at a spy convention.

"You yelled at the detectives to go talk to your neighbors. I don't know if they did, but I went over there yesterday morning."

"You did?"

"No one was there. I looked in the windows and the house was empty. Did I get the right house? Blue, 4302? Across the street from you?"

"That's Matt's house."

"Are you sure, Mr. Lane, because I looked online at the assessor's office and the house belongs to a Gladys Brodsky."

"Matt bought it last year…about seven, eight, nine months ago."

"There are no title transfers of any kind for eighteen years. Mr. Lane, I called Mrs. Brodsky. She said she rented the house to an older man ten months ago. You ever meet a man named Norman Dougherty?"

"No. There was a realtor sign in the yard. I went in the house. It was for sale. It sold really fast, but it was for sale. I watched Matt and his wife move in from my window."

GOODBYE MARIA, SORRY

"Was Maria Matt's wife?"

"No. His wife is Erin. She's like Irish or something. I saw Maria once or twice at Matt's. One day I was getting mail; he walked over and asked if I'd let her work, saying she really needed the money. I don't need a housekeeper, but, you know...I don't know. I don't even want to talk to people anymore; I guess I was just trying to get along."

"Are you that upset still about your wife's passing away?"

"Yeah, you know, we don't need to go into that. I don't want to talk about that. If you want to help, find Matt. If Maria isn't dead, then he would be the one to know where she is; find her and I can go home, right?"

"I would think so. Mr. Lane...."

"Can you just call me Danny? You're makin' me uncomfortable."

"All right, Danny. There's one other thing; I wanted to ask if you'd tell me why you told the detective the CIA was setting you up. Do you believe that?"

"I don't know." Danny kind of zoned out staring at Carol. She was attractive in her thirties: fair skin, smooth round features complemented nicely with longish, wavy dark blonde hair. What took his mind away, however, were her collarbones, just the angular beauty of them standing out slightly from her neckline. Danny really missed his wife. He used to bury his face in that part of her and just feel content, safe, loved. She was a beautiful woman, but more, she'd always just accepted him, he'd always been able to make her laugh, and they'd worked things through when times were hard, never doubting each other, and in twenty five years there had been a few of those. Danny didn't go out of the house much now because there was nothing left to go out to; it seemed that everything he did now was just wrong, he didn't fit anywhere. He had no one to really talk to since she'd gone.

"Danny?"

"Um, yeah?"

"Do you believe that? Would you tell me about it?"

He looked up to the ceiling line around the small cube. Two cameras. "You know they're recording this."

"If I'm your doctor, this is a privileged conversation."

"Are you my doctor?"

"If you want me to be."

"OK, sure; just a little weird. I seemed to have left my checkbook at home though."

She smiled gently. "Do you work for the CIA? I thought you said you were a contractor."

"I am a contractor. I don't work for the CIA, but I do this thing...."

"Go on. What does that mean? Are you undercover or whatever they call it?"

Danny smiled, embarrassed, dropping his face. "No. No. I'm nothing. It's just this little game I do."

"You guess things."

"That's right. They call it forecasting. They give you some random questions about all kinds of things around the world...."

The clang against the metal door being hit harshly was loud enough to startle him. The deputy's face in the narrow vertical window on the door, his voice over a speaker in the wall called, "Cuff up, Lane. Visit's over."

Danny looked, lost, at Carol. "I told you they were listening." He started to hang up the handset when he blurted out into the thing, "Hey Doc, can you tell them to give me something to read. I'm losing my mind in here." Her voice squawked through the earpiece, "Do you have an attorney?" "Public defender," he shouted back as he hung up the handset. She seemed bewildered, watching him back toward the closed door, looking at her while his handcuffs were installed, hanging his head in shame as the door was opened and he was escorted away.

Danny paced his eight by ten, walking to the back wall next to the stainless commode, kicking the wall with his right foot then turning to take three and a half steps to the door where he'd look out the narrow window into the hall to see what was there. Nothing was ever there, so he'd turn to walk three and a half steps to the back wall, kicking it with his right foot. The door on his tray slot squeaked and banged lightly.

"They told me to bring you this, Lane." The deputy shoved a book through the slot. Danny grabbed it, read the dust jacket: Robinson Crusoe.

"I have A.D.D. You got a newspaper?"

"No papers here."

"I've read this three times. You got anything else?"

"You want the book or not?"

"You want to hear something funny? The guy who wrote this was a spy. It's true. He was the first spy to ever write a book. But he was such a good spy, he never wrote about spying so he wouldn't give any secrets away." The door on the slot slammed shut, obscuring the sound of the word, "Fascinating." The deputy walked off.

Danny turned to the introduction and began to read as he paced his eight by ten, walking to the back wall kicking it with his right foot then turning to continue on. Soon enough his light went out. He continued to pace as his eyes adjusted to the dark room. The faint light of the fluorescents in the hall came through his window with the strength of a dying single-cell double-A. He put the page of his book in that light and his face two inches from it and continued reading.

"Cuff up, Lane. You have a visitor." Danny backed up to the slot, stepped inward as the door opened, then was escorted through the halls and into a different visitors' room. With some very aggressive persuasion from her, a few moments to check with the watch commander, he was un-cuffed and allowed to sit at a round table across from Dr. Peters.

"What happened at the arraignment?"

"Nothing. Hearing next Tuesday, no bail, P.D. didn't say anything except, 'Yes, your honor.' Are you going to come visit me every day?"

"I don't know. Am I bothering you?"

She was, in fact, bothering him a great deal. Where yesterday she'd worn a shirt with a collar open at the neck, today she was wearing a knit top thing halfway out on her shoulders, falling down into a shallow V-neck. She wore a pale blue pendant on a silver chain around her neck. He couldn't keep his eyes off it.

"No. You're not bothering me. Thanks for the book; I guess that was you." She pulled at her pendant self-consciously, put her hand flat over that part of her.

"I want to try to meet with your public defender; I would think it would be difficult to send you to trial with no evidence of a crime. Also, I called Mrs. Brodsky back. I have a number and address for Mr. Dougherty, the man who rented your neighbor's house."

"Don't you go there! Give it to the police."

"Why?"

"Well, he might be dangerous. Think about my situation."

"Well, maybe. I hadn't thought about it that way."

"You better be careful."

"I don't think it's an issue if I just take a look. Danny, I want you to tell me about the forecasting you said you do. If you think that has something to do with this, maybe there's something there to use to get you out of here." She was leaning over the table to him somewhat, keeping her voice low, resting on her arm, holding the pendant in her hand—thirty-five or so, clear smooth skin. Danny felt very old and ugly. He leaned away from her, his metal chair stabbing him in the back at just the wrong place.

"After my wife died I pretty much shut down. I stopped working. I didn't go out of the house unless I had to. Food; haircut every six months. I stopped answering the phone. My kids know how to get me so that's not an issue. Did you know I had two girls?"

"No, I didn't"

"They're both in college. We talk a few minutes every few weeks. Anyway, I read an article in a magazine talking about this website. It sounded interesting, so I looked into it. The site says it's an academic research study to evaluate the efficacy of crowd-sourcing. You know what that is, right? It's just trying to measure how accurate people's opinions are on any given subject. But the thing is being done for the CIA by all these people with half the alphabet behind their names; all of them have worked in the intelligence field for various agencies. The group is incorporated as its own entity, but the work is being paid for, done, and analyzed for use as an adjunct to normal intelligence analysis for the CIA. You following this?"

"Of course. But is this something secret?"

"No! Not at all. Anyone can participate. It's just a website. Log on and answer questions or don't answer questions, as you like. It's fun."

"What kind of questions?"

"Anything you can think of: point spreads on sporting events; closing price on gas futures by a certain date; will some second-world nation experience an armed coup by a certain date; will some pop singer be on the charts at a certain date. Anything."

"So you answer all these questions, and what...how do you know all this stuff anyway?"

"Well, that's the thing. I don't really know anything about any of this stuff. When I want to answer a question, I go online, read a bunch of newspapers or whatever I can find, and then just make up some answer that seems reasonable. I just guess."

"So, I don't get it. If anyone can do this and there's no obligation, I mean you're not an employee, why would you think that these people are trying to set you up in a murder? What would that possibly accomplish? It doesn't make sense."

"It doesn't make sense, does it? But you see, I tried to quit. It's a lot of time now. I have to read papers from all over the world. So I stopped answering questions. Later, I started getting emails to come back; I got messages that groups on the site I've never heard of want my opinion about this or that; would I join their group; one email offered me a job of some sort if I'd come back and just answer a few questions."

"But why would they do that?" She sat up straight, looking more serious than she had, possibly disbelieving this. "I can't tell if you're serious or not, but if this is what you really think, then what makes them want your opinion to the point of murder?"

He fixed her eyes firmly as he said, "I've never been wrong." For the first time she saw in him something other than a depressed man with low self-esteem.

"…Come on…never? How much do you do this?"

"I don't know exactly, eighteen months, another six of sporadic participation. Several hundred, over a thousand questions, I don't really know."

"And you've never been wrong?"

"Not once. They keep score. That's gotta be worth something to them."

The cell door squeaked and clanged as the cover on the tray slot fell. Danny continued his march to the back wall and kicked it before turning to walk the three and a half steps to look through the narrow glass at the deputy holding up another book.

"Give me the other book first."

"I gave that to the guard this morning."

"You read that whole book in one day?"

"I finished it the night you gave it to me. What's that?" The deputy shoved the book through the slot. Danny checked the spine and opened it, thumbing the first few pages. "Little Women? Are you sure you want me reading this stuff. I mean that Amy chick can get pretty wild."

The deputy looked a little confused. That was the book they'd given him to bring here. "You want the book or not?"

"Can I have a newspaper instead?"

"No papers here. Stop asking."

GOODBYE MARIA, SORRY

Danny kept the book, turned to page one and began his march to the back wall. The tray slot banged shut.

Dr. Peters threaded her way through the bodies in front of the glass entry doors of Men's Central jail, pulled a door open and unharnessed the shoulder strap of her briefcase, putting it in a gray plastic tub on the conveyor into the x-ray machine. She stepped through the metal detector when directed by the deputy standing in front of her.

Walking around people in the crowded lobby, she stepped up to the line of visitors waiting to be checked-in at the reception desk. A sign on the wall, under the clock behind the deputies, threatened prosecution to visitors bringing in contraband: cigarettes, alcohol, drugs, and weapons among other things.

"Prisoner's name?"

"Lane; 376502."

"Lane...." The deputy sitting behind the low desk typed into his terminal, squinted as he double-checked the information, then said, "He's been transferred."

"But...that's impossible. His hearing is tomorrow."

"He was transferred out this morning at eleven thirteen."

"Where?"

"I don't have that information, Ma'am. You'll have to check with the attorney or the court."

"But...."

"Just go to the court clerk. You'll find him." He leaned his head to the right. "Next!"

"Please take the ticket," the device said as it stuck out a square, orange tongue. Dr. Peters grabbed it, inching her car forward impatiently as the entrance arm lifted up. She found a parking space then double-timed it to the elevators three rows away. She emerged on the third floor with a group of people and skipped in front of some of them to get to the door of the court clerk first.

A middle-aged woman, competently bureaucratic, wire rimmed glasses on a neck chain greeted her at the counter. "Yes…?"

"My client was transferred from Men's Central, and I'd like to know to where."

"Name?"

"Daniel Lane." Dr. Peters gave the woman a docket number and leaned over the counter to see the computer monitor, earning a stern reproof from the matron.

"Who are you?"

"I'm Mr. Lane's psychiatrist."

"You have ID?"

Extending her neck tortoise-like, the clerk inspected the proffered license and business card and made a note. "Mr. Lane was transferred to Norwalk Metropolitan this morning."

"But how? His hearing is scheduled for tomorrow morning."

"Well, the judge signed the plea agreement at ten o'clock this morning. I don't know what else to tell you."

"Plea agreement? But that's insane. There wasn't even any crime committed."

"You'll have to take that up with someone else." The woman leaned her head to the left and said, "Next!"

Forced to the side in the wake of incoming people, Dr. Peters took a couple of numb steps before drifting out into the hall, checking the time on her cell phone. She walked slowly to the elevators, looking up and down the hall, a dozen or more people standing around talking, more walking purposefully along the wide swath of polished terrazzo. Near the elevators she noticed the back of a particular balding head. "Mr. Freidman!" she called out.

A good looking man in his forties, medium height, well dressed, turned to find the voice calling for him.

"Mr. Freidman. Carol Peters; I'm Danny Lane's psychiatrist."
"Of course; hello."
"What happened to Danny? The clerk said he's been transferred to Metropolitan."
"The prosecutor offered to drop all charges if Mr. Lane would voluntarily go in for observation."
"But why would you do that? There was no crime. The police said in the initial interrogation that there was no evidence of a crime. I didn't file charges so what is there to deal with?"
"Dr. Peters, please. Maybe we can go somewhere if you want to discuss this, I have a few minutes; coffee downstairs?"
"I don't care if people are looking me. What did you do to my client? He should have been released tomorrow. How can you make a plea deal when the prosecutor has filed charges for a crime that didn't occur?"
Mr. Freidman leaned a little closer, keeping his voice low. "The prosecution showed me they have good cause to request a six-month involuntary commitment based on the recordings during the interrogations and jail visits. They offered ninety days and to drop the investigation. Given Mr. Lane's fanciful descriptions of events, we felt a court verdict would not go in our favor. That's all. The judge actually reduced the time to sixty days; so I think Mr. Lane has an opportunity to put this behind him now."
"That is the stupidest thing I've ever heard! Are you actually an attorney? There is not a shred of evidence that any crime was committed. You should have stood up and told these people to…ahh, how could you do this? Why didn't you call me?"
"Dr. Peters, with respect to your professional ability, you were a victim of a crime; that you chose not to file a complaint is your business, but in the judge's chambers, you know as well as I do that I can't maintain nothing actually happened or that Mr. Lane's behavior hasn't been erratic. Besides, it's not uncommon for victims to take the aggressor's side in a defense. Just because you've developed feelings for Mr. Lane doesn't mean I can get the judge to see it that way. No. We did the right thing."

"Don't you patronize me. I found out something about the man living across the street and the woman Maria. I could tell the judge. Danny doesn't need observation. You did not approach this in the best interests of your client. Now this man will have a court-ordered commitment on his record for life. You are aware that as a mental patient he's not even allowed to pay his own bills! You've ruined him for nothing more than your expedience. I should file a complaint at the bar about this."

Her voice had been loud enough to draw the attention of the people in the hall. The elevator had dinged, but the attorney missed his car. Another arrived. He stepped toward it holding the door with his right hand. "I know something about the neighbor, too, Dr. Peters. Matt Bransford is a Realtor. He rented that house while his was being remodeled; he moved back in last week; I went there! The open house Danny says he saw was a training exercise for Realtors in Matt's brokerage. Nothing sinister in that." Carol Peters looked shocked. The elevator door started to close on Mr. Freidman, but he forced it back open to the annoyance of the three people inside it. "I did some other checking, Dr. Peters, and I found that you just advise on workers' comp cases for a living, augmenting a comfortable lifestyle with some rich neurotics on the side. I'm sorry you got caught up in this, that you feel the way you do, but there's more going on than you know. I think you should stop encouraging the man; the only conspiracy going on here is in his mind." The attorney stepped into the elevator car to the certain relief of the others, though they were admittedly fascinated with the snippet of conversation. Mr. Freidman said before releasing the door, "If you'd care to discuss this at my office, or over coffee downstairs…? I just don't feel this hallway is an appropriate place for this."

"There's nothing more to discuss." Dr. Peters turned away in humiliation masked as disgust. "Just go on with your busy little life." Most of the people watching in the hall were as uncomfortable as she was, and they turned their faces away, too.

GOODBYE MARIA, SORRY

An orderly in white, a large man, Hispanic, with a military crop, knocked at the ward door peering into the narrow glass window inset to the right. Pulling the door open he smiled at Danny pacing the length of the room, and said, "You have a visitor, Mr. Lane." A square of sunlight rested flat on his bed after Danny grabbed his shirt out from under it. He stepped toward the small mirror hanging over a small dresser, was unhappy with what he saw, un-resigned to his age. He pulled the long-sleeves on over his t-shirt, leaving it unbuttoned. Danny walked with the orderly through off-white halls, past the broad opening to the dayroom to his right and was let into a room near the end of the hall, beyond the nurses' station.

"Hi...," she said drawing the word out, standing expectantly, hands reaching nervously in front of her for his, before falling self-consciously to her sides, fluttering there with residual electricity. Danny walked into the room looking to her with relief and anxiety, just rotating his head rapidly to take in the room; no cameras, two upholstered chairs side-by-side at about thirty degrees with a small round table in front of them. The orderly walked out. Dr. Peters was wearing navy slacks and a white blouse buttoned to the top but one. Danny sat in a chair uncertain whether or not to shake her hand, hug her, or ask her to unbutton that second button. He could smell her, a faint scent, very young, nothing like most perfumes, maybe it was just the soap she used or the fabric softener on her clothes. He looked at her shirt again for the telltales of it being laundered or dry-cleaned.
"I'm sorry it's taken so long to come see you. I came here the other day but your attorney hadn't included my name on a visitors' list."
"I was wondering if we were done. I mean, you know, I didn't see you after the hearing."
"Why did you sign that? I wish you would have called me."
"I don't know...you know...I got a prosecutor and a judge staring at me, the public defender is nodding his head up and

HOWARD MANSON

down; it just seemed that two months was better than six. I don't know what it is about me, but I can't ever get anyone to just listen to me. I guess I just gave up. I appreciate your help though."

Dr. Peters leaned back in her seat, shaking her head side to side. "I didn't do anything. I tried to talk to your public defender and he just humiliated me. I haven't done a lot of legal work; I guess I made a serious mistake thinking people would listen to common sense."

"Freidman told me he felt bad about your talk at the elevator. He said you looked like you were going to cry."

"Ahh, that was so frustrating to find that out like that….Anyway, how is it in here?"

"There's a couple of guys in here that are pretty entertaining, some scary people. One guy just got out of isolation because he killed the ward cat."

"Oh, my!"

"Picked it up by the tail and swung it around while he was yelling about something, I don't know. But they won't let me read anything. Do you think you can get them to let me have a newspaper or two?"

"I can work on that." Carol fidgeted with her fingernails, uncertain how to broach her next topic.

But a loud knock at the door startled them both. The orderly stepped in, announcing kindly that the visit was over. Danny snapped, "But she just got here!"

They both stood awkwardly. Dr. Peters said with her face down, "Danny, I was thinking that maybe my visiting is bothering you."

"No! I look forward to your visits. I mean, I haven't really talked to anyone in a while; you make me feel, I don't know, this is the first time I've actually started to feel normal. I mean, if you don't want to come by anymore, you know, you're busy, I understand, but really, look, I'm in a nut house, who cares what I think, if you want to come visit…right?"

Carol Peters smiled shyly. "You're sweet, thanks. I have a conference at State Fund next week in San Francisco, so after that, I'll come by. Okay?"

"State Fund? Workers' comp? Is that what you do?"

"That's what I do…job stress evaluations. Pretty glamorous isn't it?"

The orderly cleared his throat and smiled. Danny and Carol both smiled at each other and looked down or away, quickly with the awkwardness of it all. Danny held back to allow her to go out first, where she turned to him and said, "I'll go ask about a newspaper for you. Okay?" She held his eye for a moment trying not to let her frustration show. "Bye," she said.

Danny watched her walk off to the nurses' station as the orderly closed the door on the room, checking the lock. He stepped up to Danny's side, watching Dr. Peters turn the corner out of the hall. "That's an attractive woman," he said.

Danny looked at the grinning man self-consciously and said, "She's really nice."

At the nurses' station, Dr. Peters asked the duty nurse, "Is it possible to get Mr. Lane a newspaper to read?"

"No, I'm sorry. Mr. Lane isn't allowed newspapers at the moment."

"Well, then a book or magazine? He needs more to occupy his mind."

"I'm sorry. Those decisions are made by the Chief of Staff. I'm not allowed to give Mr. Lane any reading material."

"That is really bizarre. Can I talk to the Chief of Staff then? Where is he, or she?"

"Doctor Farmingham. His office is in the administration building."

"Where is that…the big building when you drive in?"

"Yes, that's it, the three story, the tall old building when you drive in. If you parked in our lot, you might want to drive your car; it's kind of far."

HOWARD MANSON

Dr. Peters turned to look out over the day room, about a dozen clients, TV on a game show up on the wall. She frowned, checked the time on her cell phone and left the building.

In the afternoon glare of the parking lot, Dr. Peters watched a light blue Sentra come around the bend in the road. She recognized Danny's public defender and debated in anger whether to demand to know what he was doing here. She stood alongside her car watching as he parked, but as his door opened, she opened hers and climbed in, dropped her keys, then got the motor running and the air on. Uncertain of her best course, seeing in her mirror that he was getting out of his car, she backed out intending to go around the lot to avoid the man.

"Dr. Peters!" She couldn't hear him with her window up and the air on full blast, but she'd been watching him walk through the parking spaces, turn as he recognized her, and lift his right arm high into the air. She stopped, rolling down her window, staring forward as he approached the driver's window. "Dr. Peters, pleasant surprise. Did you see Mr. Lane?"

"I did. Thank you so much for putting me on the visitors' list," she said sarcastically.

"How is he doing in there?"

"Other than being wrongly incarcerated you mean, oh, he's fine." Her thumbs were banging on the steering wheel.

"Please, Doctor. That's unfair. Why don't you come by my office and we can talk about this." He held out a business card for her, something she already had. She made him wait awkwardly for several seconds before taking the card.

"Why are you here, a little guilt relief visit or are you working for them?" she said with an impotent venom.

Freidman grinned politely, the dislike showing more than he should have allowed. "I'm just getting a paper signed."

"Well hopefully, you can spend a few minutes to talk to Mr. Lane and witness the fruits of your handiwork. I have to go now." She started to roll up her window, stopped it half-way and said, "Maybe you can at least tell them to let him have something to read. He has nothing to occupy his mind."

"I'll see what I can do...." The attorney's words drowned out by the car motor roaring down the parking lane, he stood up straight, watched her drive a little too fast through the turn onto the main road around the campus toward the exit.

Dr. Peters walked from her car to the front of the administration building with a kind of passive-aggressive determination directed at the ground in front of her. She scanned the front of the old building waiting for a car to pass then hustled up the short steps to the lobby door. Inside, she made a quick appraisal; a half-dozen people walking across the foyer, a staircase to her right, a reasonable looking if mature woman working reception. "I'm Doctor Carol Peters. I'm here to speak with the Chief of Staff, Doctor Farmingham?"

"I believe he has a meeting at four, but let me check."

"Thank you." Dr. Peters looked around the foyer a second time as a small group of orderlies and a nurse descended the staircase, walked across the floor then down a hallway to her left. As she stared down that hall after them, a nearer door opened, a man stepped out into the hall, nice suit, broad smile, iron jaw. He stood there holding the door as if finishing a conversation before leaving, but then suddenly stepped back into the room, closing the door behind him. Dr. Peters stared at the empty hall in utter bewilderment. "No...way."

She walked across the lobby to the hall. The receptionist called after her, "Ma'am?"

But Carol did not answer; she walked up to the door the man had stood at, reached out for the knob. "Ma'am, you can't go in there!" Dr. Peters stepped into the room, noticed several people sitting and standing; all had been talking. The room went quiet as she turned to her left like a woman possessed, staring straight into the faces of Matt Bransford and there next to him the enigmatic, serenely beautiful Maria. "What...?" Carol Peters was momentarily dumbstruck.

The door behind her opened quickly as the receptionist blurted out, "Ma'am, you can't come in here!"

"It's all right, Ester. Thank you," the hospital director said, smiling, helping the receptionist out.

"What are you doing? Why are you here?" Dr. Peters said as she walked up to the man and woman standing silently, her initial shock turning to outrage.

Dr. Farmingham, the hospital's Chief of Staff said, "Doctor Peters, would you care to take a seat?"

"No, sir, I would not care to take a seat." Her eyes fixed the two people, though she continued to speak to the room. "I have been developing this operation for eleven months and I will not sit down while these two undo everything we've been working toward." She leaned closer to Matt and Maria and barked, "What are you doing here!?"

Matt replied uncertainly, "This was supposed to be the phase three planning meeting."

"Yes, but not for you two. Not here! You are never to come here. You realize that probably everyone on Danny Lane's ward has heard the Matt and Maria story by now. The man never shuts his mouth; everyone who knows him knows you. Months of work creating these covers and millions of dollars could be lost because some janitor or some doctor just happens to mention to him that he saw a good looking couple just like that a day or two ago. Jeez, people. Do you know his lawyer is on the ward right now; do you? You met him; what are you driving, will the lawyer recognize your car?"

"I'm not driving the Suburban today."

"I came with Matt," Maria said sheepishly.

Dr. Peters turned to a man in a suit standing alone, away from the conference table. "Who's working? We need someone on the lawyer's car; and I want it followed into LA when he leaves.

GOODBYE MARIA, SORRY

And have someone drive my car out of here, too, if the lawyer is still on the ward." She tossed her keys to the man, who stepped outside the door, reaching for his phone. She turned back to Matt and his cohort, "You two will stay in this room until that lawyer is back in LA. Change your jacket, mess up your hair, Maria needs to put her hair up; find a hat. Leave separately."

Dr. Peters pulled out a chair at the table joining the hospital director, the Chief of Staff and her operations director who asked, "Is all that really necessary?"

"Well let's see, we've got an asset who read twelve newspaper articles a year ago and predicted ninety percent of what the US government just did in Libya. How much input would he need to figure out who's pulling strings here? Not much I'm guessing. Yes, that was necessary."

"And you? How long before he figures you out?"

"I couldn't say, but he feels that he's picked me, so in his eyes, he's in control, not me. But I think we'll be lucky to get through the full sixty days, let alone a thirty-day extension we're working out with the prosecutor's office. He's not stupid." Dr. Peters turned her head behind her, "Sit down Matt; Maria, join the party."

"I was just going to use the restroom," Matt said.

"Not anymore. Have a seat," Dr. Peters replied firmly.

The hospital director leaned slightly to his right at the head of the table, to the agency's special projects director and said, "I'm getting the idea that this rather unremarkable man is worth a great deal to you."

The director replied evenly, "Our intelligence agencies aggregate a predictive accuracy of seventy-four percent. Over the last two years, Mr. Lane has demonstrated a ninety-four percent predictive accuracy. If we can learn how he does this and incorporate it into our own methodology, we could create an unimaginable advantage over any situation we encounter. Of the dozen or so predictions we've chosen to act on, his accuracy has been worth tens of billions of dollars to us, and who knows how much political advantage. He is worth a great deal to all of us."

"Why don't you just hire him?" the hospital director asked.

"We tried. He doesn't want to work for us," the agency man said ruefully.

Doctor Farmingham looked side to side between the hospital director and the agency's special projects director before facing Dr. Peters. "How then do we proceed with this plan, your phase three? Are we beginning right away since you think time is short?"

"No, Doctor. If we begin too soon, he will suspect us. I'm going to leave him on ice for a week. I'm going to stay away. While I'm gone, I'm giving him Samuel Sewall, then The Scarlet Letter, then Lady Chatterley to read. When I get back next week, we'll put him on a redacted LA Times for a few days or a week. If he's responsive to our suggestions, we'll give him limited internet."

The special projects director asked her, "That leaves you less time than you'd originally suggested we'd have to work with him. How will you get the full question list to him without raising suspicion?"

Matt spoke up for the first time. "We bury them in the articles and readers' comments for his online news." He looked to the quizzical faces of the hospital staff and offered his CV, "As the project's lead interrogator, that's my department. Some of those articles and many of those comments are us. Our profilers work up the prompts to pique his interests, ire or desires. We have a range of available options."

Dr. Farmingham surveyed the group, his first experience working at this level of subterfuge. "Doctor Peters, my experience in several hospitals leads me to wonder if this is the best approach to reach into a man's mind. Yet you seem very certain you can get him to respond to you in a short time."

GOODBYE MARIA, SORRY

Dr. Peters sat straight in her chair placing her hand on her neck, letting her fingers fall slowly down to the neck dimple just between her collarbones and linger there. "We're not here pursuing normal therapy models, Doctor, so modern clinical practices aside, we have at least one trick that has been working for thousands of years; isn't that right, Maria? I've even bought a new blouse especially for our reunion. He'll respond."

PREDATOR STRIKE
By Liam Saville

Sunday, 1 May 2011
Australian Fighting Patrol—five kilometres from Patrol Base Anaconda
Khas Uruzgan District, Uruzgan Province Afghanistan
(Twenty-four hours before the reported death of Osama bin Laden)

The loud crack-thump of the 7.62mm projectiles passing him and striking the dirt ensured Private Mark Griffith had his head in the sand well before he heard the shout of, "Contact front!" Instinctively he crawled for cover, finding a small patch of dead ground to his right. Assessing the direction of the shooter, he took aim and squeezed off several rounds from his F88 Steyr. The sound of gunfire caused the tactical radio in his right ear to spring to life, and information was quickly gathered and reported. Around him the other nine members of the section had also gone to ground. The well-oiled team had deployed into a solid, all-around defence without prompting, and significant firepower was now being brought to bear on an unseen enemy about two hundred metres ahead of them.

Griffith listened to the chatter on his radio while he continued to send rounds down range. Orders were quickly received from their platoon commander, Lieutenant Dave White, who was to the rear with the second and third sections of the platoon. As one half of the sniper pair, Griffith wasn't surprised when he and Private Bill Rankin were instructed to move to the high ground to his left to get eyes on the target.

Not needing to be told twice, the two snipers ran quickly, leapfrogging each other down a dry creek bed while the remainder of the section provided cover fire. It was a dangerous move—the small gully left by the creek made for a perfect fire lane—but it provided both cover and concealment from the enemy. Moving up to the hill on the far side of the terrain, Griffith and Rankin crawled the last twenty metres. Being careful not to expose their silhouettes over the crest, the two snipers wedged themselves in behind a large rock and got to work.

While his partner took up a shooting position behind the SR-98 rifle, Griffith pulled out his spotting scope and within seconds had eyes on the target. "Single shooter to your direct front, range two hundred and fifty metres, wind is slight and from your left," he said quietly to his partner. The shooter, who was concealed in the undergrowth, appeared to be well-trained, his continuous succession of three round bursts easily preventing the two fire-teams of the front Australian section from moving forward.

Moving his focus to the left to check for secondary targets, Griffith shook his head, blinked a couple of times, and then took another look through his scope. Twenty metres behind their target, a group of American soldiers was disengaging towards a waiting Humvee some fifty metres farther back. 'Blue-on-blue' contacts, or 'friendly fire' incidents weren't that unusual, but what stunned him was the sight of a tall Arab being escorted back to the vehicle.

It couldn't be, and yet it was; he would have known that face anywhere.

Osama bin Laden was Public Enemy Number One! He was at the top of every list of high-value terrorist targets, and while everybody was looking for him, Griffith never thought he'd actually lay eyes on him. Billions of dollars, countless lives, and hundreds of thousands of man hours had been spent trying to track down the mastermind of the 2001 World Trade Center bombings, and here he was, out in the desert with just a handful of American troops.

Thinking quickly, Griffith reached into his ammunition pouch and pulled out his camera. Clipping it into the mount on his 50x scope, he fired off a bunch of photos. The spotting scope had been specifically designed for this purpose and worked better than a telephoto camera lens, resulting in images of quite high quality. The Americans were moving briskly, and most of his photos just showed their backs, but as they reached the side of the Humvee, bin Laden turned to face the camera. It was only for a second, but that was all he needed, and Griffith snapped off a burst of photos.

At the same time, a loud shot rang out beside him. Griffith spun the scope back to the right and saw that Rankin had just taken out the gunner. "Cease fire! Cease fire!" Griffith yelled, knocking over his scope as he frantically pointed out the fleeing Americans.

"Ah fuck!" Rankin said, realising that he'd just shot a friendly soldier. "Why the fuck didn't you say something?"

"Because," Griffith replied, pulling the camera from its mounting and passing it to his partner, "I was just a bit distracted by this."

"Fuck me, that's Osama bin Laden!"

"Exactly," Griffith replied, taking back the camera and stuffing it into his webbing.

Griffith knew he urgently needed to update the boss. He crawled backwards a few metres while reaching for the toggle switch on his throat microphone.

His hand never made it.

At that very moment, a high-explosive Hellfire missile that had been launched from an unseen drone slammed into the large rock formation that was concealing the two Australians. Rankin took the full force of the blast. What was left of his charred body would be almost unrecognisable. Griffith was luckier, shielded as he was by the downward slope, Rankin's body, and a small divot in the ground. The massive percussion still threw him fifteen metres. His landing on the rocky ground below did the worst of the damage. As well as fracturing two of his ribs, Griffith also suffered a savage knock to his head, a blow that almost cracked his combat helmet in half and instantly put him out for the count.

Tuesday, 3 May 2011
Role 3 Medical Facility—Kandahar Airfield, Afghanistan
(Thirty-six hours after the reported death of Osama bin Laden)

Griffith woke with a blinding headache. He was disorientated and had no idea where he was or how he had gotten there. All he could manage before passing out again was to turn to the person next to him and ask, "Did we get the bastard?"

"Yeah, we got him." The response came in a crisp, American accent. It was all Griffith heard before passing out again with a smile on his face. It would be another twenty-four hours before he came around again, and when he did his head was a lot clearer.

"Afternoon, soldier," a familiar voice said beside him.

"Hey, Skipper," Griffith replied, turning to face Lieutenant White, who was standing beside his bed. "Where am I?"

"You were evacuated back to *Tarin Kot*, then on to Kandahar," White said. "The fucking Yanks cocked up. You and Rankin took a hit from a drone a couple of days ago. Sorry to tell you, but Rankin didn't make it."

"I remember," Griffith said solemnly, "but did we get bin Laden?"

"Yeah, a lot's happened since you've been out of it. The SEALs got him in Pakistan a couple of days ago. How'd you know? The doc said you've been unconscious almost the whole time."

"Pakistan? That doesn't make any sense," Griffith said, trying to sit up but stopping when he felt a sharp pain in his ribs. "We saw him with a couple of US grunts out in the desert just before we got hit. They were getting into a Humvee."

"What are you talking about? There weren't any friendlies out there, just that lone insurgent gunner Rankin took out."

"Skipper, I'm telling you it was him. I even got a photo through the scope. Pass me the camera from my webbing and I'll show you."

"I've got all your gear here, Private, or at least what's left of it." White held up a large bag and said, "It's what I came up to collect. I just went through it, and there's no camera."

"There has to be. I was using it with the spotting scope."

"Well, it's not there now. When you got hit, your shit went everywhere. We tried to get what we could while waiting for the chopper but could have missed it. Don't worry though; bin Laden is dead. There's no way you could have seen him in the desert a couple of days ago. You probably just heard it on the TV while you were passed out, and your mind is messing with you."

"Maybe," Griffith said, not entirely convinced.

"Just get some rest. You'll be staying in *The Ghan*, so you can come back out and join us in a while when you're mended."

Tuesday, 4 October 2011
Sydney, Australia

Sam Ryan had joined the army a little later in life than most new recruits. He'd married at an early age, and by the time his thirty-second birthday had come around, the relationship was falling apart. A friend suggested taking a little time out for himself. While the friend hadn't had anything as extreme in mind, Ryan had decided to join the army reserve.

He was already a homicide detective in the New South Wales Police Force and had a degree in policing investigations, as well as nine years of practical experience. As a result, the staff at the Australian Defence Force Recruiting Office had taken one look at his curriculum vitae and quickly steered him towards a position as a Defence Force investigator. It was a perfect match for his skills. During the selection process, his ability, prior knowledge, and experience were confirmed. Within a couple of months, Ryan was offered a direct special service officer entry as a captain with the tri-service ADFIS, or Australian Defence Force Investigative Service.

He'd never regretted it. In time he came to realise his true love was the military. With his divorce and ex-wife behind him, he'd thrown himself into his military training and the new role with gusto. About a year in, he'd resigned from the NSW Police and made the jump to full-time military service. Now, three years later, he hadn't looked back.

He was based at the Joint Investigation Office, or JIO, at Sydney's Garden Island, and he typically spent his time managing and overseeing the work of a team of non-commissioned officers, and personally investigating the more complex or sensitive matters that came across his desk. He'd also volunteered for almost every military course that was on offer and at times spent more time away from his unit on training courses than he did working with his team.

Ryan had quickly realised that policing was only a very small cog in the large military machine, a fact that suited him fine. Although he was a relatively junior officer, his superiors generally left him alone, only taking an interest in what he was doing when issues seemed particularly sensitive or shit was about to hit the fan. So when he received an unexpected call at home to attend a meeting with Colonel Rayner at Victoria Barracks, he figured something was up.

As the provost marshal of the ADF, Colonel Tim Rayner was effectively the commanding officer of the entire ADFIS and a man Ryan had only met in person a couple of times. On the last occasion, the ageing yet incredibly sharp career officer had requested an urgent briefing about an investigation into sexual misconduct on one of the Navy's frigates. Just hours later the national media broke the story. The fallout for the whole Defence Force had been huge, and as he made his way to Paddington, Ryan couldn't help but worry.

When Ryan arrived at the barracks, he was shown to the Colonel's office. Not usually the jittery type, his stomach was still doing somersaults as the senior officer dispensed with the usual military formalities and asked him to take a seat at a small meeting table in the centre of the room.

"Thanks for making time to see me this morning," Rayner began. "I know that this is a little unorthodox, but we have a situation developing, and I need your help."

"The least I could do, sir," Ryan replied, unsure that he'd had any option.

"Captain, I'm going to get straight to the point. There was an incident in Afghanistan late last night, and by incident I mean a death. Not unheard of in a war zone, I know, but unfortunately this one has a bit of *déjà vu* to it. You may recall that back in 2006 the army came under some flack when one of the 3RAR boys accidentally shot himself in Iraq."

"I take it you mean the Kovco incident?" Ryan said, thinking back to the shooting of the young infantry soldier, a case that had made international headlines for all the wrong reasons.

"That's the one. Our investigation was bungled up every which way, and it looks like it happened again."

"Another investigation, sir?" Ryan asked, confused.

"No, no, another death. We received the report earlier this morning. A soldier with the Third Mentoring Task Force was found dead in his room with a single gunshot wound to his head. Early indicators are that he most likely shot himself with his service pistol. We can't afford to stuff this up, and I need an experienced investigator that I can trust."

"Sir, sorry, I'm a little lost," Ryan said, not sure where this was going. "Are you asking me to recommend an investigator for the job?"

"No, son," the Colonel said, shaking his head and cracking a small smile, "I'm asking you to take the job. As I understand it, you're more than qualified. You even completed the Mission Rehearsal Exercise in Darwin last month with the troops heading over soon. So, what do you say, can you do it?"

"Well, I'll need some time, sir. I'll have to make arrangements with my team, and I'll need to get my personal kit squared away."

"Don't worry about your work; I'll take care of it. There is a business-class seat reserved on an Emirates flight leaving this afternoon. Fifteen hours from wheels up, you'll be in the United Arab Emirates, and from there you'll join a military transport for movement to the Multi-national Base in Tarin Kot, Afghanistan. As for kit, just take the basics; you'll be fully fitted out on arrival. So, can I count on you?"

"Who will I be reporting to?" Ryan asked, a little wary about why he was being sent from Australia when there were already investigators in theatre.

"For routine matters you'll report to the Australian commander on the ground, who, believe it or not, is a naval officer. In relation to the investigation," Rayner said, sliding a handheld satellite phone across the table, "you'll be reporting directly to me, and I'll be expecting regular updates."

Wednesday, 5 October 2011
Multi-national Base Tarin Kot (MNB-TK)

After the luxury of a fifteen-hour, business-class flight on an Emirates A380, the move to a military transport plane was a bit of a step down. Fortunately Ryan had plenty of time to stretch out and rest during the first stage of his trip because with five Bushmaster Infantry Vehicles in the cavernous cargo hold, there wasn't much leg-room left in the giant C-17. The seats too were different; gone were the plush leather loungers he'd dozed off in, and in their place he found himself strapped to a collapsible, side-mounted mesh seat that hadn't been designed with comfort in

PREDATOR STRIKE

mind. At 180 centimetres and a trim eighty kilograms, Ryan certainly wasn't large, but if he had been any bigger, the tight squeeze would have been unbearable.

Adding to the experience, about an hour and a half into the flight, just as they were coming over the mountains on approach to Tarin Kot, the pilot announced that he'd observed some surface-to-air fire. With the plane flying at less than a thousand feet, he instructed everyone to hang on while he deployed flares and conducted some standard evasive manoeuvres. The pilot then proceeded to throw the plane through a serious of sixty-degree-angle bank turns. The experience was nauseating, and by the time they landed on the dirt airstrip a few minutes later, Ryan was regretting the second helping of dessert he'd had on the A380.

Once they were on the ground, the first thing Ryan noticed when the large cargo ramp came down was the temperature. Back in Sydney the weather was just starting to warm up, but because it was now autumn in Afghanistan, there was a distinct chill in the air.

Inside the newly finished terminal, the two ADFIS investigators who'd been called in immediately after the shooting greeted Ryan. He'd met them both briefly back in Sydney months ago, before they'd been deployed to the Middle East Area of Operations. Both were competent investigators and, not for the first time, he couldn't help but wonder why he'd been flown over, given that they were already here.

Petty Officer David Cleary, a twenty-year veteran of the Australian Navy, was the older of the two and a little on the plump side. What was left of his receding hair had completely greyed, and although he was only in his early forties, he had the misfortune of looking almost sixty. His offsider, Sergeant Joseph Dunn, was just twenty-seven. He'd enlisted in the army right after high school, and unlike Cleary was a fitness fanatic. Standing together, the sight was almost comical, and, had Ryan not known better, the pair could almost pass for grandfather and grandson.

"How was your flight, sir?" Cleary asked, shaking Ryan's hand.

"Great, right up until I got off the A380 in Dubai and stepped onto the RAAF's roller coaster from hell." Cleary smiled. "Have you guys been waiting long?"

"About half an hour," Dunn said bluntly, "which isn't too bad given the lack of any real timetables into this place. At least it's warm in here. This new terminal was only finished a couple of months ago. Before that we just had a couple of old containers slapped together. They leaked like a sieve, and the wind blew straight through them."

"So what's happening with the crime scene?" Ryan asked as the three of them walked to the marked military police Land Cruiser parked outside.

"I was first on the scene," Cleary offered, handing Ryan a stack of glossy photos. "I took these the minute I got there and then sealed off the accommodation block. I have a list of everyone who was in the room before I arrived, and there's a US Marine MP corporal standing guard at the door."

"A US Marine?"

"Yes, sir," Cleary nodded. "We're really short on staffing, so we try to get help when we can. I've also asked their forensic team to come over later to help us process the scene, if that's okay with you, sir."

"Sounds fine, Petty Officer, unless either of you are qualified scene-of-crime officers?"

"I've done the course," Dunn said, "but I haven't used it much, so some help from the Yanks won't go astray."

"Okay, agreed," Ryan said, "but I want you in there supervising, Sergeant. If this turns out to be anything other than a suicide, I want to make sure we have somebody who can testify that everything has been done right. Now, as for the body, where is it?"

"Still *in situ*," Cleary said, taking the driver's seat as Ryan got in on the passenger's side and Dunn climbed into the back. "We were told you were on the way and didn't want to move it until you had a chance to take a look. The accommodation here isn't real warm, so we figured it would be almost as cold as the morgue this time of year."

"Fine, in that case, let's head straight over and have look. Then I'll get one of you guys to point me in the direction of the Q store. I'm going to need a full set of kit, as all I have is the uniform I've got on and the civvies I wore on the commercial flight."

The soldiers' accommodation at the Multi-national Base generally consisted of small, sparsely furnished, rectangular rooms with bare, plywood walls. The room that had been occupied by the deceased, Private Mark Griffith, was no exception. Along one wall at the far end sat a metal double bunk-bed similar to those you'd find in the bedroom of many ten-year olds. At the other end, a small desk with a laptop and a pile of books was positioned with a cheap, blue office chair. In between stood a collapsible, blue canvas wardrobe, and along the opposite wall were two large, green trunks: standard issue for all Australian soldiers. This didn't leave much space, and from the doorway Captain Ryan could see that the body of the deceased was lying in the middle of the only patch of unoccupied floor in the room.

"Someone's been in here," Cleary said in a low voice while looking in over Ryan's shoulder. "Have a look at the photos I gave you. When I left the wardrobe flaps were closed, those books on the desk were in a neat pile, and one of the trunks was open."

Flicking through the photos, Ryan could see that the petty officer was right. Stepping back into the corridor, Ryan approached the US Marine. "Corporal, who did you let into my crime scene?"

"Nobody, sir," the Marine replied, looking a little sheepish.

"Don't fucking lie to me, soldier!" Ryan continued, his face now only a few centimetres from the US serviceman's. "You have exactly five seconds to give me the name and rank of the person, or persons, who have been in that room, or I am going to beat the living shit out of you and have you locked up for assaulting a superior officer! Do you understand me?"

"Yes, sir."

"So, what's it going to be?"

"Naval Criminal Investigative Service, sir. Said her name was Special Agent Baker, Norma Baker. She had the correct identification, sir. Said she wouldn't touch anything and not to tell anyone she was there."

"Let me guess, Norma Jean Baker perhaps? Well? That's just fucking great! You bloody imbecile, you've just let some woman posing as Marilyn Monroe contaminate my crime scene!"

"Sorry, sir. I—I—I don't have any excuse. I—I didn't make the connection with the name."

"Get the fuck out of my sight, and tell your commanding officer I'll be over to see him about your little fuck up."

"Yes, sir."

With the hapless Marine sent on his way, Ryan turned to the two Australian investigators. "No more outside help, boys. Is that clear?"

"Yes, sir," they replied in unison.

"And, Sergeant, you'd better get kitted up to process this scene because we'll be doing this ourselves. Fucking NCIS, what do those pricks want with my crime scene?" Not expecting answers, Ryan stood there thinking for a few moments. There had to be more to this case than he'd been told.

Processing the room took the better part of half a day, and part-way through Ryan arranged for two soldiers from the Medical Corps to come down and collect Private Griffith's body. Cleary went with them to ensure that there was no mix-up at the morgue, something that had happened before and not the sort of mistake Ryan was prepared to allow to happen on one of his cases.

"Nothing here that I wouldn't expect," Dunn said as they were packing up their gear. "Angle of trajectory appears about right, and his right hand tested positive for gunshot residue. There doesn't appear to have been a struggle of any sort, and there were no defensive wounds. Judging by what we have, it looks like it was a suicide."

"I'm not sure I agree with you, Sergeant," Ryan replied, looking around the room again. "There's something missing. This guy must have had a family, and I'm thinking he'd have left a note, and besides, why would somebody impersonate a US federal agent to take a look at a suicide?"

"Maybe the note's in there," Dunn replied, pointing to the computer. "Not many messages get sent longhand these days, or it could have been taken by Marilyn."

"Could be, and we'll need to find out, but one thing's clear: we still have a lot of work ahead of us."

After finally making it to the Q store and arguing with the warrant officer running the show, Ryan was issued the kit he required. He stopped at the armoury next and got into yet another argument before eventually signing out an H&K USP pistol, three magazines, ammunition, and a shoulder rig. The pistol, developed in Germany by Heckler & Koch, was not standard Military Police issue, and therein lay the problem. Generally the H&K was reserved for Special Forces use. However, because Ryan had qualified on the weapon during the Army's Close Personal Protection Course and there were no spare Browning pistols in the armoury, he was eventually allowed to take one.

His next point of call, after dropping most of his new kit off in his room in the transit barracks, was the office of Commander Mike Sims, a naval officer who found himself in command of a unit supporting several thousand soldiers and airmen hundreds of miles away from the nearest ocean. The irony of the situation was not lost on the commander, who Ryan had met during a previous case at Garden Island.

"I figured you'd arrived, Ryan," Sims said, shaking Ryan's hand. "I've already had two WO2s complain about a smart-arse MP pushing his way around the Q store and the armoury, and I just got off the phone with an American major who wants to know why an Australian officer threatened to assault one of his MPs. Are you planning to piss anyone else off while you're here, or did you just get up on the wrong side of the bed?"

"We'll have to see how we go, sir, but as for the American, you can tell him from me that if I ever see that Marine around one of my crime scenes again, I'll more than make good on that threat."

"Yes, I heard what happened—"

"You heard…already? What, have these walls got ears?"

"Something like that. So, what do you think? Did the kid top himself, or have we got a serious issue on our hands?"

"It's too early to tell. The scene was inconclusive, and we haven't spoken to any of his colleagues or superiors yet, but something doesn't feel right. Did you know him, sir?"

"Private Griffith? No, never met the kid. I knew of him, of course. He was involved in a blue-on-blue fatality last May. The enquiry's been a real shit fight; lots of mudslinging from both sides. It's only just been completed."

"I didn't know that. What happened?"

The commander spent the next few minutes explaining to Ryan what had happened and outlined the findings of the enquiry, which essentially established that the Predator drone had malfunctioned. According to an analysis of the footage shot by the drone and subsequent diagnostic checks, there had been an error in its weapons targeting system. As a result, the Hellfire had slammed into the two Australian snipers rather than the machine gunner, who was its intended target.

"Okay, that would have been nice to know before I got here. Could have looked over the report on the flight. Do you think the two issues are related?" Ryan asked.

"Don't see how," Sims replied, "but I guess that's up to you to work out."

PREDATOR STRIKE

Thursday, 6 October 2011
MNB-TK, Afghanistan

The second day of the investigation got off to an early start. Before sunrise a group of local insurgents had decided to wake everybody early by firing off two mortar rounds that landed inside the wall of the Australian compound. Nobody had been injured, but the resulting explosion and fire all but destroyed two Land Cruisers, including the only marked Military Police vehicle on base. In response the whole compound had been immediately stood to, with all personnel taking up pre-defined defensive positions, ready to repel any resulting attack the insurgents cared to launch.

After twenty minutes it was apparent that the enemy hadn't stuck around to fight, and while the Quick Reaction Force was deployed in a vain attempt to locate the aggressors, the rest of the base was stood down to get on with their day.

It wasn't until everybody filed down to the mess hall, however, that the most devastating effect of the morning's interruption was felt. One of the main advantages of life in a large base, as opposed to the smaller forward-operating bases, was the availability of fresh, hot meals three times a day. The timing of the mortar strike, though, had coincided with the cooks' breakfast preparation, and because the cooks stood in a gun pit with everybody else, everyone had to settle for a breakfast of cereal and toast.

It was Ryan's intention to spend most of the day conducting interviews and taking statements from the members of Griffith's platoon, as well as anybody else who he'd had contact with at Tarin Kot in the days prior to his death. These would be the people that knew him best, and as such they'd be the ones to know whether or not he was in the frame of mind to commit suicide. They'd also be prime suspects if it turned out that Griffith had met with foul play, so Ryan wasn't sure how forthcoming they'd be with information.

After outlining his plan in the small, makeshift Joint Investigation Office, Ryan left Cleary and Dunn with the task of scheduling the interviews while he went off in search of the US Marine MP Company. Norma Baker was obviously just an alias used to get access to his crime scene, but whoever the impostor was, she had been after something. He didn't know what, but Ryan had a feeling it had something to do with the Americans.

Thanks to the earlier mortar strike, Ryan's options for getting down to the US compound had been somewhat reduced. He could probably have arranged to borrow another vehicle, but it wasn't far, so he figured it was just as easy to walk—a decision he regretted within the first few minutes. According to the thermometer outside his building, it was a cool eight degrees Celsius; factoring in the wind chill, however, it felt closer to zero.

The Marine MP Company was located by the entrance to the American compound. Security, not surprisingly, was tight, but after confirming his identity, the soldiers on duty at the main gate quickly pointed him in the direction of the company commander's office.

The Americans, unlike their Aussie cousins, were very well-equipped. As if to rub it in, not one, but a small fleet of military police Humvees were parked in front of the company HQ. When he stepped inside, Ryan could have been forgiven for thinking he was walking into a fully-equipped, civilian police station back in Sydney. The corporal manning the front counter immediately left whatever he was working on at a nearby desk and approached the Australian officer. "Can I help you, sir?" the Marine asked in a thick, Southern accent.

"Yes, I'd like a few minutes with your OC if he's available."

"I'll see if Major Tan is available. Who should I say is here to see him, sir?"

"Don't worry, Corporal, I've got it," a slim, Asian officer said, stepping into the office. "Captain Ryan, I presume, I'm Major Mike Tan. Come through to my office."

Ryan followed the American officer past the counter and into one of about half a dozen offices at the rear of the building. Tan's office wasn't large, but even so it was at least twice the size of the whole JIO back at the Australian compound. "So what can I do for you, Captain?" the American said, taking a seat and motioning for Ryan to do the same. "You haven't come over to threaten any more of my Marines have you?"

"No, sir," Ryan replied. "I just wanted to have a chat, but now that you mention it, your man cocked up yesterday, and as a result my crime scene was compromised. I was fairly angry about it, but it was out of character for me, and I'm sorry."

"Well, yes, I can see you had your reasons, and I'd have been pretty pissed too. So apology accepted. Now, to the reason you're here, I ran the name Norma Baker through our system, and we don't have any NCIS agents by that name. I don't know who that woman was, but to be honest I wouldn't have associated the name she gave with Marilyn Monroe either."

"That may be the case, sir, but his instructions were clear," Ryan said, not letting the issue go, "and they were not to let anybody into that area. Even if she'd been a real special agent, she had no business being in my crime scene."

"Well, I guess I have no argument there. As you said, he cocked up. I'll see to it that the corporal is suitably reprimanded, but believe me we have no idea who that woman was, and her actions weren't sanctioned by us."

"At least not officially, hey?" Ryan said, standing up to leave. "Thanks for your time, sir."

"Is there anything else I can do for you, Captain?" Major Tan inquired, choosing to ignore Ryan's remark.

"Not unless you work out who that woman was," Ryan said. "She had to be American."

"Look, Ryan, don't push it. I've already told you she wasn't one of ours, and what makes you even think she was even American?"

"Well, if she's not she really should be in show business because her accent clearly fooled your guy." Ryan turned and walked out of the office without waiting for an answer.

As luck would have it, in the short time he'd been at the US compound, the sun had made an appearance. It was still cold, but the wind had also dropped, so it wasn't bone-chillingly so. Just as well too; the way he'd left things with Tan, he doubted very much that the Americans would have offered him a lift in a blizzard.

Back at the Aussie compound, Cleary and Dunn had arranged the interview schedule and had started taking statements off some of Private Griffith's section mates. They'd organised it so Ryan would interview his roommate, his close friends, and his section and platoon commander, while they concentrated on anyone who Griffith dealt with on a daily basis but in the larger scheme of things were a bit further removed. The first cab off the rank was Griffith's platoon commander, Lieutenant David White. At first impression the 191-centimetres, pencil-thin lieutenant seemed a little geeky, almost clumsy, and he didn't fit the mould of the typical combat-hardened infantry officer. Like all the members of his platoon, White had been at Tarin Kot for about a little over a week when Griffith had been shot. The platoon, he told Ryan, had rotated back to the rear echelon base after a six-week stint at Patrol Base Tinsley and in two days would be heading out again to Patrol Base Anaconda.

"He was never quite the same after he was injured," White said, in response to a question about whether he thought Griffith's death was an accident. "Just couldn't get back in the saddle, always seemed to be a bit distant, suspicious of everything, maybe even a bit paranoid."

"What do you mean by paranoid?" Ryan asked.

"He had it in his head that this whole thing was a big conspiracy. He thought he'd seen Osama bin Laden out in the desert just before he was hit. Couldn't get the idea out of his head."

"And what, the missile was a deliberate attempt to cover it up?"

"Yeah, something like that. But it couldn't have been; it's impossible. The SEALs killed him the next day in Pakistan. Griffith must have heard the news or something while he was semi-conscious, and then twisted the story in his mind. The problem was that he honestly believed it."

"So do you think the paranoia was enough to make him want to kill himself?"

"I wouldn't have thought so, but I don't see what else it could be. As far as I knew he was looking forward to heading home soon, as we all are."

For the remainder of the day, Ryan heard variations of the same story from everybody he interviewed. By all accounts Griffith was a competent soldier who'd been affected by a tragic accident that had cost the life of his mate. His family life had been normal, and there had been no recent bad news from home, but everyone had heard a version of the story about Osama bin Laden. Some said they'd all noticed a change in their colleague, but none of them really believed that this had led to Private Griffith taking his own life.

The last interview Ryan conducted that day was with one of Griffith's close friends. Private Chris Smith had attended recruit training at *Kapooka* with Griffith, and the two had been tight ever since. The interview with Smith had taken longer than most of the others. This was typical: those closest to the deceased always had a far greater insight into what had been going on in the person's life. What struck Ryan as odd, however, was that Smith, unlike everybody else, didn't raise the missile attack or the way it had affected his friend until he was directly asked. Even then he got the impression Smith was holding back, almost as if he was feeling him out on the issue before deciding to talk about the topic. Ryan could understand somewhat and sympathised with the young soldier who had just lost a good mate, but he needed the full picture, and he knew he'd need to conduct another, more frank discussion with the private at a later time.

It was 1830 hours by the time Ryan met with Cleary and Dunn in the JIO to go through the events of the day. "So what do we think?" Dunn asked between sips of the largest protein shake Ryan had ever seen. "Was he so screwed up by the incident last May that he took his own life?"

Ryan shook his head, clearly not comfortable with the idea. "I'm not seeing it. Nobody I've talked to has given us any indication that the kid was depressed. Sure he was a bit screwed up by it all, but I don't see that leading to him blowing his brains out."

"So what about this story about the bin Laden sighting?" Dunn asked. "Sounds a bit out there, but by all accounts Griffith believed it was true. Maybe he just got sick of everyone laughing at him about it behind his back."

"Well, there had to be one hell of an investigation into the incident," Ryan said. "I mean, you don't just accidentally drop a Hellfire missile on two guys on your own side and then sweep it under the carpet. We need to get a hold of a copy of that investigation report, and we need it yesterday. Can you make it happen?"

"Definitely, sir," Cleary said.

"I also want to talk the doctor who treated him in *Kandahar*. They signed off on him returning to active duty, so they must have had an opinion on his mental state." Ryan stood up and moved towards the door. "Here's what we do tomorrow: you guys stay here and finalise the interviews and statements. They're moving out to Anaconda the day after, so we need to finish up. Also, don't forget to get me a copy of that investigation report. I don't care where it comes from, but I need it quickly."

"I don't think it's going to say that Osama bin Laden was in the middle of Afghanistan the day before his death," Dunn said.

"You're right, it won't, but we need to be sure we're not missing something here. While you guys are doing that, I'm going to jump on the morning transport to Kandahar to see what I can find out at the hospital. Now, unless there is anything else that's pressing, let's get some chow and call it a night."

Friday, 7 October 2011

Unlike the previous morning, Friday got off to a considerably more civilised start. The local insurgents had obviously decided not to press their luck with another attack, and Ryan was able to sleep until 0600 hours. He'd made arrangements the night before to hitch a ride with a Chinook crew that was making the trip from Tarin Kot to Kandahar Airfield at 0900 hours, so he had a bit of time on his hands.

Ryan headed to the mess for a hot breakfast after showering, and then he phoned through his first report and left a voice-mail message for Colonel Rayner back in Australia.

When he returned to his room on his way to the flight line to pick up his cold-weather jacket, Ryan was surprised to find an envelope addressed to him under the door. Ripping it open, he found a short, handwritten note from Private Smith inside:

> *Sir,*
> *Sorry I couldn't tell you yesterday. Mark Griffith didn't shoot himself. He gave me something two weeks ago and said I'd know who to give it to when the time came. We need to meet again but in private because I think I'm being watched.*
> *—Private Chris Smith*

Ryan read the note twice. He'd figured the soldier had been holding back, but he hadn't expected this. Placing the envelope in his jacket pocket, he locked the door and headed out. Pulling Smith in for a second interview had just become more important, and he made a mental note to send a message to Cleary and Dunn from Kandahar to set up a private meeting for later that night.

Despite the slight delay at his room, he was still an hour early when he arrived at the terminal at 0800 hours. Dunn's comments about the unpredictability of flight times were still fresh in his mind, and he didn't want to miss his ride. As it turned out, however, he needn't have worried because the crew was content on exercising the time-honoured military tradition of 'hurry up and wait.' At 0930 hours he was finally asked to head out to the aircraft, where he took his seat while the pilots carried out their pre-flight checks. When the aircraft was still on the ground fifteen minutes later, Ryan figured that they must have found a problem. The crew hadn't said anything, and it was left to one of the ground technicians to tell him that they were waiting for a civilian passenger. The technician didn't know who it was, and it wasn't until she arrived that Ryan learned that the person holding them up was an American journalist.

Her dark, wavy hair was tied back in a ponytail, and Ryan guessed she was in her late twenties or early thirties. Even in the loose-fitting cargo pants and an oversized army surplus jacket, there was no hiding the fact that she had an absolutely smashing figure. When she caught his eye, she flashed a flirtatious smile as she climbed aboard, and it was suddenly clear why the pilots had been in no hurry to leave. Good looks, it seemed, could get you places—even in a war zone.

The twenty-five minute, 115-kilometre flight was thankfully uneventful, and Ryan used the time to take in the view, both of the largely barren desert terrain through the small bubble window next to him and of his gorgeous fellow passenger on the other side of the cargo hold.

The moment he stepped off the Chinook and onto the apron at Kandahar International Airport, Ryan was lost. The airport, which was located about 16 kilometres to the southeast of Kandahar City, was one of the largest in the country. Over the past decade the sprawling airfield had grown exponentially, to the point where it was now the largest base in this part of the country and the nerve centre for the International Security Assistance Force in southwestern Afghanistan.

Ryan had been told that the hospital was housed in a modern, custom-built, and fortified building close to the airstrip. The only problem was that this description fit half the buildings he could see, and he didn't know which way to turn.

"You look lost, Captain," a female voice behind him said.

Turning to see the journalist from the flight behind him, Ryan smiled. "Yeah, I'm looking for the hospital. It's probably one of the biggest buildings here, but I have no idea where I'm going."

"I was like that my first time. This place is a city, but you're in luck: I'm going there myself. Doing a story on a trauma team from my hometown."

"And where's that?" Ryan asked.

"What, my hometown? Washington."

"Not exactly a town."

"Well, no, but it is home," she said, flashing him another smile while holding out her hand. "I'm Erica by the way, Erica Daniels."

"Sam Ryan, but call me Ryan; everybody else does," he said, shaking her hand and holding her gaze momentarily. "I'm all yours; lead the way."

It only took a few minutes to stroll from the flight line to the hospital complex, but Ryan was chatting with Erica as they walked, and he wouldn't have cared if it had taken a few hours. Feeling like a schoolboy with his first crush, Ryan was almost disappointed when they parted ways at the main entrance, and he couldn't help but hope he'd run into the gorgeous journalist again.

Quickly snapping back to reality, Ryan approached the front desk and was pointed in the direction of the Australian medical team's office. There he was asked to take a seat while the doctor who'd treated Griffith was contacted. Not having an appointment, or even any idea when the doctor was working, Ryan wasn't surprised when, after several minutes of waiting, he was asked to come back in a few hours when the doctor would be on duty.

Ryan headed to the cafeteria to kill some time. Grabbing a magazine and a coffee, he took a seat where he could see the TV while he flipped through the month-old edition of TIME.

"Mind if I have a seat?" Erica said, walking up to his table a short while later. "I need to talk to you."

"Please do," Ryan replied, smiling as he put down his magazine and turning to face her.

"I'm afraid I wasn't entirely honest earlier," Erica admitted, sitting down and pulling her seat in close. "It's about your investigation. Private Griffith didn't kill himself; he was murdered."

"Okay," Ryan said, leaning back and crossing his arms, "now you've got my attention. What do you know about my investigation?"

"A confidential source at the CIA told me that the missile strike that injured him in May wasn't an accident. He and the other sniper saw something that they shouldn't have."

"Go on," Ryan said, still a little in shock.

"He agreed to talk to me on the record. Said he could give me proof that Osama bin Laden was in Afghanistan and in US custody the day before he was killed."

"And what exactly did he tell you?"

"Nothing, that's the point: he was killed the day before we were to meet."

Ryan sat in silence, not knowing how to respond. "It doesn't make sense," he said after several seconds. "If he was already in custody, why stage a raid in Pakistan? What aren't you telling me, and who are you really?"

"Nothing, I'm just journalist following up on a story, as I told you."

"Yeah, but now your story is about my investigation, not some trauma team. Slight difference, wouldn't you agree?"

"Yes, and I'm sorry," Erica said, looking down at the table. "I don't know who to trust on this."

"You didn't know who you could trust? Just who do you think you are? I can't talk to you about an ongoing investigation, and even if I could, you still haven't answered my question. Why did they conduct the raid in Pakistan if bin Laden was already in custody?"

"It's complicated, but basically the CIA has had him in Syria since two-thousand-two."

"Syria?"

"Syria is a no-brainer," she said. "His mother and first wife were Syrian, he spent time there as a kid, and the Syria government was happy to come to the party. But when the relationship between Washington and Damascus began breaking down earlier this year over the Syrian uprising, the CIA started to get worried."

"What, that the whole world was going to find out about their little white lie? Oh yeah, sorry for all the fuss and all folks, but we forgot to mention that we caught the fucker ten years ago! That's not going to go down real well, and I can see how they might be worried. So do you have any proof for any of this shit?"

"Yes," Erica said. "I've got documents and eyewitness reports that put him in Syria, but Private Griffith's sighting was the only definitive link to the US government's involvement."

"I want a copy of your research. If you have information that relates to the murder of an Australian soldier, I want a copy."

"I can't do that."

"Oh, I think you can, unless you want to get arrested for impersonating an NCIS agent, which I assume is a fairly serious offence in your country. I'm sure the Marine you bluffed your way past at my crime scene will recognise your photo."

"Okay, okay, there's no need for threats. I'll let you have a copy, but you have to keep me informed about your investigation. If anything comes up that links into my story, you have to tell me."

"Not a chance. You don't walk in here, bat your eyelashes, and get everything you want. Oh, and one other thing, I want to know what you removed from my crime scene."

"Nothing, nothing at all. It was stupid of me to go there, I know. I thought he might have a diary or some notes, but there was nothing there."

Ryan went silent again and put his hand on his jacket to feel the letter from Smith through the thick material. Getting back to Tarin Kot to speak with the young soldier just got a whole lot more important. Right now, however, both Smith and his interview with the medical staff at the hospital would have to wait. His priority had to be getting the information from Erica, if that was even her name. He didn't know what information she really had, but if it was even half of what she said, he couldn't risk letting her out of his sight.

"So, do you have a copy of your research here at the base media centre?" Ryan asked.

"No. I didn't want to leave it lying around. I've got it with my laptop, locked in the safe in my room in the city."

"You're not staying on base?"

"No. I prefer to be independent. I even have a local driver who gets me around."

Ryan was skeptical. Who was this woman, and what wasn't she telling him? For all he knew, she could be CIA herself, or even the person who shot Griffith. Could he trust her? Probably not, but what other choice did he have?

Kandahar City, Afghanistan

After a twenty-minute ride in the back seat of a local taxi, Ryan found himself in the city centre outside the Continental Guest House. Erica had told him while they'd been driving that the guesthouse was one of only a handful of hotels still operating. This one in particular, she'd said, was popular with journalists because it offered an Internet connection in each of its thirty-seven rooms. Was that the truth? Again, he had no idea. When they pulled up at the rear of the hotel, Erica handed the driver an American twenty-dollar bill and asked him to wait.

Walking up the well-worn hallway towards Erica's room, Ryan couldn't help but notice that all the furnishings were tacky Western knockoffs with no hint of the rich, local Afghan culture. Personally he didn't understand it, but maybe the owners thought it would be more appealing to their international guests.

As they approached Erica's room at the end of the hall, it became obvious that something was wrong. The door, although closed, was broken, and the surrounding doorframe was in a similar state. The cause of the damage was equally evident: right next to the handle, on the otherwise white door, was a large, black boot mark.

"I take it this isn't how you left it?" Ryan whispered, drawing his pistol.

"No, it was fine when I left yesterday," Erica replied.

Half suspecting a trap, Ryan pushed the door aside and stepped in, pistol up in a two-handed grip. There was nobody there, but the room had been turned upside down. All of the furniture had been upended, Erica's clothes were on the ground, and even the mattress had been slashed open.

"Where's the safe?" Ryan asked.

"On the floor in the robe," she said, stepping over her clothes and opening the wardrobe. "Or at least that's where it used to be."

Ryan walked over and looked in. It seemed the safe had been prised from the floor.

"That would have taken some effort," he said, looking at the cracked concrete. "I think you'd better get your bags packed. I'll arrange a room for you at the base."

They stopped at reception on their way out, and Ryan confirmed that the room had been intact when the housekeeper had made her rounds at 1100 hours. As for CCTV footage, he wasn't surprised to learn that the hotel manager didn't know that such technology existed. Ryan checked his watch. It was just after 1300 hours, meaning the room had to have been ransacked sometime in the last couple of hours.

When they stepped out the hotel's back entrance, Ryan saw that the taxi was still waiting. The twenty dollars had obviously been enough to buy the driver's time, yet something wasn't right. As they got closer, he saw that the taxi's two front tyres were flat, but it was the sight of their driver slumped in his seat, with blood and brain matter sprayed all over the inside of the windshield, that confirmed his fears.

Erica screamed.

Stepping in to shield the panicked journalist from the view, Ryan took a closer look. There was a small, neat bullet hole on one side of his head and a large, messy exit wound on the other. At least it had been quick. The taxi, like Erica's room, had been turned over. The glove box was open, its contents and all the driver's belongings spread out through the front.

"What are they looking for that wasn't in that safe?" Ryan asked, turning back to Erica. She looked pale.

"I have no idea. All my notes were in the safe. I haven't got anything else."

Ryan didn't have time to argue because at that moment the glass window beside him shattered. The sound of the impact made him duck, and as he did a second round went whizzing past his head. Moving on instinct, Ryan crash-tackled Erica, forcing her down and around to the rear of the car. "Get the fuck down!" he shouted, shoving her to the ground again as she tried to get up, and he drew his weapon. "Just keep your head down!"

Looking around the side of the car, Ryan couldn't see the shooter, but he had to be close. Both rounds had come from a silenced pistol—probably the same one that had been used to kill their driver. They'd been caught by surprise, and their enemy had the initiative.

The immediate problem was the shooter's location. Ryan had an idea of direction and distance, but in the urban, Afghan landscape, he could be anywhere. His preferred option would have been to take cover in the hotel and wait for reinforcements but being stuck behind a taxi on the other side of the car park made that a little difficult. "We're going to have to run for it," he said, turning his attention back to Erica momentarily. "Any problem with that?"

Erica shook her head.

"Okay, on three we move around the corner," he said, pointing to an alcove in a building behind them. "One, two, three: move, move, move!"

Sprinting toward the corner, Ryan was half expecting to feel the biting pain of a bullet in the back, but thankfully it never came. From the alcove he checked again: still no sign of the shooter. He was just about to move again when two men, both carrying pistols fitted with suppressors, darted out from the corner of the next building, headed for the taxi. As they ran, one took aim in his direction. The bullet went high, chipping the brickwork about a metre above his head. Firing on the move wasn't easy or accurate, but the shot had the desired effect, and Ryan was forced to pull back behind the corner while the men were moving. Peering out again over the sights of his pistol, Ryan waited. He knew where they were, and he was happy to wait for them to make the next move. Less than a minute later, one of the shooters stuck his head up. In contrast to the nail-gun-like pop made by the silenced pistols, the sound of the two rounds exiting Ryan's H&K echoed out across the neighbourhood. An experienced shooter, Ryan's well-aimed shots passed through the already damaged windscreen and slammed into the forehead of his target.

Ryan didn't wait for the body to hit the ground. He pushed Erica up and then sprinted to the next alcove. From there it was just two metres to the corner of the building. Covering her as she moved, Ryan sent Erica around the corner with instructions to return to the front of the hotel and hide until he returned.

With Erica safely out of the way, it was time for a more proactive approach. Firing three more rounds, he ran towards a line of parked cars on the other side of the driveway. As Ryan changed position, the remaining shooter also moved, leaving his partner's body lying where it was, and hastily retreating back around the opposite corner of the building.

Ryan maintained his momentum and sprinted down the line of cars, past the rear exit of the hotel before hitting the deck at the corner. From a crouching position, he edged his way forward and around the corner, pistol up, to confirm that the shooter wasn't standing there waiting for him.

By the time Ryan cleared the corner, the remaining shooter was in full retreat, at least thirty metres down the road and moving away fast. Within moments he'd reached the end of the block, where an old, silver Mercedes, screaming hard under brakes, slid around the corner. The vehicle was stationary for just seconds before taking off again, leaving Ryan with no chance to close the distance. Running hard as the Mercedes sped off, Ryan let fly another quick succession of shots. He had no idea if he was even hitting the car and only stopped when the slide on his pistol locked back, indicating his magazine was empty. Ejecting the used mag, Ryan slammed home a new one, released the slide, and held the pistol up with a two-handed cup-and-saucer grip, covering the street. Once he was satisfied that the Mercedes wasn't coming back, he holstered his pistol, stowed the empty magazine, and returned to the rear of the hotel.

Back at the taxi, a crowd of locals had surrounded the body of the shooter. Ryan pushed his way through the group to reach the body, rolled it over, and confirmed the man was dead, then patted him down, finding a Croatian passport in one of his pockets. Confirming the photo matched what was left of the dead man's face, Ryan copied the man's name, date of birth, and passport number into his notebook then, using the tail end of the man's shirt, he wiped down the document and stuffed it back into his pocket. The Croatian's pistol was nowhere to be seen. The second shooter could have taken it, but more likely it had already been souvenired by one of the first locals to arrive at the scene.

The Afghan National Police arrived quickly. Supported by four Canadian MPs and two Humvees of US soldiers, they'd responded to reports of gunfire and had come equipped to carry on the fight. Under the direction of a Canadian corporal, half of the local police contingent and the US soldiers spread out, forming a secure perimeter around the scene. When the locals were moved away, Ryan approached the Canadian.

"Is everybody okay on our side, sir?" the MP asked.

"Yeah, just the two of us," Ryan said, pointing to Erica, who was seated on the step of the hotel's door, "and we're fine."

"If you don't mind me asking, sir, what the hell were you doing out here alone?"

"It's a long story, Corporal, but the short version is that we'd come here to pick up some information about an ongoing investigation. We walked out the back to where our taxi was waiting, and this guy got the jump on us. I think he killed our driver too."

"Any idea why he'd want to do that, sir?"

"No idea at all," Ryan said, lying and deliberately leaving out the second shooter and the silver Mercedes. "Don't think it's anything I'm working on."

"Eastern European by the look of him," the MP said. "Probably came over to join his Jihad buddies in the fight against us infidels. We've seen a few of them in recent months. He must have picked you for an easy target. Looks like he was wrong."

While Ryan was talking with the Canadian, the Afghan police got to work photographing the scene and questioning a few of the onlookers. No coalition troops had been injured or killed, and Ryan was certain that after a cursory report was filed it would be the end of the investigation. It was, after all, still a war zone.

Turning back to Erica, he could see she was still shaking and looked as pale as a ghost. Putting his arm around her shoulder, he led her back into the foyer. At least he knew she wasn't a cold-blooded CIA killer.

"What did you tell him?" Erica asked a few minutes later as they sat together waiting for the investigation to wrap up.

"Nothing, just said we got jumped by the guy as we came out of the hotel."

"What if they start asking questions? How do we explain my room?"

"They won't. He didn't buy my story about us being here as part of an investigation," Ryan said.

"What, why not? It's the truth."

"It might be, but he'd have taken one look at the two of us coming out of the hotel and assumed we were here together for a whole other reason. I know I would have in his situation."

"Oh, well, right now I could think of worse things."

After wrapping up their investigation of the scene and arranging for the bodies to be removed, the Canadians gave them a lift back to the airfield.

"So now what?" Erica asked, taking a seat at her desk in her paper's small office in the media centre. "They have my laptop and all of my research."

"Who are 'they'?" Ryan asked a little impatiently. "You feed me a story about Griffith being killed because he saw bin Laden and was going to talk, your notes get stolen, and now we get shot at. This is just un-fucking-believable! Do you have a copy of your research?"

"Yes, back in Washington, but my laptop had the only copy of my story."

"Oh, well, at least they didn't shoot you," Ryan said. "Just rewrite it, or better still, don't and go home because next time they might not miss."

"I can't do that anymore than you can," Erica said. "This is a huge cover-up. Don't you get it? The only reason troops were sent to Afghanistan was to get bin Laden. It's all been a lie!"

"Maybe, and I can see your story means a lot to you, but chasing it down almost got you killed, and it still might."

"I know, I should have been more careful. I saw what they did to Private Griffith, but it didn't occur to me that they'd come after me like that." Erica stood, grabbed her jacket, and walked over to the door. "So are you coming?" she asked. "I don't know about you, but I could really do with a strong coffee. My nerves are shot."

From the media centre, they made their way to the recreation centre of the airbase known simply as The Boardwalk. The wide, covered, wooden walkways that formed a mini town centre had originally been built by the Americans and since then had been expanded upon by the various coalition forces. Each nation had added something new, and it now included a gymnasium, rows of local and international stores, and various restaurants and coffee shops. Thanks to the Canadians, it even had its own hockey rink.

"You can buy just about anything here," Erica said as they strolled along the wooden walkway, "from clothing and trinkets from local vendors to televisions and other electrical items at the American PX. There's even a KFC."

Stepping inside the TGI Friday's restaurant, Ryan was impressed. If the idea was to make the troops forget where they were for a few minutes, the place was a success. The restaurant's walls were covered with various sporting, music, and movie memorabilia, and while normally he'd consider the decor tacky, somehow here it worked.

"So what was it that you were really after in Griffith's room?" Ryan said, taking a seat in one of the corner booths. "And don't give me that shit about a diary or some notes. I don't buy it. Those guys at your hotel had your research, but they were still after something else, and I need to know what."

"Maybe they just didn't find the safe until after they'd turned over the room," Erica offered.

"Possible," Ryan said, "but unlikely. If they had what they wanted, they wouldn't have waited around to ambush us outside the hotel. It was too risky. They had to be after something."

"I'm sorry, but I don't know. I—"

"Drop the crap, Erica. This is only going to work if you're honest with me." After a few moments of silence, Ryan stood up and started to leave.

"Wait," Erica said, looking up at him. "You'll help me with my story?"

"I can't promise anything, but if we release anything to the media, I'll make sure you'll get it first."

"All right, I guess I can accept that. It was a camera, I was after a camera. He told me there was a camera with some photographs on it that could prove it was bin Laden he saw just before the Predator strike."

"Okay," Ryan said, taking his seat again, "that makes more sense. So do you have it?"

"No. I was hoping he was going to give me a copy of the image when we met, but as I said, he was shot before we had a chance to meet."

Ryan nodded. He had a fairly good idea where the camera might be, but that wasn't something he was about to share.

The two of them sat in silence for a few minutes, lost in their own thoughts as they finished their coffee. As unbelievable as it was, her story was starting to make sense.

"What I still don't get," Ryan finally said, "is if they had him in Syria and the plan was to move him to Pakistan to kill him—"

"Why was he in Afghanistan?" Erica said, finishing his sentence.

"Exactly. It doesn't make any sense."

"I couldn't see it at first either, and I racked my brain over it for weeks, but I came up with the answer. It took a lot of digging and a fortune in bribes to government officials, but I was able to get a copy of the tower log from Damascus International Airport."

"And?"

PREDATOR STRIKE

"And it shows that a US civilian Learjet left at five thirty in the morning local time. It didn't show the destination, but if it was headed for *Jalalabad*, it's only four hours by car across the border to *Abbottabad*."

"Okay, so why was he in *Uruzgan*? That's nowhere near Pakistan," Ryan asked.

"Something happened to the plane. It was forced to make an emergency landing."

"And you have proof of this?"

"No, not directly, but there is no record of that plane ever landing or taking off again, and I mean anywhere. Planes don't usually disappear without a trace."

Ryan didn't respond. It was possible—unlikely, but technically possible. If the Learjet had gone down unexpectedly as Erica was suggesting, it would explain Griffith and Rankin's sighting and the excessive response by the Americans, but that meant that the CIA had deliberately murdered two Australian soldiers. So much for being on the same side.

"If this is true," Ryan said, "you know you are in real danger. We need to get copies of all your research, and then I'll stash you away somewhere until I get to the bottom of this."

"You can't just sideline me!" Erica exclaimed. "This is my story, remember?"

"Yes, and if you want to live to write it, you need to let me help you," Ryan said, standing up. "So are you coming or what?"

"Looks like I don't really have a choice," Erica said, following Ryan out of the restaurant.

Back in Erica's office, Ryan used the satellite phone to call Cleary back at Tarin Kot. Not wanting to explain the whole story over the phone, Ryan stuck to the basic details and instructed Cleary to send Dunn to Kandahar on the first available transport for a couple of days of close personal protection work.

While Ryan was on the phone, Erica logged onto her newspaper's secure network in Washington. Thankfully her archive file was still intact, and within minutes she was printing two new copies of her research on the laser printer on the other side of the office. Ryan picked up a copy when it finished and flicked through the documents. The pile, which was about a centimetre thick, contained a mix of foreign papers, translations, interview transcripts, photographs, and pages of typed research notes.

"That everything?" Ryan asked as he placed his pile into a plastic document folder that Erica handed him.

"That's it," she said. "So now what?"

"Now we wait until my guys in Tarin Kot get back to me."

"Thanks," Erica said.

"For what?"

"For staying so calm and keeping me alive today. Somehow I think things would have turned out somewhat differently if you hadn't been there when I got back to my room."

The call came about twenty-five minutes later. Cleary had done his best, but he wasn't able to get Dunn on a flight until first thing in the morning, and one soldier making the trip alone by road would be suicide. He'd also tried getting Erica a last-minute seat on the military transport Ryan was due to take back later that night, but that wasn't going to happen either, and so he'd taken the liberty of organising them some accommodation. Figuring Ryan would want to stay off the radar, Cleary had called in a favour with a civilian contractor and had arranged an off-the-books room for them at an engineering firm's compound. After copying down the details, Ryan thanked him and promised a full update when he got back in the morning.

At the compound Ryan tracked down Cleary's contact, who showed them to the accommodation block. Unlike the rows of cheap prefabricated huts that most military personnel lived in on base, the Australian contractors had fairly good accommodation. Making use of the tools and equipment that they'd brought in to help rebuild the nation, they'd turned a row of concrete archways from a pre-Taliban building into comfortable living quarters. The room they were given was accessed through a roughly built wooden staircase that took them to the top level under the first concrete arch. It was furnished with a single bed and second mattress on the floor as well as three folding chairs and a small bookshelf. The room wouldn't pass for a suite at the Hilton, but it would be more than comfortable for their short stay.

Ryan gave Erica some space to start redrafting her story, and he spread his copy of her research and documents across the spare mattress. He started with her detailed notes, which he saw were referenced back to her source documents. It was immediately apparent that Erica had been very thorough in her work. It took almost two hours to read through all of the material, but at the end Ryan was convinced. While the evidence she had was largely circumstantial, it made for compelling reading.

"So," she said, seeing him file the papers back into the plastic sleeve, "what do you think?"

"I think I need to use the bathroom," Ryan said, "and then I need something to eat."

"Yeah, okay, but I was talking about my research."

"There's definitely something there, but it doesn't matter what I think. Everything you've come up with so far could, and probably will be, explained away. It will make a great conspiracy theory, but I don't think you've got enough to prove anything, at least not yet."

Stopping only momentarily to make use of the compound's toilet facilities, the two of them walked over to the DFAC Luxemburg, one of the many dining facilities where food was provided to troops free of charge. With her media credentials and a smile, Erica had no trouble getting in either, and they soon found themselves in one of the two hot food lines.

The food wasn't fantastic, but they hadn't eaten any lunch, so neither of them was going to complain. Filling their plates with a mix of roast beef, overcooked vegetables, and salad, they found an out-of-the-way table where Ryan could keep an eye on the door and most of the room. He didn't expect any trouble at the

DFAC, but after the incident in the city, he wasn't taking any chances.

"So what's your story?" Erica asked between mouthfuls of roast beef.

"What do you want to know?" Ryan countered, putting down his cutlery and leaning back in his chair.

"Single, married, family? I don't know, how about how you ended up here doing this? Anything really, just tell me about yourself."

"It's not that interesting," he said. "Divorced, no kids, career cop, and all this just fell in my lap. A few days ago, I was back in Sydney looking forward to a few days off at the beach, but that seems worlds away now. What about you?"

"Single, definitely single. My job tends to get in the way a bit. Never been married. I came close once, but it didn't work out. Story of my life really: a lot of things get started and never get anywhere, which I guess is why I want this story so much."

"Even if it gets you killed?" Ryan asked.

"Hopefully it won't come to that, but there aren't too many people who'd miss me if it did."

"I find that hard to believe. You must have family and friends back in the States."

"A few friends, but I'm away from home so much. As for family, I'm an only child, and my parents have passed. I have an uncle, my dad's brother; he calls me a couple times a year and sends a Christmas card, that sort of thing. I guess if he didn't get a card he might notice I was missing."

"Sorry to hear that. For what it's worth though," Ryan said, "I've just met you and already I'd be pretty upset if something happened to you. So don't go jumping in front of any stray bullets, okay?"

"Yeah, okay."

After finishing their meal, Ryan decided to take a roundabout way back to the contractor's compound. It would take longer, but it was the best way to make sure they weren't followed. Despite both having warm jackets on, the icy wind was brutal, and by the time they got back to their room, both he and Erica were chilled to the bone.

"I suppose this isn't a good time to tell you the heating isn't working?" Ryan said, trying to turn on the wall-mounted air-conditioning unit in their room.

Erica walked over and looked at the device over his shoulder. "Any chance you can fix it?" she asked, her hands lingering on his hips.

"Not likely, unless one of these gets it working," Ryan said, noticing her closeness as he abandoned the remote and tried the controls under the machine. "Might have to get the contractors to take a look in the morning, but it's going to be a cold night."

As Ryan turned, Erica leaned in and kissed him lightly, her lips soft and moist against his. "You know," she whispered, "there are other ways to keep warm."

"Are you sure that's a good idea?"

"Why not? We do, after all, have the place to ourselves," she said, giving him that same flirtatious smile he'd seen in the chopper that morning. Leaning forward, she kissed him again, only this time longer and more passionately.

Surrendering, he wrapped his arms around her and returned the kiss, his hands exploring the small of her back and the nape of her neck. They held the kiss for minutes, several of them, before Ryan stepped back, dropped his jacket on the floor, and pulled his shirt off over his head.

The temperature of the room was now completely forgotten.

Kissing his neck, Erica kicked of her shoes and removed her jacket, adding them to the pile of clothes growing on the floor before taking his hand and leading him to the bed.

LIAM SAVILLE

Saturday, 8 October 2011

Dunn arrived at the contractor's compound early, and after a quick round of introductions, Ryan briefed him on the situation.

"So, if Griffith didn't kill himself, who the fuck did?" Dunn said, getting straight to the point. "It had to be somebody with clearance, or they couldn't have gotten into our compound, so that rules out your two shooters from yesterday."

"It's not that hard to get in," Erica said, "and wouldn't be a problem for the CIA. After all, I did it with a fake badge and a smile."

"If this thing is as messed up as you say," Dunn added, looking over at Erica, "you really ought to take Captain Ryan's advice and head back to Washington. You're not going to be safe here, even with us looking out for you."

"I'll be fine as soon as my story is published," Erica replied, not about to be cut out of the story. "Once my article goes public, there will be no reason for anybody to target me, but until then I'm probably not safe anywhere, let alone back in Washington."

Leaving Dunn to babysit Erica, Ryan headed back to the hospital. He was desperate to get back to Tarin Kot and speak with Private Smith, but interviewing Griffith's doctors had been the whole purpose of his trip, so he'd have to take care of that first.

Thankfully the doctor who'd cleared Griffith for a return to active duty was on shift this time, and after a short wait, a young Australian doctor came up and introduced himself as Captain Darren Savage.

"Savage, bit of a tough name for a doctor," Ryan said light-heartedly after introducing himself and showing his badge.

"Yeah, if I had a dollar for every time I heard that one…" Savage said, stuffing his hands into the pockets of his jacket.

"Sorry, didn't mean to offend. I need to talk with you about one of your former patients. Is there somewhere we can talk privately?"

Savage ushered Ryan into one of the nearby consulting rooms and took a seat, offering Ryan to do the same.

"I won't take up much of your time," Ryan said, sensing the doctor was in a hurry.

"Thanks. Unfortunately we're pretty busy in here today."

Ryan outlined the purpose of his visit, and Savage turned to the computer on the desk. "You have to understand," he said, typing Griffith's name into the PC as he spoke, "we see so many patients here that it's impossible to remember them all."

Referring to the notes, Savage gave him a quick summary of his recovery. "By all accounts," he said, "when Private Griffith returned to his unit, he was fully fit. He would have had a few sore ribs for the first couple of weeks, but other than that he appeared to suffer no significant injures. He was one of the lucky ones."

"What about his mental state?" Ryan prompted. "There is a suggestion he might have committed suicide. Apparently he was obsessed with the idea that he'd seen Osama bin Laden just before he was injured. Was there any sign of post-traumatic stress or anything else that could have triggered this?"

"No. Nothing in the notes, but now that you mention it, I remember the soldier you're talking about. He was a little confused is all, not unusual when you take a knock like that to the head. We've had people in here telling us they've seen all sorts of shit."

"Okay, doc, thanks for your time. I didn't think there would have been an issue here, but we still had to check," Ryan said, standing and moving towards the door. "Is there any chance I can get a copy of his medical file?"

"Sure. I'll have one of the admin staff print it off for you. Now if you'll excuse me, I'm due in surgery."

His business at the hospital finished, Ryan added the medical notes to the pile of papers Erica had given him and headed back to the flight line. There, he quickly found the flight crew Cleary had arranged for him to fly back with and was surprised to see it was the same crew that had flown him down to Kandahar the day before. This trip, unlike the first, unfortunately, wasn't delayed by the late arrival of a good-looking female journalist, and they lifted off the tarmac at Afghanistan's busiest airport right on schedule.

Sitting in the rear of the long, cigar-shaped Chinook, Ryan flicked through the medical report and went through the events of the last seventy-two hours in his mind. What had started out as a possible suicide was now looking more and more like a murder involving the government of one of Australia's closest allies. Erica's motivation in all this also had him concerned. Taken at face value, she was after the story; an exclusive like this had to be a once-in-a-lifetime opportunity for a journalist, and there was no way she was going to back off. Yet what if she was actually part of it all? From her reaction during the firefight outside the hotel, he was certain she wasn't a CIA field agent, but he couldn't be sure she wasn't involved in some way, and despite what had happened between them, he made a mental note to check her background when he got a chance.

After touching down at Tarin Kot, Ryan headed straight to the JIO. He needed to place a call to Sydney and update Colonel Rayner. He'd specifically asked to be kept informed, and a lot had happened since Ryan had last been in touch.

Ryan greeted Cleary as he walked in and then dialled the Colonel's direct office number on the satellite phone. It was a little after 1300 hours in Afghanistan, making it about 1830 hours back in Sydney. Despite the time, Rayner was still at his desk and answered the phone within two rings.
"So what do you propose doing next, Captain?" Rayner asked bluntly without a hint of surprise in his voice after listening to Ryan's account.
"Well, sir," Ryan replied, "I was hoping you'd tell me. This looks like it's turning into a major international incident, and I

want to make sure we're all on the same page before I press any further."

"It's your investigation, Captain," Rayner said after a few uneasy seconds of silence. "So investigate. Do your job and find out who's responsible for Griffith's death. Just do it quickly and quietly, and whatever you do keep that journalist on ice."

Ryan hung up and slid the phone across the desk. "Well, that wasn't the response I'd expected," he said.

"Why, what did he say?" Cleary asked, having only heard one side of the conversation.

"Nothing really, which is odd given the likelihood of this turning to shit. He pretty much just told me to carry on as if there was nothing to it. I'd have thought he'd want to send in the cavalry, a team from Foreign Affairs or maybe some ASIS spooks. It's like he doesn't care, and I can't help but wonder why."

"Maybe that's just his style?"

"Not unless he's had a whole personality change. You should have seen how he micromanaged a sexual misconduct investigation I did last year just because it got some media attention. He was all over it like a rash. Something very odd is going on here, and I'm not so sure I like it."

Tossing the situation around for a few minutes, Cleary and Ryan discussed their options for moving the investigation forward.

"It's time we got somebody a little higher involved here on the ground," Ryan said, thinking aloud. "I need to have a quick chat with the boss. Can you find Private Smith in the next half hour or so? I should be back by then, and I have a feeling he has something that's going to make things a little more interesting around here."

Ryan walked straight to the base commander's office and knocked on Sims's door. "Captain Ryan," Sims said, looking up from a pile of paperwork. "I heard you had a bit of an incident up in Kandahar yesterday, something about a fire fight in a local square and a good-looking American journalist." Sims smiled and shook his head while pointing to the seat on the other side of his desk. "I thought you were here investigating Private Griffith's death, not getting your rocks off in some fleabag motel and stirring up trouble. Every time my phone rings lately it seems you've pissed off somebody new. You know I have more to worry about than your shenanigans, don't you?"

"It wasn't like that, sir," Ryan said, taking a seat. "We were the ones that were attacked, and both the hotel and the journalist are related to the investigation."

"Likely story, Casanova. Care to explain?"

"Exactly why I'm here, sir," Ryan replied.

During his initial meeting back in Sydney, Colonel Rayner had told Ryan that he'd be reporting to Sims for day-to-day issues. He hadn't gone so far as to say he could read the commander in on the details of the investigation, but that was exactly what Ryan intended to do. Bringing another senior officer into the loop made sense because it made the whole investigation harder to deny—and besides, he trusted Sims.

Not surprisingly, Sims found the conspiracy theory a little hard to swallow.

"So you're saying everything the kid was spouting on about when he got back from hospital was true?" Sims asked.

"It's looking like that, sir," Ryan said. "But one way or the other, I've been tasked to find out."

"How? If what you say is true, this is an extremely high cover-up. The Yanks aren't going to let you anywhere near it."

"We have some ideas, and there has to be more evidence. We just need to find it."

"What can I do to help?"

"Well, I'm not sure at this stage, but we may need local support, boots on the ground sort of thing. And someone watching our backs could be useful."

"Understood," Sims said, reading between the lines. "This organisation is great at hanging people out to dry, but don't worry, I'll keep an ear to the ground for you, and you know I'll move heaven and earth to help you track down anybody who killed one of our guys."

"So how did getting a hold of Smith go?" Ryan asked, walking back into the office a few minutes later.

"You're not going to believe this," Cleary said, "but they headed back out to Anaconda this morning."

"Weren't they due to leave later tonight?"

"Yeah, but orders came through late last night apparently."

"Well, let's just hope Private Smith keeps that package safe until we can get out there. That camera could be the key to all this."

Determined to keep the investigation moving, Ryan figured that the best use of their time would be to take another look at the crime scene. He grabbed a crime scene kit from the cupboard, and the two of them headed down to Griffith's room. When they'd gone through the first time, he'd been looking at it from a purely forensic point of view, and their search of Griffith's personal items was limited to anything that may have indicated why he'd shot himself. This time, however, he was looking for something else entirely. He didn't know what just yet, but he was betting that Griffith hadn't handed all his cards over to Smith for safekeeping. There had to be something in that room that could tell him more.

Breaking the military police seal, Ryan opened the door and just shook his head. All of Griffith's kit had been spread around the room; every cupboard, drawer, and footlocker was open, tipped out, and gone through. Even the mattress on the bed had been cut open and its contents added to the pile on the floor.

"Fucking pricks!" Ryan said, turning to Cleary, who was standing behind him at the doorway. "When was the last time we can confirm the scene was secure?"

"I checked the seal myself last night, boss. It was fine, but nobody's been inside to check since we conducted the initial search."

"And the rest of the barracks were reopened, correct?"

"Yes. Right after the body was removed and the search completed. There was an infantry platoon living outdoors while they were closed, so we had to get them open again."

"Okay, that doesn't help. Let's just get some photographs and start going through this mess. It could be that whoever did this missed what they were looking for."

The second search of the room took them a couple of hours. Ryan and Cleary went through everything, but even so the scene revealed little.

"I thought you said a platoon of grunts moved back in here after we reopened it?" Ryan said as they walked down the hall heading back to their office. "Looks deserted."

"They did. The guys in Griffith's platoon were using these rooms. A new group will rotate in later tonight."

"Right, so not only could it have been one of them in that room, but just about anybody else could have walked in unnoticed after they left. I guess that increases our suspect pool somewhat."

"Looks that way."

Back at the JIO, Ryan pulled out the laptop they'd seized from Griffith's room during their original search. He switched it on and waited for the operating system to load. "Have we got a copy of Griffith's personnel file?" he asked.

"Sure do," Cleary said. "Had it sent over yesterday while you were in Kandahar. Nothing in it was useful though."

"Maybe, but who has he got listed as his next of kin?"

"His parents, why?"

"Does it list his mother's name?" Ryan asked.

"Yeah, Anne."

"Is that A-n-n or A-n-n-e?"

"A-n-n-e."

"Got it, thanks," Ryan said, typing the name into the laptop and hitting "enter." "Bugger! Not that, what about his date of birth?"

"Seventeen October nineteen eighty-eight."

Ryan entered several variations of the date into the computer, hitting "enter" after each. After the last, 1-7-O-C-T-1-9-8-8, he smiled. "Nine times out of ten," he said, "they always pick a simple password."

The operating system finished loading and a picture of a smiling, older couple appeared on the screen. "His parents no doubt," Cleary said as he pulled up a seat and looked at the screen. "What are we searching for?"

"A photo," Ryan said. "He might have handed the camera over to Smith, but I'm hoping he kept a copy of it." Clicking on the "My Computer" tab, Ryan navigated to the search bar, typed '.JPEG,' and hit 'enter.' The page filled with thumbnails of hundreds of photos, at least half of them porn. Scrolling through the thumbnails, Ryan could see that none of them were what he was after, so he repeated the search this time for '.RAW' files, followed by '.TIFF,' '.PNG,' '.GIF,' and '.BMP' picture file formats.

"Well, he could have them hidden on here somewhere," Ryan said after closing the last of the photos, "but we'll need someone with more of an idea than me to have a look."

"So now what?" Cleary asked.

"Now we go to the source. We need that camera, and because Smith is out at Anaconda, it's time to call in a few more favours. I'm going to need a ride."

LIAM SAVILLE

Sunday, 9 October 2011

Unable to sleep, Ryan was up early, and by 0530 hours he'd had breakfast and was down at the armoury signing out a rifle. His pistol was fine within the confines of the rear echelon bases, but the plan was to head out to a forward patrol base, so he'd need a bigger bang stick. Having learned from his previous run-in with the armoury staff, he'd had Commander Sims forward his request for a rifle the night before, and the sergeant on duty didn't even raise an eyebrow when he signed out the M4A5, the Australian variant of the American M4 Carbine, along with a range of ancillary equipment and ammunition.

With his new kit sorted, his next stop was the range. The rifle he'd been given had no doubt been fully checked over, but only a fool would take a weapon into a combat zone without going over it. After pulling it apart and checking each component, he reassembled the rifle, checked its action, and then mechanically zeroed it. Satisfied, he made his way up to the firing point and, under the watchful eye of an infantry corporal, zeroed the rifle. His first three shots grouped nicely, although high and to the left. After adjusting the front sight four clicks anticlockwise to lower the elevation and then the rear sight five clicks to the right, he took up a position again at the firing point and squeezed off another three rounds. Like before, the grouping was tight, and this time they fell smack on the centre of the target.

Getting out to Anaconda was going to be a bit tricky. Had there been a resupply flight heading out, he could have hitched a ride, but as luck would have it, there wasn't one due for another two days. The solution, therefore, was to go by road, and Ryan had arranged through Commander Sims to tag along with a joint Afghan National Army and Aussie Special Forces patrol heading out that morning.

"Captain Ryan," a deep voice said from the depths of one of the four Bushmaster vehicles being prepared for the patrol, "who let you loose to play in the Ghan?"

Sticking his head in through the open armoured door, Ryan's eyes quickly adjusted to the darkened interior. "Sergeant Weber," Ryan said, identifying the familiar face of Matt Weber, a Commando sergeant who'd been the weapons instructor on Ryan's close personal protection course a few months earlier. "I thought I recognised that voice."

"So I hear you're looking into the barracks shooting. Was it really the Yanks?"

"Where'd you hear that?" Ryan asked, genuinely surprised by the question.

"You know how it is, word gets about. Also heard you had a bit of a dust up in Kandahar."

"Yeah, well, the prick had it coming," Ryan said, "but I'd love to know where you get your information."

"You know I could tell you, but…"

"Yeah, yeah, I know, you'd have to kill me."

"You know," Weber continued as he stepped down out of the Bushmaster, "if there is anything we can do to help you get the pricks that did this, just let us know."

"Thanks, I hope it doesn't come to that, but the offer is appreciated. Now where do you want me and my shit?"

Weber helped Ryan get his gear aboard the second Bushmaster and then got back to preparing the vehicles to head out. Despite there only being fifteen members of the patrol, sixteen if you counted Ryan, the four Bushmasters were full to the brim. Typically you'd get nine infantry soldiers and all their gear into just one of these vehicles, but the Commandos needed to be self-sufficient for extended periods, so the extra kit they carried necessitated extra vehicles.

With all the equipment stowed and checked, the patrol mounted up. Surprisingly Weber climbed into the rear of the second vehicle with Ryan and, after securing the door, got on the radio and gave the command for the patrol to head out. As the patrol commander, Weber usually would've taken the front passenger's seat. This position would have given him a much better view and made it easier to maintain command and control if the patrol came under attack. The fact that he climbed in the back suggested to Ryan that he wanted to talk, and it didn't take a genius to work out what about.

Located eighty kilometres as the crow flies to the northeast of Tarin Kot, Patrol Base Anaconda wasn't all that far away. The Bushmasters each weighed over twelve tonnes and had a top speed of over one hundred kilometres per hour. On patrol, however, they wouldn't travel at anywhere near that speed, and the trip, assuming nothing happened along the way, would take about half the day.

At first Ryan was a little reluctant to talk about his investigation, particularly those aspects that related to bin Laden and the involvement of the CIA. However, Weber was persistent and readily agreed to keep the information confidential.

"I figured it was something like that," Weber said bluntly, after Ryan outlined the basic premise of the bin Laden theory.

"What?" Ryan said, giving Weber a puzzled look. "Did you just say you were expecting me to tell you Griffith's death was related to something like that?"

"Yeah, so?"

"Yeah, so? Is that all you're going to tell me? What on God's Earth would have led you to that conclusion?" Ryan asked.

"It's classified."

"It's classified. I just gave you the detail of my investigation into the death of a digger, and you're seriously going to sit there and tell me the information you have is classified? Why the fuck did you even bring it up?" Ryan sat back in his seat and shook his head in disbelief. Weber sat in silence.

"Okay," Weber relented after a few minutes. "I'm only telling you this because I trust you, but my involvement or the fact I gave you anything can never appear in any report you write, and you'll have to verify it all for yourself. Are we clear?"

"Crystal."

Leaning forward so he could hear clearly over the noise of the Bushmaster's engine, Ryan took out his notebook. "So what do you know?"

"We had a static OP in place," Weber started, "about twenty clicks from Anaconda back in May. We were dug in on a hillside for a couple of days, watching a road below, because there was intel that the Taliban was using it to move opium and resupply local insurgents. Anyway, just after sunrise one morning, we hear the whine of a jet coming in low. I could tell straight away that something was wrong; it just didn't sound right. When I got sight of it, I saw it was civilian, and it was lining up to land on the road right below us. As it got closer, I could see smoke pouring out of both engines, and just as it touched the road, the one on the left exploded. Caused the plane to spin to the left, and it hit the deck hard."

"What happened then?" Ryan asked, too enthralled by Weber's account to be taking any notes at this point.

"Nothing for a few minutes. It just sat there with the whole back end on fire. After a while the door at the front flew open and four guys climbed out. I was watching through the spotting scope, and I recognised two straight off from some work I did with the US Special Forces, and one looked like a pilot. Then I look over at the fourth guy, an old guy based on the way he walked."

"And was it bin Laden?"

"Couldn't tell you, they had a hood over his head, but it sure looks like it might have been now, though."

"So what happened next?"

"Well, I know these guys tend to operate under the radar, and we were in a perfect overwatch position, so we just held tight and prepared to give them fire support in the event any insurgents turned up."

"You didn't call anyone?"

"No. We were maintaining radio silence," Weber said. "The party on the road below was fine, and I figured somebody would come and collect them sooner or later."

"And did they?"

"Yeah. About four hours later, two Humvees and a bunch of US grunts turned up. They loaded the prisoner into one of the vehicles, set some charges, and drove off. A couple hundred metres away, they stopped, blew the plane up, and kept going. That was the last I thought about them until a few weeks later. That's when I heard about a digger going on about seeing bin Laden and being hit by a US missile. I did some checking and the timeline matched, so I kind of put two and two together."

"Did you report this to anyone?"

"Report what?" Weber said. "My suspicion I saw bin Laden? Who to? As soon as we returned and put in our report about the plane going down, our whole mission was classified. Even telling you could get me booted out of the army and locked up. You know this shit could bring down the whole US government if it gets out? That would break apart the whole coalition, which would be a major victory for terrorists the world over."

"So why tell me?"

"Because I trust you, Ryan," Weber said. "I know you're a soldier, and you'll do what you're told, but at the end of the day you're also a cop, and you'll do the right thing to make sure these bastards are brought to justice."

Several hours later, as they approached Anaconda, Ryan stuck his head out of the gunner's roof hatch and took a look around. The landscape was dry, barren, and dusty, and the sand-filled HESCO barriers that fortified the base gave it an almost medieval look. The barriers, which had first been designed for flood protection, had proven more than successful in recent years at securing buildings and constructing fortified walls in the desert environments of both Iraq and Afghanistan. Arriving as flat packs, the collapsible, steel-mesh barriers had heavy fabric liners, and worked much like sandbags. Just a few soldiers could easily spread them out and link them together before filling them using a backhoe.

At each corner of the base, above the barriers, stood elevated gun towers that were manned twenty-four hours a day with numerous weapons, including a fifty-calibre machine gun.

Dismounting from the Bushmaster inside the walls, Ryan could see that the living conditions were pretty rough. Clearly there was no working sewage system because he was instantly hit by the pungent smell of burning human faeces coming from drums on the other side of the base.

"Captain Ryan," Lieutenant White said, greeting the newly arrived group, "what brings you out here?"

"Private Smith, actually," Ryan replied. "I need to have a chat with him ASAP. Is he about?"

"Yeah, he just came in from a patrol. He's been acting real weird since you spoke with him last time. Is there something I need to know? I mean, it's a long way to come just for a chat."

"Not at the moment, Lieutenant, but I'll let you know if that changes. Now where's Smith?"

"I'll track him down and send him your way."

Within minutes Smith appeared at the rear of the Bushmaster. "I got your note, Private," Ryan said. "Have you got the package?"

Smith nodded, reached into his jacket, and pulled out a plastic map case. Inside was a small, white envelope.

"I've kept this with me the whole time since Mark was killed," he said, handing over his map case as he took a seat in the back of the vehicle. "I figured it must have been important, so I didn't want to let it out of my sight."

"Is that it?" Ryan asked, opening the envelope and finding nothing in it but another handwritten note. "He didn't give you his camera or maybe even a memory card?"

"No, nothing like that, just the letter."

Ryan unfolded the letter and read through its contents while Smith waited.

To whom it may concern,

> *My name is Private Mark David Griffith, and if you are reading this it is because the government of the United States of America has murdered me.*
>
> *On 1 May 2011, I was on patrol in the Uruzgan Province in Afghanistan when forces believed to be local insurgents engaged my platoon. During the contact Private William Rankin and I were ordered to move to higher ground in order to identify the location and size of the enemy force. Whilst scouting the area with a spotting scope, I saw and photographed several US soldiers withdrawing from the contact in company with al Qaeda leader Osama bin Laden.*
>
> *Just moments later Private Rankin and I were hit by a missile fired from an unmanned drone aircraft. The missile killed Rankin and injured me. This was their first attempt to silence me.*
>
> *Since the incident everybody has tried to tell me what I saw can't be correct, that I must have imagined what I saw. I did not. I have a clear recollection of exactly what happened, and when I woke in hospital I found that my camera was missing. I don't know where it went or who took it, but there are photos on it that can prove what I saw.*

"Have you read this?" Ryan asked, folding the letter and putting it back in the envelope.

Smith shook his head. "Made me promise not to, and I wouldn't betray his trust like that."

"Okay. Did he ever say anything to you about a missing camera?"

"No, not really. I mean, I know he lost one when that missile hit him. He had to fill in an L&D form for it, and we were joking that the government would probably make him pay for it."

"Did they?" Ryan said.

"Nah, just wrote it off as being lost."

"So what do you know about his alleged bin Laden sighting?"

"The same as everyone," Smith said. "He'd tell anyone who'd listen to him about seeing Osama, but nobody believed him."

"What about you, did you believe him?"

Smith paused. "Yeah, I do. I wasn't sure at first, but I know he'd never kill himself."

Ryan nodded and waited to see if Smith would keep talking. "Okay," he said after several seconds of silence. "Is there anything else that you can tell me?"

"Only that I hope you get the pricks that did this, sir. He was a good man and my mate."

After dismissing the young soldier, Ryan read through the letter again. He'd been certain that the package Smith had was the camera or at least a memory card, which would have been the proverbial smoking gun and proof of the cover-up. Now, however, he was back to square one, and he had absolutely no idea where the camera was or even where to start looking.

"Lieutenant White," Ryan said a few minutes later as he walked into the reinforced blackout tent that was being used as the command post, "do you have time for that chat now?"

Taking a seat on one of several collapsible chairs in the patrol base's briefing room, the young lieutenant seemed concerned. "So, do you think Private Smith was involved, sir?" he asked.

"Involved in what?" Ryan said.

"In Griffith's death. I need to know if one of my soldiers is a murderer."

"Ah, no, that's not what we're thinking at the moment. Why, do you suspect something?"

"No, just like I said before, he's been acting really weird since the first time he spoke to you."

Ryan nodded his head. "I think it's safe to say that Smith wasn't involved in that way. He did, however, have a letter that Griffith had left with him."

"A letter, oh, okay, I see," White said with a surprised look on his face. "So it was a suicide then. He shot himself."

"Could be, but it's still too early to tell," Ryan said, not wanting to share his theory with Smith. "By any chance did Griffith ever talk to you about a missing camera after he was injured in the predator strike?"

"You're kidding me, right, sir?" White said defensively. "This whole crap about bin Laden hasn't come up again has it? I thought that was put to bed with the enquiry."

"It's been mentioned," Ryan said, "and I need to look at every angle."

"With respect, sir, I've already answered all these questions, several times over. Besides, it's all in the report."

"I know, I've already read it," Ryan lied, "but reports get twisted. So if you could just indulge me for a minute that would be great. Now tell me about Griffith's camera."

"Well, he said he had taken some shots on the camera and that it went missing after he was hit. Probably came out of his webbing when he was thrown down the hill," White said. "I mean, don't get me wrong, sir, Griffith was a good soldier, but this incident really messed with his head. He was adamant that he saw bloody bin Laden out there, but that was impossible."

Ryan nodded.

"Even so, just to be sure I asked around, you know, to see if anybody else could confirm he had the camera earlier, before the incident."

"And?"

"And nothing. None of them saw it, so it was probably missing before that patrol. Griffith just used the incident as a chance to have it written off. It happens all the time, gear always mysteriously goes missing during a heavy contact with the enemy."

"Okay, thanks," Ryan said. "Good to know."

Ryan wasn't convinced. If Griffith had simply wanted to write off equipment, making up a story about having photos of Osama bin Laden didn't help his case. There had to be a more logical solution.

"What happened to Griffith's gear when he was medevac'd out of the field?"

"Most of it, except for his weapons, went with him. It was all secured at the Role Three hospital in Kandahar until I collected it a couple of days later. Why, do you think one of the doctors took the camera?"

"No," Ryan said, "just trying to eliminate all possibilities. But is it possible that somebody at the hospital could have taken it?"

"Suppose so, sir, but unlikely. They get all kinds of gear going in with injured soldiers, and they have a pretty good system of securing it. I've never heard of anything going missing."

After dismissing White, Ryan made use of the privacy of the briefing room and placed a quick call to Cleary back at JIO. Without explaining, he gave the petty officer the general coordinates of the area where Weber had seen the plane go down and then instructed him to source satellite imagery of the area the day before and the day after the missile strike. The images shouldn't be hard to get, but if for some reason they were, Cleary had enough sense to have Sims place some high-level pressure. Secondly he asked him to contact Dunn in Kandahar and have him check on security procedures for injured soldiers' equipment at the hospital. In particular Ryan wanted any records that could be located for the equipment Griffith brought in with him.

In return Cleary reported back that he'd discreetly started checking some of the information provided by Erica. The task was proving difficult, but so far the basics around her timeline of events and the movement of aircraft and personnel were checking out. He also confirmed that Dunn was still with Erica and that she'd been spending the time working on her article. So far there hadn't been any more threats to her safety. Satisfied with the progress, Ryan ended the call and went in search of Matt Weber.

He found the Commando in the back of the Bushmaster. Not one for wasting time, Weber had drafted his orders for the next leg of the patrol and was now busy double-checking his map coordinates.

"Got time for a quick chat?" Ryan asked, climbing into the back of the vehicle.

"Sure, what do you need?"

"This might be a bit to ask, but I'm hoping there isn't a set route that you need to take when you head out later. I wouldn't mind checking out a couple of sites."

"Let me guess: the plane crash and the site of the missile attack?"

"Yeah, what are my chances?" Ryan asked.

"I figured you'd want to take a look for yourself, so I've already factored it in," Weber said, tapping his map.

"Excellent. Then I'll head out with you guys when you go. Thanks."

1600 Hours. Sunday, 9 October 2011
Australian Reconnaissance Patrol—near Patrol Base Anaconda
Khas Uruzgan District, **Uruzgan Province, Afghanistan**

Once the vehicles were positioned around the site, and the Australian and accompanying ANA soldiers had taken up defensive positions, Ryan was free to take a close look at the wreckage. There wasn't much of the aircraft left; the explosive charges or the resulting fire had destroyed most of it.

"You're sure this is the plane?" Ryan asked as he and Weber sifted through what had been the tail section of the aircraft. "Identifying it is going to be a bitch."

"Yeah, unless someone took a shot when it landed, that is," Weber said, with a big grin on his face.

"What are you saying? Did you get a photo of the registration?"

"It was a recon patrol; we got photos of everything that went down that road, including the plane. But before you ask, no, I don't have a copy. I handed in the memory card the minute we got back."

"Shit," Ryan said. "Then they're as good as buried. There's no way that report will be released, particularly if it went to the Yanks."

"Well, it's lucky I made notes as well then."

"Surely you had to hand them over too though?"

"Yeah, of course, but—"

"But what? How is that lucky?"

"If you let me finish, boss, I'll tell you. Seeing a plane landing here like that was a bit unusual. I'd certainly never seen anything like it, and I thought at the time it might be important. I knew I'd have to hand in all my notes, so I wrote the registration down on the inside of one of my ammo pouches, got it right here, in fact."

Weber pulled a couple of magazines out of one of the pouches on his vest, turned the material inside out, and there in faded black ink was the registration number: N221SG.

"Why the hell didn't you tell me this earlier?" Ryan asked, copying down the number.

"You didn't ask."

"So is there anything else you haven't told me? You didn't happen to keep a copy of your photos, did you?"

"Nah, I would have, but I didn't have the equipment to copy them," Weber said, returning his magazines to the pouch. "Fact is, I actually forgot about it until we got here. Seeing the wreckage just brought it back, I guess."

Ryan shook his head, slung his rifle over his shoulder, and spent the next few minutes photographing the crash site. Even the best of them, it seemed, let things slip occasionally.

Satisfied he had all the information he was likely to get from the site, Ryan let Weber know he was good to go, and within minutes the whole patrol had mounted up and was moving out.

Before making the fifteen-kilometre journey from the crash site to the site of the missile strike, Weber had an important task that had to be taken care of. One of his mission objectives was to collect and relocate a couple of remote sensors from a nearby road. The sensors, which were activated by the vibration of vehicles, were an efficient method of monitoring traffic along known insurgent routes. Set a specific distance apart, the data they captured could tell them a lot, including the number of vehicle movements, the approximate size of the vehicles, and their direction and speed of travel. Moving them was not, however, a simple task, and in order to ensure they were not detected by anybody using the road, they needed to be installed and removed under the cover of darkness. The task was going to take some time, but Ryan was simply tagging along with the patrol, so he could hardly object.

After concealing the patrol's vehicles under cam nets in a large *wadi* about one kilometre from the sensors, Weber set out on foot with three of his men just after dark. It would take a couple of hours to slowly and discreetly approach the sensors, and another couple to remove and then install them at another site along the roadway.

While they were gone, Ryan and the remaining members of the patrol took the opportunity to get some sleep. After digging a shallow shell scrape at his allotted point around the perimeter of the vehicles, Ryan climbed in and curled up in his sleeping bag for some rest. His sleep, however, was short-lived. Just a couple of hours later, he was woken for his shift on the gun piquet. Even though he was the most senior officer on the patrol, Ryan was still expected to pitch in with security, and that included taking his turn manning one of the heavy machine guns atop one of the Bushmasters.

Ryan had only just returned to the warmth of his sleeping bag after his watch was over when the whole patrol was woken by movement just outside the perimeter. It was a slow and tense couple of minutes while four figures came closer to the patrol's location, and eventually a verbal challenge was made. Fortunately the correct response came back, and Ryan breathed a sigh of relief as Weber and the three soldiers he'd gone out with moved back inside the circle.

Monday, 10 October 2011

After standing to for half an hour at first light, Weber had the patrol up and moving again early. It was his intention to head directly over to the location of the missile attack in order to give Ryan as much time as he needed at the site. Although, given the time that had elapsed since the incident, they both figured it was extremely unlikely that they'd find anything of value. Even so, Weber understood Ryan's desire to walk the ground himself, and after hearing about the missing camera, even he was hoping for a miracle.

Dismounting from the vehicles on the high ground near where Griffith and Rankin were hit, Ryan was surprised to see that they were not the only patrol at the site. On the other side of the wadi, he could make out the silhouette of two other Aussie Bushmasters. Pointing this out, Weber made a quick radio call and confirmed that a platoon-strength fighting patrol from Anaconda was also at the location.

"It'll be that pencil-neck White for sure," Ryan said under his breath. "I spoke with him yesterday about the camera."

"And what, he's out trying to put this thing to bed for his guy? He didn't strike me as the type to give a shit," Weber said.

"Could be. I actually got the impression he didn't believe Griffith even lost it out here, so who knows what he's doing."

Leaving their vehicles and half the patrol in a covering position, Ryan and Weber took the remaining troops and made their way on foot to the top of the hill on which Griffith and Rankin had been hit by the missile.

"Morning, Lieutenant," Ryan said as he walked up to White. "Come to make sure you didn't miss anything when you pulled out after the contact?"

"Something like that, sir," White replied. "As I said yesterday, I thought all this crap about bin Laden and the missing camera was done and dusted. Guess I figured I owed it to Griffith to have a look, though."

"Well, thanks for coming out. We could use your help," Ryan said, fighting hard to hold back what he really thought.

Spreading about a dozen soldiers out into an extended line, the group made a series of systematic sweeps over the area. A half an hour later, however, it was clear that they weren't going to locate the camera on the hill.

"You know, it's strange," White said between swigs on his water bottle when they'd finished, "when we medevac'd Griffith and Rankin out of here, there was a fair bit of kit strewn around. It was nothing important, so we left it to save time, but I'd have thought there'd be a bit still lying around. It's only been a few months. I checked and nobody's been back to collect any of it."

Ryan looked around and noted that the lieutenant was right. The only sign that the Aussie troops had been there at all was the scorched rock face where the missile had landed.

"Maybe the insurgents came and gathered it up to see what they could use, gain some intel, that sort of thing," Ryan said.

"It's possible," Weber replied, listening in on the conversation between the two officers. "How far away is the closest village?"

"Just down the next valley," White replied. "You can see it from the crest where we've got our vehicles. Why?"

"Well, it's pretty common for the local kids to come up and scavenge around after a fire fight," Weber said. "They'll take anything that's left behind and either keep it for themselves or pass it on to their local insurgents, depends where their loyalties lie. Something like a digital camera, however, would be a pretty cool souvenir for one of these kids. I doubt they'd get rid of it."

"You're a genius, Weber," Ryan said, thinking back to the pistol that went missing after the firefight back in Kandahar City. "I think it's time to take a drive down for a chat with the locals."

PREDATOR STRIKE

"I can take care of that for you, sir," White said. "I've dealt with the elders there a few times and can probably get them to hand it over if they have it."

"I appreciate the offer, Lieutenant," Ryan said, wondering why the young officer was so keen to help, "but this is one I'd like to do myself. If we get a hold of that camera, I won't be letting it out of my sight."

"No problem. It's just that our vehicles are already on that side of the valley. I thought we could get there quicker and take care of it, but if you prefer, we'll head over and RV just out of town until you get there."

"Sounds like a plan," Ryan said, leaving it to Smith to identify the RV point. "Once we're all there, we can put together a small group to go in and speak with the elders."

Sitting on the far side of the wadi, it would take less than twenty minutes for White's platoon to drive down to the small village of *Hossani*. Ryan's group, on the other hand, first had to navigate a deep, dried-up creek bed and a deep ravine, which added another half an hour to the trip.

"Why didn't he just wait and provide cover for us as we came across?" Weber asked as they made their way back to the vehicles. "I mean, shit, what's the rush? He's going to leave us out in the open so he can wait around at the other end for us to arrive. The guy has no fucking idea."

Same Day
Hossani Village, Khas Uruzgan District
Uruzgan Province, Afghanistan

Bringing his patrol to a halt at the designated RV some two hours later, Weber turned in his seat. "Sure this where they agreed to meet?" he asked, obviously still pissed off. "There is nobody here but us."

Standing in the back of the vehicle and looking out the top hatch, Ryan looked around and checked his map. "Yeah, this is the place," Ryan said. "He even picked the fucking location. You don't think anything could have happened to them, do you?"

"Nah, they were a fair way in front, but we'd have heard if they got in any shit."

Concerned by the apparent disappearance of the mounted infantry platoon, Weber moved the vehicles and his soldiers back up the high ground and into an all-round defence. He wasn't sure what was going on, but he wasn't impressed. According to his hastily made plan, White should have been waiting here for their arrival. Something wasn't right, and Weber didn't like it one bit.

Leaving three of the Bushmasters as well as two-thirds of their troops behind, Weber and Ryan took a handful of Commandos and made their way into town. Driving through the main street, they were instantly swamped by a group of local kids who started following the Aussies, hoping for handouts. Instructing his driver to stop for a moment, Weber got out and spoke with a couple of the kids in broken *Dari*.

"What did they say?" Ryan asked as he got back in the vehicle.

"I just asked them if they'd seen any other people in a vehicle like ours."

"And?"

"Said they had. Three of them came through just a short while ago, heading to the village elders' house."

"That fucking prick!" Ryan said, angry that he hadn't at least insisted on travelling with White in the first group of vehicles. "He just can't fucking help himself."

Finding the other vehicles and the soldiers from White's platoon a short way up the road, Weber told his guys to stay put while he and Ryan went to find White. The search didn't take long. Alerted to their presence by the sound of the vehicle, Lieutenant White came out of a small house and compound down the road.

"I've just met with the village elders," White began as he walked up to Ryan. "No one here has the camera. Looks like I was right. Griffith must have lost it before that patrol."

"What about the RV?" Ryan said, not hiding the anger in his voice.

"What do you mean?"

"You know what I mean, Lieutenant. You came up with the fucking plan. We were all meant to meet at the RV and come in together."

"Well, yeah, sorry about that, but I changed the plan, I figured—"

"You figured nothing, you snot-nosed prick!" Weber said, stepping in and landing a solid right cross that connected with White's jaw, knocking him to the ground.

Dragging himself up, White looked shocked and was clearly dazed. "Your career is finished, Sergeant," he mumbled, holding his jaw with one hand and pointing at the big, muscular Commando with the other. "I'll have you charged for that."

"For what?" Ryan interjected. "I didn't see anything, did you, Sergeant?"

"Just Lieutenant White falling over his own feet and hitting his head," Weber said.

"Well, let's hope the bump knocked some sense into him," Ryan said, brushing past the lieutenant and heading for the compound. "Let's go, I want to go speak with the village elder."

"I've already spoken to him!" White protested.

"That's great," Ryan replied, "so you can just fuck off then. We'll have a conversation about this back at Anaconda with your OC."

Leaving White to skulk back to his platoon, Ryan and Weber headed for the house. Outside, Weber knocked on the door, and they waited while the women and children were ushered out of the house and into the private rear courtyard. Weber explained why they were there in his broken Dari, and Ryan was relieved to hear a response in English.

"Thanks for agreeing to see us," Ryan said, taking the lead now that the language barrier had been broken. "We are looking for the same camera the other soldier was after. I know you told him you don't have it here in the village, but we need to be sure."

The English speaker translated and the group of elderly men in the room instantly broke into animated discussion.

"Well, this is interesting," Weber said quietly to Ryan. "I can't understand it all, but things aren't what they seem."

"I'm sorry, but there must be a big mistake," came the reply a few minutes later. "As we said to your comrade, the camera you are looking for is here. It was found by a young boy, who has it at his home. The other soldier paid the village one thousand US dollars for its return. We are going to go with him to the house now to give it back."

"Oh shit!" Ryan said, realising what was about to happen. "Where is the house? You need to show us quickly, the family may be in danger."

Following the Afghan, Weber and Ryan ran up the street in the direction the elder had pointed. The house, similar in style to the one they'd just come from, was surrounded by a mud-walled compound, and before they reached the door a single shot rang out, narrowly missing Weber.

"Is he fucking kidding?" Weber said, taking cover outside the building.

"We know you're in there, Lieutenant!" Ryan called out. "You need to give it up now before this gets any worse!"

Another two shots rang out.

"Well, I guess that's his answer," Weber said, pulling out his radio.

Within minutes heavily armed Australian and ANA Commandos surrounded the building. Taking command of the situation, Ryan ran back to where White's platoon was waiting and, without explaining exactly what was going on, ordered them to form an outer perimeter around the whole village block. Then he arranged for several of the ANA soldiers to go house to house to evacuate the neighbouring residents before he rejoined Weber.

"There's no telling how many people he's got in there with him," Weber said. "I can send my team in, but if he's got hostages, it's going to get messy."

"Lieutenant!" Ryan called out again. "It's still not too late to end this peacefully."

"Fuck you!" White replied from somewhere in the compound. "My life is fucking over now because of you! Why couldn't you and that dickhead Griffith just let things be?"

"I'm not sure I'm following you, Lieutenant, but if you come out peacefully we can talk about it!"

While Ryan kept White talking, Weber went to work with his team and planned an impromptu assault on the building.

"I'll come out when I've got the camera," White replied over the sound of furnishings being tipped up and smashed inside the house."

"You know he'll destroy it if he finds it," Weber said quietly. "We're ready to go in if you want."

"Okay. Get him out of there, but remember, he is an Australian officer, so do what you can to bring him out alive."

Weber nodded. "We'll try, but ultimately it will be up to him."

Ryan took a deep breath and tried to steady his nerves.

When it started, the Commando assault on the house went off with a bang—or, more correctly, three of them—as three flashbang grenades exploded almost simultaneously, having been thrown through windows and doors in different parts of the building. A split second later, an explosive charge punched a hole in the side wall of the mud-brick building, and four heavily armed soldiers stormed in.

The loud blast and blinding light given off by the grenades was designed to stun rather than harm, and that was exactly what had happened. Speed and aggression was the key to success, and the Commandos quickly found White, who was taking cover behind an overturned bookcase. Two shots rang out, both roughly directed at the first soldiers through the door. Instinct and training kicked in, and any hope of bringing Lieutenant White out alive evaporated with several short bursts of automatic gunfire.

After clearing the house, Weber called in Ryan, and the two of them got to work searching for Griffith's camera. Fortunately it only took them a few minutes. In a large wooden cupboard in the main bedroom, Ryan found the ruggedized Panasonic Lumix wrapped in an old rag on the top shelf.

Relieved, he unwrapped it fully and dusted it off. The camera looked intact, but there was really only one way to find out. Ryan pushed the small power button on the top of the camera and waited, but nothing happened.

"Fucking hell!" Ryan said, annoyed that the camera wasn't working. He turned the camera over and opened a small panel; at least the SD card was still in place.

Quickly calling for another camera from Weber's team, Ryan took out the card and inserted it into the camera he'd just been handed. Switching on the second camera, Ryan's initial concern that the card may have been damaged gave way to dread. The memory card was less than half full, but it contained a couple of hundred photos of Afghan boys playing in and around the village.

Not willing to give up hope just yet, Ryan thumbed his way through the images to the start of the card; there his heart skipped a beat. In three groups of burst shots, Ryan found the photos he was looking for. Of the twenty or so photos taken by Griffith, most showed the backs of a group of US soldiers and an elderly Arab walking towards a couple of Humvees. Two, however, were crystal clear images of the Arab's face, confirming Erica's theory in an instant.

PREDATOR STRIKE

Monday, 17 October 2011
Victoria Barracks, Paddington
Sydney, Australia

After being shown in to Colonel Rayner's office by one of his staff, Ryan took a seat at the meeting table and thumbed through his report while he waited. The colonel was expected back any minute, and he'd sent a message ahead asking Ryan to make himself comfortable while he waited. He'd only been back in Sydney for a couple days, and in that time Ryan had spent almost every waking hour writing and rewriting his report in anticipation of this meeting.

After locating the photos of bin Laden in the village, Ryan had flown back to the Multi-national Base with the Black Hawk crew that was called in to evacuate White's body. Back at the base, he and Cleary had made solid work of fitting all the pieces together, and in a couple of days they'd mapped out a clear picture of exactly what had happened.

The final piece in the puzzle had come when they'd checked White's finances. For a young man with no financial means outside the army, White had a lot of cash in his bank account; with their audit uncovering a series of $50,000 payments made just after Griffith's death. Totalling half a million dollars, the money was easily traced with the assistance of AUSTRAC, Australia's anti-money-laundering and counter-terrorism financial regulator, to a small US corporation from Rehoboth Beach, Delaware.

Long suspected as being a CIA front company, the same corporation also turned out to be the last registered owner of the US-registered Learjet N221SG, an exact match to the registration Weber had given Ryan in the desert, and also the same plane Erica had traced leaving Syria on the first of May. The satellite imagery Cleary had obtained at Ryan's request also confirmed the timeline, and by comparing images taken on April 29 and May 3, 2011, they were able to see that an aircraft had crash landed right when and where Weber had said it did.

When Colonel Rayner entered his office, Ryan sprang to his feet but was quickly waved back down by his superior. "So what have you come up with?" Rayner asked, taking a copy of Ryan's report as he sat down on the other side of the table.

"Sir," Ryan said, "as we discussed when I got back, it's clear what happened. Private Griffith, as unfortunate as it is, was responsible for his own death. There is absolutely no evidence of foul play or anyone else's involvement. There's also no evidence it was a suicide, so this one falls into the category of an accidental shooting."

"And what of the camera you gave me the other day?"

"What camera is that, sir?"

"Good response. There may be a future for you in this army after all, Captain. You know, of course, that if the truth ever came out it could bring down the US government, and the flow-on effect would be felt all the way to Canberra?"

"I realise that, sir," Ryan said.

"So how did you deal with the journalist, Erica whatever-her-name-is?"

"She won't be a problem, sir. As you suggested, I met her in Kandahar before I came back. I told her we'd checked out what she'd given us but couldn't confirm any of it. Her evidence is all circumstantial, and she knows it."

"How did she take that?"

"Slapped me in the face and accused me of selling her out," Ryan said. "She wasn't happy, but what could she do? She'll write her article, but without any real evidence, it will be easily dismissed. I had Sergeant Dunn escort her back to *Dubai*, and for her own safety he stayed with her until she boarded a United flight back to Washington."

"Okay, and the mess with White?"

"Shot by an insurgent during a village clearance. According to the senior non-commissioned officer at the scene, he was leading from the front when he stepped around a corner and walked into a hail of bullets, it could have happened to anyone."

"Very good, Captain, very good," Rayner said, getting up and showing Ryan to the door.

"Oh, and, Captain," he said, calling out to Ryan as he walked off down the hall, "you might want to take a look at today's Telegraph. It appears the current trade negotiations with the US are going better than expected. For some reason the Yanks are agreeing to everything we've asked for."

Later That Day

Strolling along the Haymarket end of Pitt Street, Ryan found what he was looking for down a dimly lit laneway. He'd spent the last hour and a half getting on and off various buses and trains around the city, checking the faces of those around him, and noting those that got on or off with him. Satisfied that he wasn't being followed, he'd made his way here. Known for its basement karaoke venues and sleazy all-night games rooms, these narrow back lanes on the outskirts of Sydney's Chinatown were generally avoided by the mainstream public. Here, just about anything could be bought for a price, up to and including the girls serving the drinks. Tonight, however, all Ryan wanted was anonymity.

Pulling his baseball cap low to shield his face from the CCTV camera above the door, he walked into the dingy internet cafe. This establishment, like its neighbours, had once been part of an industrial warehouse that had long since been divided into smaller commercial lots.

Walking up to the counter, he handed over a ten-dollar note and then found a seat at a private terminal in the corner of the room. Navigating to the Hotmail website, he created an anonymous account, opened his new mailbox, and created a new message. Ryan paused, took a deep breath, and typed in Erica's email address, then, after checking that nobody was watching, he plugged in a USB memory stick and uploaded just two photographs. In the message window he typed a short note: "I found the attached in the desert; somebody said you were looking for them." Then he clicked Send.

Confident it wouldn't take Erica long to realise that the metadata in the photos had been GPS coded, he didn't need to tell her anything else. Even a simple Google Earth search would show where they were taken, and that would be enough.

Ryan shut down the computer and walked out of the cafe, up the laneway, and back onto Pitt Street. There he snapped his memory stick in half, throwing one half into the back of a passing garbage truck and the other into the next bin he came across. Smiling, he continued down the street. Trade concessions were one thing, but Weber was right, somebody had to pay for what had been done.

UNDER COVER OF DEATH
By Howard Manson

(*With a nod to Robert E. Howard*)

Adham squinted down the blue barrel of his Lee-Enfield, called devoutly on *Allah* and sent a bullet through the brain of the pig running toward his door.
"*Allahu Akbar!*"
The big Arab shouted with righteousness, waving his weapon above his head, "God is great! By *Allah*, I will send another American pig to Hell!" His companion peered patiently over the rim of his spectacles, through the window cut from the mud-brick wall, seeing two men now walking toward him. He was a tall and wiry commander known only as Rafiq.
"Be patient, Adham. Put that down. Not every American is the enemy."
"This one, Rafiq, is spying on us. I saw him talking with the Americans in *Say'un*. He is not faithful. He is a pig."

A boy in uniform pushed the door open for the man dressed as the others in camo, so thoroughly worn it was indistinguishable from sand. He wore a red and white *keffiyeh*, now pushing it aside to have something to do while he appraised the tension in the room.
"Look, Rafiq, he is hiding his fear!" Adham stood closer, boldly, and shouted at the new arrival, who was changing his

posture with the spread of his feet, preparing to thrust his hand up under the man's larynx to shut him the hell up.

"*Assalamu Alaikom*, Rafiq. Why is Adham singing like a fly on a horse's ass?" said Jal, in nervous bravado.

"By *Allah*, I will see you dead, American. Today I wished to be the day, watching as my bullets went home. Go, Rafiq! I want to teach this pig what it means to be a spy. I will cut him down!"

Jal noticed that Adham had stayed two good steps back. Adham was a big man, could easily wrestle Jal to the floor. But Jal had made a point of displaying his passion for violence with his quick reflexes. No man yet had beaten him, and this fat sluggard wasn't going to be the first. It seemed clear that, despite his bluster, Adham was aware of this too. But it was the rifle, with the psychopathic, twitchy finger, that turned Jal to his mentor, Rafiq.

"Brother, *I seek forgiveness from Allah*, but what have I done? What did I do last week, or the week before? Are you sympathizing with this madman?"

Rafiq put his arm around Jal's shoulder, turning him to a chair near his desk. "Adham is my right hand, my wife's nephew. He is hot blooded, but I trust him. Put that down!" This last said as Rafiq stepped around to sit behind his desk, seeing Adham aiming his weapon at the back of Jal.

Jal turned with purpose to face the rifle barrel. "Shoot me! You son-of-a-bitch, I will come back from the dead to kill you." Jal again began to sit down but stood a second time as he saw the rifle swinging back at him.

"PUT IT DOWN!"

Adham lowered his weapon, staring boyishly at Rafiq. "Tell him, Rafiq…."

"Shut-up or get out!"

Rafiq let the silence spread within him before speaking calmly; "Adham saw you talking with Americans in Say'un the day before yesterday. He thinks you are giving them information about us."

Jal grimaced painfully with self-reproach. He shook his head, about to speak, the words and thoughts colliding in the back of his throat. He made a sound, put his palms up while shaking his head. Rafiq smiled with paternal, yet tight lips. Adham was about to speak, but Rafiq shook his head to the side once, silencing the man for the moment. He appraised Jal.

"Well...?" Adham shouted in frustration with the long silence.

Jal stood out of his chair. "Well what, you fat idiot? Every week you come tell Rafiq that I'm spying for the Americans. Every week you tell every man in this camp that I'm spying for the Americans."

"You talk to them! You come from America. How did they know to send their drone into THIS *wadi* last week? How! I'll tell you how. YOU!"

"You fucking moron. You and your men put up so much radio chatter and put down so many tire tracks in the middle of nowhere—if you could write, you should make them a sign. *Allahu Akbar*, but the Americans have satellites. Have you heard that one?"

"I'm going see you dead, brother...."

"DON'T you call me brother!" Jal spat, venom and saliva flying to the dusty floor.

Rafiq asked quietly, now behind Jal, who was still staring down Adham, "What did you talk about with the Americans in Say'un?"

Jal began his answer before turning his eyes away from the ape, "Two men came to me in the market. One of them said he worked for the CIA. He knew my name." Jal now took his eyes off Adham, turning his back to sit in the chair facing Rafiq.

"What did they look like?"

"Tall, white man. Military look, dark hair. The other man was Arab. He didn't give me a name."

"What was the Arab man dressed like?"

"He wore blue jeans and a shirt. He dressed like a westerner, not in Arab *thawb*.

"What did you want in the market?"

Jal raised an eyebrow but answered naturally, matter-of-fact, "You know, I went in for tea and bread and gum."

"Were you alone?"

"I was with Mika'il, Rafiq...."

"Did you buy these things?"

Jal looked strangely at Rafiq. "Yes."

"And how did you carry them out of the market?"

"Rafiq...?"

"It's a simple question."

"I mean, do you mean...how? I just carried them out. I guess I put them in my pack."

"Perhaps Mika'il helped to carry them out with you."

"He'd gone off on his own. I haven't seen him since. I asked you two days ago where he went, but you haven't told me."

"So you put your tea and bread in your pack?"

"Yes. It's like a backpack. You know, hangs on your shoulder."

Adham circled the opposite side of the desk from Jal. "That is your lie! I saw you at the market. You had nothing in your hands, no bag with you. I saw you with the white man and the Arab. You did not have a bag with you!"

"But I had the bag. It could have been on the ground, the truck...I don't know what you saw, but...."

"There! You see! He is thinking of something to say. That is the same excuse Mika'il made...."

"What are you talking about? Where is Mika'il?"

"This is what I'm telling you, Rafiq. He has nothing to hide behind. He went to Say'un to talk to the Americans, because he is working for the Americans."

"The Americans talk to everyone! They ask everyone from the camp to tell them something. They will give ten American dollars to anyone who walks in their building and gives them a name."

"That! Why do you say that?" Adham demanded.

"Because they told me.... Ask the men. They talk to everyone, probably even you!"

UNDER COVER OF DEATH

Adham shouted, "*Laa, laa, laa, laa, laa, laa!* Not me! I saw you. You are trying to wriggle out of this by blaming me. *Ya Allah!* But I saw you...."

"Rafiq, those men told me that this camp is being watched. I learned this from them. Ask the men. I believe the honest men will tell you the same I am saying." He turned inimical eyes on Adham, "It is the man with something to hide that would need to deny it."

Adham lunged across the width of the desk, shouting incoherently. Jal was up and skirting the onslaught, but late. Adham's arms slipped down the waist of Jal, but he grabbed the man's leg and twisted him painfully down to the floor. Rafiq was up shouting. Jal twisted his upper body back around toward his attacker, driving his shoulder to the floor for purchase, then firing off a jackhammer burst of wicked sets into the back of Adham's neck. The grip on his leg freed as Jal did a breakdance kind of thing, spinning around on his back, fiercely kicking out with the hope of sending Adham to hell or *Allah*, either was fine as long as he went.

A pistol shot cracked through the scuffle.

"Enough! Stand up." Rafiq let his pistol hand down to his side. Jal stood without dusting himself, stepping out of reach of the man on the floor.

Rafiq spoke sternly if evenly, "Adham is my family. I've known him his entire life. You have been here six months. As much as I like you and want to believe you are my brother, there are others who feel the way Adham has spoken."

"Rafiq...."

Shaking his head, denying the interruption, "I will give you two chances to prove your loyalty."

"*Jazaka Allahu Khairan*, my every breath is at your command...."

Adham stood up, shaking himself back together. He rubbed the back of his head and neck. Rafiq fingered the release on the old *Makarov*, checked the clip, and slid it back in with an exclamation before handing it to Adham. "Give it to him."

The Arab gorilla stepped forward, but Jal stepped toward him as well, keeping his eyes on the man's in case he needed to disarm him. But the ape shoved the flat side of the pistol toward Jal's chest, trying to startle or hurt him, though Jal just fielded the gun with two hands.

Rafiq was matter-of-fact. "I want to see the items you bought at the market. We'll go to your quarters."

With the certainty of the righteous, Jal nodded, gesturing to the door, "Of course. We'll go right now. I want to clear this up once and for all." Rafiq smiled politely, looking as if he intended to agree. Adham picked up his rifle, finger on the trigger, taking a position behind Jal.

Outside the door into the hallway, Rafiq turned to Jal, put his hand on the man's shoulder and said, "It has occurred to me that you will probably have the items that Adham clams he did not see you with. If you are a spy, such a lie would be foolish. I know you are not foolish. What is it that people say, the best liars only tell the truth?" Rafiq squeezed and rubbed Jal's shoulder with affection. "Still, even the best men make small mistakes now and again." Looking down, speaking as if measuring out words to his own son, "I believe in you, Jal. I want to believe in you. You are American, it's true—we have others here. But you are an Arab, and I know in my heart you are one of us." Rafiq continued to massage Jal's shoulder. It was becoming an annoyance, a sort of communication that Jal didn't want to hear. "I believe you, Jal. I do. That is why I want you to show Adham that my trust in you is well-founded."

"I will, Rafiq. You can trust me.

"I know. I know I can." The hand stopped massaging, but remained gripped firmly. "Mika'il is in the room there. The storeroom. Take the gun and shoot the traitor for us. Show Adham that you are one of us."

"But Rafiq, What do…Mika'il is not a traitor! I can't do that."

"I'm very sorry to hear that, my friend. Because if you don't walk in that room and kill Mika'il in the next ninety seconds, Adham is going to shoot you. This is the act of good faith our leaders have said they will accept."

"But Rafiq, anyone can...."

"Your time, along with my trust and the remaining days of your life, is slipping away. Go now." Rafiq crossed his arms before turning his back.

Jal made the six or eight steps hesitantly down the hall, stood outside the door, looking toward Rafiq's back. "*La hawla wala quwata illa billah.*" He burst through the door into the storeroom.

Adham pulled down the hammer on his museum piece, taking one step toward the door before hearing Rafiq say sullenly, "Wait. Give him one more minute...then you must go in and shoot him."

"*Ya Allah!*" Jal burst through the door into an image painted with pure barbarism.

"*Bismillah Arrahman Arraheem.* In the name of *Allah*, the most gracious the most merciful." He shouted automatically, more as segue into critical thought. Mika'il was standing at the small room's center with his arms tied to a beam over his head, beaten and bloody, his weight borne by the twisted ankle of one foot as his other had been splintered into three angles. His chest and arms bore the engravings of a sadist. His eyes and lips had long ago swollen shut and hardened. "*A-ozu billahi mena shaitaan Arrajeem!*" Jal shouted. He decided then that when Adham opened the door, he would turn and shoot the bastard, come what may.

"Mika'il! Can you hear me?" Jal whispered into the ear of the fleshy *piñata*. His face was close to his friend. His flat hand caressing the wounded cheek without moving. Jal looked around the small room for inspiration, anything, a miracle.

But there were only boxes and a small window opening cut into the mud-brick wall, big enough for a man to squeeze through, but about five feet up the wall. "Mika'il! We have one minute!" Jal drew a pocketknife and reached up for the ropes around his friend's wrists. His only thought now was to get out. He could shove Mika'il through the window, carry him into the wadi, wait for the night to return to steal a truck. Or he could wait, shoot Adham as he walked through the door in the next minute, use the pistol and the rifle to kill Rafiq and any guards, then get outside to a truck.

The only thing clear to Jal now was that he was going to *Allah*, and Adham was not going to be the Angel of Mercy about sending him there. If they knew about Mika'il, they knew about him. The Egyptian's cover had been perfect. Though they'd met and trained with NCS together, preparing to infiltrate this group, Mika'il had gone on alone to Egypt to begin the long work of creating the life of a believer. So immersed in his cover when they'd met again, there had been uncertainty and distance between them when he'd arrived at camp last year. But Mika'il was the truest of men, and the six months of friendship here together, along with the purpose of their unspoken work here for the agency, had rekindled the affection for their former friendship.

Perhaps it was the emotion that had turned the rope to steel. Perhaps it was the certainty that he was about to fail as a field agent and a friend. But whatever the reason, the rope would not cut quickly. He reached up with a second hand to hold it taut.

The unreality of the hoarse whisper stalled its meaning, "Don't tell Kathryn what happened to me."

Jal reached down with a hand behind the neck of Mika'il, pulling himself close to the face, his lips touching the blood-caked cheek. "Can you walk with me if I carry you?"

Mika'il shook his head a millimeter. "I don't feel my legs."

"If I put you through that window, you will fall, but you can't make a sound."

"I'll try...."

Jal put a stout wooden box at the base of the window, thinking he might stand on it to roll the injured man off his shoulder, then shove him through. Facing the back of the camp, there was but one small building between them and the escarpment a hundred yards away. There were caves enough for hiding if he could get them there. Jal returned to his task at the ropes.

"I told them about me, Jal. Everything. But he didn't stop."

"What did you tell them?"

"He knows pain. He didn't want information, he wanted tears."

"Adham did this?"

"He has the devil's fingers."

The shuffling boots of that Arab primate scraped the floor in the hall outside. The laconic, moaning oath worming its way through the cracks in the door foretold the fate awaiting them. "*Allahu Akbar!*" sung with the undertones of satisfaction that only a psychopathic murderer can conjure.

Jal stood just in front of Mika'il, but turned to face the door, planted his feet, sighted down the stubby black tube above his two-handed grip. The lever on the door moved and stopped. There was no other way out.

"They don't know about you or our mission." Mika'il's speech was as quiet as thinking.

Jal did not take his sight off the door, yet part of his mind disconnected to look back on his friend. He wanted to hear more—there was an answer in there somewhere, but the door flew open with a violent kick and a sickly grin revealing filthy teeth. But this awareness did not distract Jal from seeing the rifle being brought to bear on him and then hearing the basso profundo, "*Allahu...*" Jal felt his finger taking up slack at the long-pull position on the Mak's trigger.

Without removing his eyes from Adham, Jal drew his right hand holding the pistol back across his body as an archer would, drawing a bowstring. But he continued outward with it to extend his arm, the pistol now aimed at Mika'il's face. Jal's empty left hand extended toward Adham with his fingers compelling the brute to a second's stillness.

Jal felt himself in two parts, watching from behind as he twisted his head to his friend, taking aim, and then again as he searched the eye behind the swollen slit of an eyelid now struggling to open. There was a message there for Jal, something of recognition, and the unspoken words of purpose, 'Mission first.' His heart dove into that one brown eye; he felt himself crying out, "I will tell Kathryn what I've done. I love you, brother." Jal sent his bullet through the center of Mika'il's face. A brain-stem shot that relaxed all tension without reflex. The body now hanging limp from its bonds.

"*Astaghfiru lillah!*" Jal shouted in rage.

The dissociation of Jal's mind went completely outside himself. He watched himself from above, yet perceiving his goal through a narrow conduit, focusing his hatred on Adham. Jal watched as he flung himself at the giant man, stepping inside the rising rifle barrel, twisting the ape's wrist to its threshold of pain, driving the bulk of Adham back into the wall, and shoving the muzzle of the pistol viciously hard into the skin at the side of the nose. But there had only been one bullet, and Jal had not noticed the locked open slide. Only a dozen pulls on the impotent trigger brought him to the point that he smashed the side of the gun into Adham's temple, and then as the man tottered, thrust up with the heel of his other hand, square into Adham's nose. The back of the man's head brutally hit the wall before his body crashed to the floor.

The bright hot sun lancing his eyes and his head jerking down to avoid that brought him to the awareness of the arm around his back and the hand gently massaging his shoulder. There was a firm squeeze accompanying the words, "Did you kill Adham?"

"I don't know."

"I'm sorry about Mika'il. I know you were friends. I liked him, too. I truly did. I don't know if he said those things to stop Adham or if they were true."

Jal said nothing; Rafiq's words, meaningless. But he felt the pressure on his back guiding him to walk. So he walked.

Rafiq talked to the blue sky, "Walk with me. You can make me tea in your quarters. Things are different today, my brother, and the time has come that we need to discuss your new mission with us."

Jal was aware that his mind was disengaged and seriously struggled with himself to get it to refocus on his vague feeling of imminent danger, yet try as he might, he could not bring his attention to bear on the situation. What mission? And for the life of him, he couldn't recall the last time he'd even bought tea. He didn't drink tea.

---

http://gutenberg.net.au/ebooks06/0601741.txt
Title: The Fire of Asshurbanipal Author: Robert E. Howard * A Project Gutenberg of Australia eBook * eBook No.: 0601741.txt

BREAKING IN
By Stephen Leather

HOUSE-BREAKING was a victimless crime, pretty much. That was what Richie Grout thought about his chosen profession. For a start he almost never did any actual breaking when he did the entering. There were more than enough unlocked doors and open windows around, even in South London. Nine times out of ten, his method of choice was to shin up a drainpipe and into a bathroom window. Most people seemed to think that windows above ground floor were somehow unreachable. Big mistake.

And when he was in the house, he never – repeat never – hurt anyone. That was an absolute rule. If there was someone moving around, he left. Like a bat out of hell. He'd never had a confrontation, and he never would. But he knew that if he was ever confronted then he'd either run or he'd raise his hands and surrender. Grout was a thief, not a mugger. He didn't carry a weapon of any kind, not even a knife.

Not that he'd even come close to being caught in the act. Grout was too clever for that. Too clever and too prepared. He'd ended up in court, that was true. But that was always because he'd been shafted when he was trying to unload the stolen goods. And a couple of times he'd been caught by CCTV. But he'd never been caught red-handed and he planned for it to continue that way.

The things he stole were insured most of the time. And if they weren't insured then that wasn't his fault, was it? Insurance wasn't expensive and if you couldn't be bothered taking out insurance then you shouldn't start whining when someone takes your stuff.

So all in all, there were no victims. Just the insurance companies. And they were worth billions, so screw them. He looked up at the drainpipe and took a couple of deep breaths to steady himself. He was wearing his usual house-breaking gear – black jeans, black Nikes and a grey hoodie. He had on tight-fitting leather gloves and a small black Adidas backpack in which he had a small Magnalite torch, a set of night vision goggles, a mobile phone jammer and a nylon bag that, when unrolled, was big enough to hold a 32-inch flat screen television. That was one of Grout's favourite items. Televisions, BluRay players, laptops, anything like that was an easy sale. But he knew a fair bit about antiques and paintings so he always had a good look to see what was on the walls and in display cases.

He tended not to get jewellery because people kept stuff like that in their bedrooms and Grout broke into houses when people were asleep. That was when they left windows open. When they went away on holiday they locked everything and set their alarms. When they were asleep in their bedrooms they felt secure and they let their guard down. That was when Grout would move in.

His technique rarely varied. Up the drainpipe and through the window. A quick check of the upper floor to make sure no one was awake. Then downstairs, keeping close to the wall to minimise squeaks. He'd unlock the back door, then do the same with the front door. That way he had his escape routes ready. If anyone came downstairs he'd be on his toes and away, no fumbling with keys or bolts or chains.

The next step was to check for car keys. His van was parked close by but if he could find the keys then he was more than happy to relieve the owners of their vehicles. Some people took their car keys up to the bedroom but most left them in the kitchen or the hallway. The people in the house he was about to burgle had two cars. The guy drove a BMW 3 Series and his wife had a

BREAKING IN

red Mini Cooper. The BMW was in the driveway and the Mini was parked in the road. Grout would be happy with either. Stealing cars was another victimless crime, he reckoned. Anyone who didn't have their car insured for theft was just asking for trouble.

Then it was time for a quick look around for valuables, then off into the night. Simple. And nobody got hurt. He'd arrived at the house at just after two o'clock in the morning and all the lights were off. The couple were always in bed by midnight, regular as clockwork. He took another deep breath, rolled his shoulders, and grabbed the drainpipe. He climbed easily, letting his legs do most of the work, and within seconds he was alongside the bathroom window. He reached for the latch, unhooked it, and slipped inside.

He stood by the shower for a while, his head cocked on one side as he listened intently for any sound that the occupants were awake. If he did hear anything he would be back out of the window and down the drainpipe. But there was nothing. He smiled to himself. It was always during the first few minutes of entering a house that he had to fight the urge to burst into the bedroom and shout "Surprise!" at the top of his voice.

He knelt down, took off his backpack and opened it. He slipped on the night vision goggles and switched them on. Soon everything was bathed in a greenish light. He took out his mobile phone jammer, a cigarette-sized stainless steel box with three aerials of varying lengths, and switched it on. It would neutralise any mobile phones within fifty feet. He put his backpack on, stood up and listened carefully again and then eased open the bathroom door and stepped out into the hall. His heart was racing so he forced himself to breathe slowly and evenly, in through his nose and out through his mouth. He kept his back to the wall as he tiptoed down the stairs.

He stopped when he was halfway down. There were three doors leading off the ground floor hall. One led to the kitchen, one to a dining room and the third to the sitting room. The sitting room door was open. Grout stiffened as he realised there was a man standing by a large sofa. He was wearing a pair of night vision goggles similar to Grout's.

Grout froze, wondering what the hell was going on. The man with the night vision goggles was holding something. A knife.

Grout took a step back up the stairs and a board creaked. The man in the goggles turned to look in his direction. He was a big man, wide shouldered and with bulging forearms. He was wearing a black nylon bomber jacket and tracksuit bottoms. And on his feet, the sort of paper shoes that forensic scientists wore on the cop shows that Grout loved to watch.

The man with the knife straightened up. Grout turned to run back up the stairs. That was when the man standing behind Grout slammed something hard against the back of his head and everything went black.

When Grout opened his eyes his head was throbbing. He started to lift his right hand but realised that it was taped to the arm of a wooden chair. So was his left hand. He blinked his eyes, wondering what had happened. The lights were on and the curtains were drawn. His night vision goggles were on the coffee table. There was a flatscreen TV on one wall and a Bang and Olufsen stereo on a shelf but Grout was no longer thinking about what he could steal.

The Big Man stood next to the table. He had taken off his own goggles but was still holding the knife. It was almost a foot long with a wooden handle. A carving knife maybe. Something that belonged in the kitchen. There was blood along the length of the blade. Grout realised that the man was wearing pale blue surgical gloves. He frowned. All the thieves he knew wore gloves, but he'd never heard of anyone wearing latex ones.

"He's awake," said the Big Man. His head was shaved but there was enough hair growing back to suggest that even if he didn't shave he'd be pretty much bald. He had pale blue eyes, thin bloodless lips and large, slab-like teeth. He moved to the side and Grout saw someone else sitting on the sofa. It was the guy who lived in the house, the driver of the BMW. His head was slumped on his chest and there were flecks of blood on his shirt.

A second man walked in front of Grout. He was short, just over five six, and wearing a brown leather jacket that looked as if it was a couple of sizes too big for him. Like the Big Man, he had paper covers over his shoes and was wearing blue surgical gloves. He peered at Grout and nodded. "Told you he'd wake up sooner rather than later."

Grout tried to move his legs but realised that they were also taped to the chair.

"You could have killed him, knocking him down the stairs like that."

"I didn't have time to do anything fancy," said the Little Man. He was holding sheets of kitchen roll. He had a pinched, rat-like face and some sort of growth on the side of his nose.

"Stairs clean?"

"Done and dusted," said the Little Man. He gestured at the knife in his colleague's hand. "Are you planning on taking that with you?"

The Big Man grinned. He went over to the sofa and took a close look at the man slumped there.

"Is he dead?" asked Grout.

"Not yet," said the Big Man.

"Who are you?" asked Grout. "And what the fuck's going on?"

"We were about to ask you the same thing," said the Little Man. He opened Grout's backpack and took out the phone jammer. He switched it off and showed it to the Big Man.

"Nice bit of kit," said the Big Man.

"Stops people calling the cops," said Grout.

"You don't say," said the Big Man.

The Little Man put the phone jammer and the backpack on the coffee table next to Grout's goggles. "Got all the gear, haven't you?" he said. "The jammer, the goggles. You're a real pro."

"I do my best," said Grout.

"Where did you get it from?"

"The internet," said Grout. "You can get anything on the internet."

"And you're doing what? A bit of thievery?"

"That was the plan. Take what I can, hopefully lift one of the cars. Look, you can just let me go, I won't tell anyone."

"How did you get here?" asked the Big Man.

"Why?"

"Why? Because I want to fucking know," said the Big Man. He raised a shovel-like gloved hand. "And if you're not a bit more forthcoming you're going to be getting a slap."

"I drove," said Grout quickly. "My van. Renault. Outside."

"Keys?"

"My pocket."

The Big Man lowered his hand. "That's better." He turned to look at the Little Man. "What do you think?"

"It doesn't matter what I think, it's up to her, right?"

"Are you going to call her?"

The Little Man nodded. "I'll have to." He bit down on his lower lip. "She's not going to be happy."

"Shit happens," said the Big Man. "She gets paid to make the big decisions."

"What decisions?" asked Grout.

The Big Man pointed at Grout. "Speak when you're spoken to or I'll knock you out again."

"I'll call her now," said the Little Man. He took his phone out of his pocket and walked into the hallway.

"You can just let me go, I won't say anything to anybody," Grout said to the Big Man.

"It's not as simple as that."

"Look, you broke in, I broke in, you and me are the same. Live and let live, hey?" Grout forced a smile. "Honour among thieves, right? Professional etiquette they call it."

"We're not thieves, sonny," said the Big Man. "What's your name?"

BREAKING IN

"Grout. Richard Grout. My friends call me Richie."

"Yeah? Well, Richie, you chose a hell of a time to go housebreaking."

"I think of myself more as a cat burglar than a housebreaker," said Grout.

The Big Man chuckled. "Do you now?"

"Yeah, I don't usually break in. I'm the Drainpipe King, me. Always take the easy option, that's my philosophy. Why smash a window when there's usually one open?"

"Makes sense," said the Big Man. "And you've got the figure for it. What do you weigh? Sixty kilos?"

"Just about," said Grout.

"See now, that's perfect for shimmying up and down drainpipes. Unless they're plastic. So what do you do? Case the place before?"

Grout nodded. "Yeah, I walk around, see what's what. Make notes in a little notepad I carry. During the day I see what windows are open and then I check at night. Then I look to see what time they go to bed. Try and see who lives there, too. If there's a baby then they'll be up and down all night. If there's an old fella then he'll be going to the toilet every hour or so. Trick is to find someone on their own with a job because they go to bed early and sleep through the night. Couples are okay, best if they've both got jobs. But no kids. If I see that a house has got kids then I give it a wide berth."

"And you make a good living?"

Grout shrugged carelessly. "Can't complain." He looked over at the man on the sofa. His head was slumped on his chest as if he was sleeping. He grimaced and looked back at the Big Man. "So who are you, the cops?"

The Big Man grinned. "Do we look like cops?"

The Little Man came back into the room. "She'll call us back," he said.

"How did she take it?"

"Mad as hell, but it's not like it's our fault. I told her the little bastard came in through the bathroom window."

"Who are you?" asked Grout. "And what are you doing here? What's going on?"

The Little Man walked over to Grout and stood looking down at him. "We're the ones asking the questions," he said. "That's why we're walking around and you're tied to the chair." He looked over his shoulder at the Big Man. "We need to get it done, the timing's got to be right," he said.

"What about him?" said the Big Man, gesturing at Grout.

"Whatever we do with him, we still have to take care of business," said the Little Man.

"Yeah, you're right," said the Big Man. He knelt down, placed the knife in the right hand of the man on the sofa, then slowly drew it across the man's left forearm, a deep cut that went from the inside of the elbow to the wrist.

Grout yelped. Blood spurted from the wound, over the man's shirt and trousers. The Big Man released his grip on the man's hand and straightened up.

"What the fuck?" shouted Grout.

"Keep your voice down or we'll gag you," said the Little Man, pointing at Grout's face.

Blood continued to pump from the wound and Grout's stomach lurched. He shuddered and closed his eyes.

"Don't like the sight of blood, huh?" asked the Big Man.

Grout took a deep breath, fighting the urge to be sick. He turned his head from the sofa and opened his eyes again. The two men were standing in front of him, smirking.

"So you're like what, MI5?"

"Doesn't matter who we are, sonny," said the Little Man.

"Yeah, you're MI5. Spooks. Like that TV show."

"We're nothing like Spooks," said the Big Man.

"More like James Bond," said the Little Man.

"Yeah, but Daniel Craig, not Roger Moore," said the Big Man.

"He was good in Moonraker, that was a fun film," said the Little Man.

"But not real."

BREAKING IN

"They're films. It's all make-believe."
"But that's what you are, right?" said Grout. "Spooks."
"We don't call ourselves spooks," said the Little Man.
"Agents, then," said Grout. "Secret agents."
"We're secret, that's for sure," said the Little Man, and he laughed. "Secret fucking squirrel, that's what we do."
"You break into places, don't you? I could help you. I could sign up."
"Sign up?" said the Little Man. He laughed again and turned to look at his companion. "Did you hear that? He wants to sign up. Have you got an application form with you?"
The Big Man laughed.
"I'm serious," said Grout. "I could help you. I'm the most prolific housebreaker in Croydon. No one breaks into more places than me."
"Is that right?" said the Big Man.
Grout nodded enthusiastically.
The Little Man looked at his watch. "She's taking her time."
The Big Man shrugged. "She has to clear it at the top. Close to the top anyway. That means getting someone out of bed."
"Look, you could use someone like me. I could get you into places." Grout could hear the uncertainty in his own voice. He tried not to look at the body on the sofa.
"Yeah?" said the Little Man.
"I can get in anywhere, pretty much," said Grout. His mouth was dry and it hurt when he swallowed.
The Little Man pointed up at a sensor in the corner of the room. Red and green lights were winking. "What would you do about that? It's a motion and heat sensor. Sets off the alarm. And the alarm here is linked to the cops."
"Not a problem," said Grout. "I always break in when they're asleep and if they're in the house then the alarm is switched off." He grinned. "Easy."
"Yeah, but what if the alarm is on? Suppose you get in and the alarm is beeping which means you've got fifteen seconds to enter the four-digit code. What do you do?" Grout shrugged.

The Little Man grinned and took something out of his pocket. It was about the size of a small phone.

"You need one of these. If you haven't got one of these then you're fucked with a capital F." He put the gizmo back in his pocket. "And what about the lock? You can pick a lock, can you?"

"Some," said Grout, but he could hear the uncertainty in his voice.

"So, take the lock to this place," said the Big Man, gesturing at the door. "It's a six pin cylinder and saw-resistant lock with a triple striker. You could pick that, could you?"

"Probably not," said Grout.

"Well I can," said the Big Man. He nodded at the Little Man. "And him, he can reverse engineer any lock to produce a key in less than two hours. Now that's the real skill."

"Why do you need a key if you've already broken in?" said Grout.

"Sometimes you have to go back, and lock-picking is a pain in the arse," said the Big Man.

"You mean steal the TV and then go back for the stereo?" said Grout.

The Big Man chuckled. "Something like that," he said.

"I could learn stuff like that," said Grout. "I'm a quick learner."

"Did well at school, did you?" asked the Little Man.

"Nah, I was crap at school. But the teachers were tossers. Wasn't my fault. But getting into houses, that I'm good at."

"Yeah, pity they don't teach it at university," said the Big Man. "Get yourself a BSc in house-breaking."

"You know how much I made last year?" said Grout.

The two men shook their heads.

"A hundred and twenty grand," said Grout. "That's what I got in my hand, cash, for what I took."

The Big Man nodded, impressed. "That's more than I earned," he said.

"But we get a pension," said the Little Man.

BREAKING IN

"There is that," said the Big Man. "And job security, of course."

"What I'm saying is, I can work for you. I could be a big help."

"Yeah, but how many times have you been in court?" asked the Little Man.

"Never been caught," said Grout. "Not red-handed, anyway."

"I said in court. You've been in court, right?"

Grout grinned. "Loads of times," he said. "But never been sent down. Always wear a suit to court, I do. And my old mum turns up and says what a tough childhood I had because my dad left, and that I'm about to join the army, and I get a letter from one of my old teachers saying what a good kid I was, so I get a slap on the wrist and that's all."

"But that's your problem right there," said the Little Man. "You're in the system. You're known. The whole point of what we do is that no one knows us. We're the grey men. You're too high-profile."

"So? So what are you going to do? You're going to have to let me go sometime, aren't you? Just let me go and I won't say anything. Why would I? I broke in, didn't I? It's not like I'm going to tell anyone, is it?"

"Yeah, but you're a talker, Richie. You can't help but run off at the mouth. You'll tell someone."

"I won't, I swear."

The Little Man laughed. "Like you swore on a stack of Bibles in court that you were innocent, right? You're a thief and a liar, Richie, there's no way we can believe a word that comes out of your mouth."

"So what are you going to do?" asked Grout.

The Little Man shrugged. "That's not my call."

"At least tell me what you're doing here."

"That's need-to-know. And you don't need to know."

"What's the harm?" said the Big Man. "No matter how this pans out, telling him won't make any difference."

"You tell him, then," said the Little Man.

The Big Man shrugged. "Do you know who he is?" he asked Grout. He jerked his thumb at the body on the sofa. "The guy whose car you were going to steal. Have you any idea who he is?"

"Works in an office, doesn't he? Always wears a suit. Carries a briefcase."

"Surveillance not your strong point, then?"

"All I care about is when he gets home and what time he goes to bed."

"And you don't know where he's from?"

"Don't care."

"Yeah, well we care," said the Big Man. "He moves money around the world. Money that gets used by terrorists. Money that's used to kill people."

"So you've killed him, is that it?"

"Somebody had to stop him, and stop him quickly," said the Big Man.

"So why are you still here? Why didn't you just do it and leave?"

"Because we have to set the scene," said The Big Man. "That's what we do."

"And we're bloody good at it, too," said the Little Man.

"I don't understand," said Grout, his brow furrowed.

"Of course you don't," said the Little Man. "Why would you?"

"We tell a story," said the Big Man. "We tell a story to explain why he killed himself."

"But you killed him?"

"Yes, we did. You know that and we know that, but when PC Plod arrives he's going to put two and two together and get four. He's going to find a woman upstairs who's been stabbed in the chest a dozen or so times. He's going to find a man on the sofa who has cut his own wrists with the same knife. Then he's going to look a little deeper and see that she wrote on her Facebook page that she was about to leave him. And on his Facebook page they'll see that he wrote that he'd never let her go, that he'd rather kill her than let her go to another man."

"There's a dead woman upstairs?" said Grout. "His wife? She's dead, too?"

"What we call collateral damage," said the Little Man. "But she was as bad as him. Birds of an Al Qaeda feather."

"So you killed them both and made it look like he killed her and then killed himself?"

"That's what we do," said the Little Man.

"And you do that for the Government?"

"Depends what you mean by The Government. I doubt that the Prime Minister knows we're here. Or his deputy. Probably no one in the cabinet knows the nitty-gritty. But we're G-men, all right. Bought and paid for."

The Little Man's phone buzzed and he fished it out of his pocket. He pressed the phone to his ear and turned away. Grout heard him say "okay" three times and then he put the phone back in his pocket.

"What?' asked Grout. "What's happening? What did they say?"

The Little Man ignored Grout and turned to look at his companion. "She says green light."

"That's that, then," said The Big Man. He bent down and picked up a black leather holdall.

"Green light?" said Grout. "What does that mean?"

The Big Man put the bag onto a table and unzipped the top. He took out a roll of duct tape and a polythene bag.

"Doing it here?" asked the Little Man.

"Be easier to handle as a dead weight," said the Big Man.

"Guys, come on," said Grout. "You don't have to do this."

"We do," said the Little Man.

"It's what we get paid for," said the Big Man. "Just relax, it'll be over soon." He put the polythene bag under his arm and tore off a strip of duct tape. Just as Grout started to scream, the man slapped the tape across his mouth, pulled the bag over his head and began to wind duct tape around his neck.

Grout struggled but with his arms and legs bound to the chair he could barely move. His chest heaved as he fought to breathe. His lungs were burning and there were tears running from his eyes. The Big Man continued to wind the duct tape around Grout's neck, tighter and tighter. Condensation on the polythene blurred Grout's vision but the last thing he saw was the Little Man looking at his watch, an annoyed frown on his face. Then everything went black.

THE DEATH TOLL AUTHORS

THE DEATH TOLL AUTHORS

Now that you've met everyone, stop by Amazon and have a look at the great titles available from these fine writers.

http://amzn.to/YUg5Y1

Stephen Leather is one of the UK's most successful thriller writers. He was a journalist for more than ten years on newspapers such as *The Times*, the *Daily Mail* and the *South China Morning Post* in Hong Kong. Before that, he was employed as a biochemist for ICI, shovelled limestone in a quarry, worked as a baker, a petrol pump attendant, a barman, and worked for the Inland Revenue. He began writing full time in 1992. His bestsellers have been translated into more than ten languages. He has also written for television shows such as *London's Burning*, *The Knock* and the BBC's *Murder in Mind* series.

http://amzn.to/XqWSyW

Alex Shaw spent the second half of the 1990s in Kyiv, Ukraine, teaching Drama and running his own business consultancy before being head-hunted for a division of Siemens. The next few years saw him doing business for the company across the former USSR, the Middle East, and Africa. He is the author of the #1 International Kindle Bestselling 'Aidan Snow SAS thrillers' *HETMAN* and *COLD BLACK* and the new *DELTA FORCE VAMPIRE* series of books. *DANGEROUS, DEADLY, ELITE* - The third Aidan Snow Thriller will be available in July 2013

Alex, his wife and their two sons divide their time between homes in Kyiv, Ukraine and West Sussex, England. You can follow Alex on twitter: @alexshawhetman or contact him via his website: www.alexwshaw.com.

THE DEATH TOLL AUTHORS

http://amzn.to/ZbeWOE

J.H. Bográn, born and raised in Honduras, is the son of a journalist. He ironically prefers to write fiction rather than fact. José's genre of choice is thrillers, but he likes to throw in a twist of romance into the mix.

His works include novels in both English and Spanish, short stories, contributor to *The Big Thrill* magazine, and screenwriter for Honduras domestic television and movie reviewer for *La Prensa*.

He's a member of the *International Thriller Writers* where he serves as the Thriller Roundtable Coordinator.

http://amzn.to/10xLxde

Stephen Edger is the author of four books, *Integration*, *Redemption*, *Remorse*, and *Snatched*. He lives with his wife, Hannah and daughter Emily in Southampton where each of his books are set. Stephen was born in Darlington in NE England but was raised in London. He moved to Southampton to study Law at University in 2000, but after graduation decided his future lay outside of a courtroom. Stephen has worked in the finance industry ever since. His fifth book *Dead Drop* is due in 2013.

THE DEATH TOLL AUTHORS

http://amzn.to/ZbfEf2

Liam Saville lives in Sydney Australia with his wife, two children, and their German Shepherd.

He is a former member of the Australian Army and has studied at the Royal Military College Duntroon. Liam also served for several years as a police officer in his home state of New South Wales, and currently works full time in a regulatory and enforcement role with a public sector agency in Sydney. *Predator Strike* is his first book, and the first in a series of planned novellas featuring Australian Defence Force Investigative Service officer, Captain Sam Ryan. **Sam Ryan is returning this May in Liam Saville's *RESOLUTE ACTION***

http://amzn.to/12hQvzZ

Jake Needham practiced international company and finance law until he grew up and began writing, first screenplays and eventually novels.

He is the author of six published crime novels (or maybe they're legal thrillers...who the hell knows?) set in the cities of contemporary Asia: *THE BIG MANGO, LAUNDRY MAN, KILLING PLATO, A WORLD OF TROUBLE, THE AMBASSADOR'S WIFE,* and *THE UMBRELLA MAN.* The print editions of his books are available in Asia, Europe, and the UK. The e-book editions are available worldwide. Mr. Needham, his wife, and their two sons divide their time between homes in Bangkok and New York. You can learn more about Mr. Needham and his crime novels at his official website, www.JakeNeedham.com.

Thank you for buying our book.

If you have a minute, we'd love to hear your thoughts and comments.

www.deathtoll.co.uk

And visit EspionageMagazine.com, short thriller fiction, non-fiction, mystery, and suspense from new and emerging writers, and a few pros, too.

www.espionagemagazine.com

Printed in Great Britain
by Amazon.co.uk, Ltd.,
Marston Gate.